BLACK RANGE REVENGE

COLTON BROTHERS SAGA

BLACK RANGE REVENGE

MELODY GROVES

FIVE STAR
A part of Gale, a Cengage Company

Farmington Hills, Mich • San Francisco • New York • Waterville, Maine
Meriden, Conn • Mason, Ohio • Chicago

LIBRARY OF CONGRESS CATALOGING-IN-PUBLICATION DATA

Names: Groves, Melody, 1952– author.
Title: Black Range revenge / Melody Groves.
Description: First edition. | Farmington Hills, Mich. : Five Star Publishing, [2018] | Series: Colton Brothers saga
Identifiers: LCCN 2017047649 (print) | LCCN 2017050094 (ebook) | ISBN 9781432837136 (ebook) | ISBN 9781432837129 (ebook) | ISBN 9781432837266 (hardcover)
Subjects: | BISAC: FICTION / Historical. | FICTION / Action & Adventure. | GSAFD: Western stories.
Classification: LCC PS3607.R6783 (ebook) | LCC PS3607.R6783 B58 2018 (print) | DDC 813/.6—dc23
LC record available at https://lccn.loc.gov/2017047649

First Edition. First Printing: March 2018
Find us on Facebook–https://www.facebook.com/FiveStarCengage
Visit our website–http://www.gale.cengage.com/fivestar/
Contact Five Star™ Publishing at FiveStar@cengage.com

Printed in the United States of America
1 2 3 4 5 6 7 22 21 20 19 18

For Colton, Mykie and Zayden

Couldn't have done this without help from:
Myke Groves
Judy Avila, Sherri Burr, Phil Jackson,
Sarena Ulibarri and Kathy Wagoner

CHAPTER ONE

September, 1863

Black Range Mountains, southwestern New Mexico Territory

Like every other morning for the past month, he'd crawled out of his canvas tent, slurped a cup of what passed for coffee— bitter and black water—and went to work. Pan in the water . . . slosh, slosh, slosh. Pull it out. Inspect. More water . . . slosh, slosh, slosh.

Until five minutes ago.

Gunfire, whoops and screams shattered the symphony of chattering birds and gurgling water.

Hunkered down behind a rock, a juniper bush covering him, he held his breath and listened hard over the flutter of dried leaves stirred by a light breeze. He sent pleas heavenward. Would this be the day he died? Now shallow spurts, his breathing matched his gaze as it darted from tree to bush to rock and back. Muscles wound until he knew they'd coil in on themselves, at least they would let him run the hundred miles back to Mesilla if he could.

Would his hiding place protect him? He'd heard about the Warm Springs Apaches and their retaliation for the January murder of their leader, Mangas Coloradas. But they'd already wiped out the camp of Birchville twice earlier this year. Wasn't that enough?

Enraged Apaches had slaughtered innocent men. Enraged, rightfully so. But was murder the answer?

Screams. More screams. Some closer, others fading. Grateful to have set up camp a mile from the others, Andy Colton hoped he'd chosen a spot far enough away. He cringed, squeezing his eyes closed, then realized he'd have to stay vigilant. They opened.

Off to his left, branches snapped. Couldn't be his horse. She was hobbled farther up the creek, out of sight, he hoped. How small could he make himself? He plastered his body against the boulder, tucked in his arms and curled in tight. Hooves pushed fallen leaves aside, a few crinkling under the weight. Slow, methodical clip clops inches away. He braced himself for a knife or arrow to slash through his muscles, and perhaps end his life.

Even if the juniper covered him, he knew the Indian would be able to hear his heart pound. Andy tried to swallow, but only the acidic taste of fear filled his mouth.

Fallen leaves being spread apart by hooves, the sound slowed, then stopped. Did he dare peek around the boulder? No. Movement of any kind would prove fatal. The sound began again. This time moving away from Andy. He waited until he heard nothing. No birds, no small critters scurrying for brush, not even screams from camp. Licking his lips and taking a deep breath, he uncurled and peeked around the boulder. No Apache waiting.

Should he leave his hiding place? His boulder? He wanted to stay, needed to stay until dark, at least, but his legs said otherwise. Andy unfolded like a caterpillar emerging from a cocoon, his long legs grateful for freedom. He brought his body up to its full height, then sprinted for an aspen. How its narrow trunk and leaves above his head would serve as protection he knew was pointless, but standing against it gave him more security.

Waiting, listening, he cocked his head. Again, no sounds. He knew what that meant. It wouldn't be pretty, but as a survivor, it was his obligation. Help the wounded, dead and dying. He blew out air, gave one last look and started for camp.

CHAPTER TWO

September 1863,
Birchville, Black Range Mountains

Andy rubbed his eyes. Nothing would erase the images. Arrows at attention in men's backs. Blood where hair used to be. The smells. Gunpowder. Smoldering hair. Burnt skin. Would it erase the creak of timber as a house caved in on itself? He scrubbed at the nightmare. Would that erase the blood on his hands? Would it bring back the twenty-three men murdered? Mutilated?

No.

A deep breath, a sigh, another breath, then Andy ran his fingers through his shoulder-length hair. His sooted hand scrubbed his face stubble. Hadn't he shaved just yester—. . . days, weeks, months ago? Not since the attack on Birchville. One eye pried open, he leaned forward and realized he was propped against the headstone of Thomas Marston, killed some ten years or so before. Killed courtesy of Apaches. Marston, he'd been told, had the dubious honor of being the first to occupy this cemetery. To his right stood the beginnings of a church, if a stone foundation was any indication. Maybe, if it had been built, the Indians wouldn't have attacked.

Right.

Knowing he had to get up, but knowing also if he did, he'd do nothing but wander up and down what was left of the main street, talking with the survivors. A few buildings remained standing. Of those, the most important was the Buckhorn Saloon.

"Get up, Andy."

He glanced right then left. Who'd said that? The cemetery was empty, except for the dead he and the survivors had recently buried along with the ones who'd preceded them. The place was filling up.

"Not doin' any good sitting here. Get up."

Andy picked up his hat. It *was* time for moving on. First, he'd get some sleep, then pack his clothes and mining supplies. He'd have to buy another horse since his was missing—either run off or stolen by Apaches. Most importantly, he'd shake off this blood-stained fog and get on with his life. But go where?

"Go home."

Andy regarded his hat as if it spoke. What the hell had he been thinking? Leaving the safety of Mesilla, New Mexico Territory, on the off chance he'd find gold nuggets like the ones he'd heard about. Like the one he'd seen back home in Mesilla, courtesy of a miner showing off the results of his hard work. Andy had believed that prospector bragging in Sam Bean's saloon. Hell, the old man had said he'd spotted something glinting in the water over on Bear Creek and damn, when he picked it up, that nugget caught the sun's light and almost blinded him. At least, that was his story. Andy saw the gold—didn't get to touch it, but admired it inches away. Enough to catch "the fever."

"Go on."

Snugging his wide-brimmed hat onto his head, he sat up straight, shoulders back. He froze. That voice was *his*. He gazed up into the sky. Maybe he was crazy.

He rolled onto his hands and knees, used Marston's cross to push against, then wobbled upright. Andy was tall, a good few inches above the heads of most men, but this afternoon his body sagged like a broken old man. As he knew he would, as he'd done too many times in the past few days, he ambled toward the Buckhorn, thanking someone above or whoever was in charge, that it had survived.

"Another beer, Andy?" The barkeep held up the empty glass, one lone bubble of suds sliding down the inside.

Andy nodded. Another one would chase the first three. Maybe these would numb him. Maybe not. But then again, is that what he wanted? To live his life numb? *Brace your backbone and forget your wishbone.* Pa's words circled his brain. How can one man stand against Apache attacks?

Maybe he could be more like Mangas Coloradas, the Apache chief who'd come into this camp, white flag in hand. He wanted peace with the Americans, he'd said. He wanted his own people to be able to live their lives without threat of war. He wanted to understand the "white" man.

And what did it get him? Double-crossed and killed. The army didn't want peace with the Indians. Apparently, they had wanted it all—the land for Americans and the Apaches eradicated. Andy tugged on his lower lip. The insanity and lack of respect the army showed was so wrong. In many ways, he was embarrassed to ever have been a soldier.

A refilled glass appeared in front of him. His gaze traveled the length of the bar. Men like him lined along it. Men alive, but not living. He regarded the amber nectar, which promised an escape. He turned the glass right, then left, lifted it, then put it down. No more living here, always afraid of Indians. Hell, he hadn't found much gold to speak of. Others had been luckier than him. What the hell had he been thinking? Chasing up here to the Black Range, specifically the Mogollon Mountains. Giving up a good job for what? His head wagged before he could stop it. That's what he'd always done. Change his mind. For as

long as he could remember, he'd get distracted and not follow
through. He'd done it so often, his family had become ac-
customed to it. Dammit! He gritted his teeth. Choose a path
and stick with it. Mind firmly made up, he pushed the beer
glass away, stepped back from the bar and dropped a coin on
the wooden counter. He nodded to the bartender. "Guess I'm
done, after all, Al." Andy adjusted his hat and shook hands with
the man. "I'll be heading out first light. Maybe I'll see you
around."

"Heading out? Where you going?" The man's thick eyebrows
ran together as he frowned. "Thought you'd found a decent
claim."

"Decent enough, I reckon." Andy cocked his head. "But I
don't think it's decent enough to get killed over."

"Gold is!" a man at a table hollered.

"Hell, I wouldn't turn tail and run just 'cause some red devil
might ride in and lift hair," another man said, raising his glass.
This brought more upraised glasses, hoots and salutes from
others in the dim room.

The barkeep leaned across the wooden bar top. "You really
going?" He clutched his wiping rag.

A third man, on his way to the door, wheeled around and
elbowed his way to Andy. "Since you're runnin' scared back to
Mama, can I have your claim? And your tent?"

"I didn't put paper on the claim. So anybody's welcome to
it."

The man at Andy's shoulder lowered his voice to a near
whisper. "Where'd you say it was?"

Andy clenched his jaw. "I didn't."

Another voice behind him, close to his ear. "Well, then, me
friend. *I'll* be buyin' it from ye, I will." The man leaned forward,
addressing the first man. "Go on now. Me friend and I have
much to be discussin'."

Andy flinched, bumping into the fella at his right shoulder. Thomas O'Malley, formerly of Kilkenny, Ireland, and now of Birchville, New Mexico Territory, and a bit more than an acquaintance, stood grinning. "I'll pay yer good coin, Andy, me boy. Then I'll pull ever' last nugget outta the stream." He produced a wide grin, one tooth missing. "And I'll be rich! The richest Traveler what ever come over from the ol' sod."

Andy had to laugh. O'Malley's grin proved contagious and it felt good to smile again. Here was someone Andy would miss. His stories of Ireland, growing up in a family of ten siblings, their sheep shearing shenanigans, then wool spinning—all fascinating. Andy could sit and listen beer after beer. And he had. Back before . . .

A hand on his shoulder pushed Andy forward. "It's a drink I'll be buyin' ye," O'Malley said. "Then back to your brothers ye can be goin'."

"I'll take the drink," Andy said. "But how'd you know where I was heading?"

The bartender, no longer interested in the conversation, handed each man a shot of whiskey, then moved down the bar.

"How'd I know, Andrew?" O'Malley held up his glass. "Here's to ye and yer family. It's back to them ye're goin'. That's all ye talk about." He threw his whiskey back, plunked the glass on the bar. "It's Mesilla ye'll be returnin' to and bein' a copper, it is."

The whiskey flowed down Andy's throat, the fire to move on, all but extinguished. Getting the hell out of town while he was still on his feet . . . was that the answer? To run and hide behind his sheriff brother's reputation? To hide behind the badge declaring Andy a deputy?

Before finding an answer, more whiskey filled Andy's glass. O'Malley leaned against the bar and half turned to Andy. "Just exactly where is this magical place full o' gold ye've been tellin' me about? I'll be headin' to it first light."

"You ain't considering leaving? I mean with Cochise and the other Apaches raiding, attacking, you're willing to stay? Maybe end up without your hair?"

O'Malley leaned way back, his laugh filling the smoke-clogged room. "A funny one ye are, Andrew Colton." He whipped off his bowler revealing a thin ring of hair running from ear to ear. "I'd like to see 'em try 'n get ahold of this!"

Men whooped and hollered, offering suggestions of what the Indians *could* take instead of his hair. Andy laughed, too, although his question had been deadly serious. At almost nineteen, he had a lot of living yet to do, and he sure as hell didn't want it cut short by greed or by his recent impulsive decision to head out on his own. Hell, he'd already done something like that when he'd joined the Union army two years ago. Lying about his age, he and an older brother had marched from Tucson clear to California and back. He'd been shot by a Reb in Yuma. Shot and survived. He'd been lucky then, but would he remain lucky?

A long look at the men standing shoulder to shoulder at the bar. Andy glanced at the three tables all occupied with men, weary men, wounded men. They weren't running. They weren't whining. They were going to their diggings in the morning. Talking about what their gold would buy when they found enough. They were thinking about the future.

Andy straightened his shoulders and brought himself up to his full height. By damn, he'd stay, continue working up the hill and find gold. When he was truly satisfied he'd panned as much as he could, then he'd turn south, return home to Mesilla. He nudged O'Malley.

"Tell you what, Tommy. What say you and me go in together? Your claim's showing color, but I think together we'd make more money." Andy studied his friend's bearded face, his brown eyes wide. "And one of us could watch for Apaches."

O'Malley grew serious, his eyes narrowing. "Ye're proposin' then, me friend, is a merger? Like partners?"

Andy nodded.

"And we split everythin' fifty-fifty?"

Again a nod.

"Even the cookin'?"

Andy smiled.

O'Malley's gaze swept the room, then settled on his whiskey glass. A few rises and falls of his chest, the mud-streaked vest straining at the buttons, he whistled between his front teeth.

"Here's to us!" O'Malley held his glass high. "May the road rise up to meet us!"

"And what my Irish ma says," Andy held up his glass. "And may the wind always be at our backs!"

They clinked glasses.

CHAPTER THREE

November, 1863
The Black Range
Andy breathed out crystal fog as he sat on a boulder near the campfire, his fingers gripping a tin coffee cup. He'd tried blowing on his icy hands, hoping the warmth of his breath would thaw the stiffness. He'd flexed two fingers, both refusing to do more than quiver. His breath hadn't been enough to do much good. Maybe the hot cup would loosen his hands a bit. Cold this morning. It had turned damn cold earlier than expected. He sucked in frosted air; his lungs tingled. Maybe he should leave his diggings and head for the much warmer Mesilla.

The cold's frigid tendrils hugged him tight, much like a frozen mistress. He couldn't shake himself warm. He glanced to his right. His partner wasn't in any better spirits than he was. O'Malley squatted against a tree, his gloved hands outstretched over the fire. That Irishman hadn't said three words all morning. Andy guessed by day's end they'd both be pulling up stakes and heading somewhere warmer. Somewhere with gold. Gold? Hell, he'd settle for sunshine about now. Anything to break up the murky sky matching his dark mood.

The past few weeks had shown slight profit. O'Malley had the "gift of gab" as his ma had said about Andy's older brothers, and the Irishman had turned out to be a passable good cook. At least he hadn't burned the beans and bacon. Both men had worked hard side by side and found a slew of flakes along

19

with a few nuggets. Nothing worth hollering over yet, but Andy knew, just like the sizable trout that had evaded his hook, substantial nuggets were in the water. The stream running near camp gurgled as if telling him exactly where to look, but Andy failed to understand the strange language.

Andy clenched his jaw until it ached. What was he waiting for? Time to come down off the mountain and head somewhere sunny and warm. He'd come back in the spring, after the thaw, and plunge his pan into Bear Creek again. Maybe by then, the Apaches would have marauding out of their system, and Andy and the other prospectors could work without fear.

All right. That's what he'd do. Pack up his bedroll, tent, lantern and pan, his scant food supplies, load his horse and then head downtown for a final beer or two before riding home. A quick sip of coffee slid down his throat, warming his chest. He spoke over his cup.

"What say we pack up and head to Mesilla?" Andy pointed his cup south and then sipped again. He spit out coffee grounds. "I'm thinking we're done for the winter." He waited for his partner to say yea or nay . . . anything. Instead, he got one raised eyebrow.

"Hell, O'Malley," Andy said. "We're not finding anything. Besides, I can't feel my fingers to put that pan in the water." He paused until his friend turned his eyes to him. "And look at all the ice hugging the bank. Pretty soon we'll be breaking ice just to get to the river."

O'Malley blew on his hands. His silence drew Andy's full attention.

O'Malley spit coffee grounds and coughed.

" 'Tis a fine time we've been havin', Andrew. A fine time." O'Malley rubbed his hands together and stood. "But ye're right, lad. A warm house and woman's cookin' suits me down to me toes."

A long foggy sigh escaped Andy's chest. Good. It was settled. They'd come back in the spring. Hopefully, some other prospector wouldn't stake this claim. They'd never filed proper papers on it, leaving it open for anyone. Not that it was better than other spots, but he knew this part of the river. He'd hate to come back to find someone squatting on it. But with miles of stream available, he'd find another part to pan in.

"Let's get our poke assayed in town." Andy poured the last swallow of coffee onto the fire. "Then I'll buy you a beer. We can head out from there. It's only three days or so to Mesilla."

O'Malley smiled. "I'll take that beer," he said. "But only if it's hot."

Andy and Thomas O'Malley stood shoulder to shoulder at the Buckhorn Saloon. Andy turned his back to the bartender and leaned against the bar. Inside the Buckhorn was one of almost every walk of life: Scots, French, a couple Mexicans off by themselves, more than several Irish, all jabbering in their native tongues. In the mix stood one woman who served drinks. Word was she was no "painted cat," just a server, her accent from somewhere in the south. Tennessee, Andy had heard. But he wasn't interested in such women. The "soiled doves." They were nothing but trouble, his brothers had explained. In detail. No good comes from cavorting with them, they'd said. And he believed them. He'd seen fights break out and heard men talk about the diseases they'd picked up.

No, he'd wait. Although it was becoming more difficult.

A hardy slap on his back pushed him forward. "Drink up, me boy. Time to get goin' it is."

Andy downed the remainder of his beer, turned and put the glass on the bar. "Let's go see what the assay office says. Maybe we're rich and don't even know it!"

They pushed through the men until they stood outside on

what passed as a boardwalk. Mostly mud with a chunk of wood underneath. Instead of keeping feet out of the muck, it usually succeeded in tripping boots, the corners of the wood turned up or missing. Andy preferred walking in the street. There, road apples were about the biggest hazard.

The assay office bustled with men. At least it was warm inside. Andy turned sideways near the front and sidestepped up to the counter. A man, white apron snugged around a skinny waist, hollered over the crowd.

"Can I help ya?"

"Yes, sir." Andy pulled off his hat, swiped at a loose strand of hair, then ran his hand down his coat front, the small bulge of gold dust in his vest pocket bringing a smile. "Got some findings that need weighting."

"Be another minute or two," the man said. "Been busy."

Andy cut his eyes sideways at O'Malley. Both shrugged. As the man stepped away, Andy threaded his way through the men, pacing from door to back of the room then over to a counter full of scales, ore samples and small picks. He pulled out his pocket watch, checked the time, then closed the cover. He paced.

Andy pulled out his watch again. Before he could check the time, the man marched in from a back room, leaned over the counter and waved to Andy.

O'Malley arrived steps ahead of Andy, who dug into his vest and extracted the sack. He handed it to the assayer, watching as he dumped the dust, flakes, and a few small nuggets into a dish. He placed it on the scale.

After adjusting a couple of weights, sliding them up and down a bar, the man raised one eyebrow. He eyed O'Malley and then Andy. "You wanna sell? I'm buyin'."

"How much?" Andy and his friend spoke in unison.

"Twenty-five."

"Dollars?" Andy leaned in.

"You heard right." The assayer held up one hand. "Thirteen dollars an ounce." He twirled his meaty finger over the gold. "You got here just about two ounces. And not the best quality, neither."

" 'Tis robbery, it 'tis. Hell, I heard the goin' rate is nineteen!" O'Malley frowned at Andy and then turned on the man. "You're nothin' but a gurrier, a liar and a pollywagger, ye are. I won't be sellin' my hard-won gold to the likes of ye."

"Suit yourself." The man shrugged. "I know it's not what you wanted to hear. Take it or leave it."

"Damn right we'll leave it!" O'Malley scooped the gold out of the dish, eyeing each grain as they poured back into the bag. He tied the leather pouch with a thin strand of rawhide, then clutched it to his chest. "Let's go, Andrew. We'll find an expert who knows quality gold when they see it."

Andy turned on his heels and marched through the door behind his partner. Was this assayer telling the truth, or not? No way of telling since this assay office was the only one within fifty miles. When they got to Mesilla, surely there was an honest assayer who would give them the true value of the gold. Hell, they'd worked day and night for weeks, months and for what? Twenty-five dollars? His aggravation grew into outright anger by the time he and O'Malley walked across the street, headed again for the Buckhorn. One beer, his nerves would be calmer, and then they'd start out for Mesilla. Another hour wouldn't make any difference.

The two marched across the road, but, before they reached the saloon, shouts behind them turned both men around. A clot of people, pouring out of the assay office, stampeded into the street. Whoops and hollers filled the cold air, their cheer echoing off the hills and rolling into the valley.

Swept into the crowd, Andy dodged eager men and then elbowed his way toward O'Malley. "What's goin' on?" Andy shouted over heads.

"I'm rich!" A man shrieked. "Found gold. Biggest damn nugget you'll ever lay eyes on!"

Men, along with a couple of women, crowded around.

"Where'd you find it?"

"How big?"

"What's it worth?"

"Show us!"

The man, sunburnt face, heavy cotton pants, and mud encrusted coat, held up a piece of paper. "Got this from the assay office over yonder." He thumbed over his shoulder. "Says my nugget's worth . . . well, more money'n you'll see in your whole lives!"

"Where?" The crowd moved in like a cougar pack ready to attack. "There any more?"

"More?" the man hollered back. " 'Course there's more. Up in them Mogollon Mountains, over by Silver Creek."

Maybe he should head over to Silver Creek. Andy had heard it was a day or two trip over the mountain, but he'd also heard there was some sort of trail or path. A fella named Cooney had started a mine over in that area and was becoming rich. At least that's what he'd heard.

O'Malley elbowed Andy. "It's goin' we should be. Up to Silver Creek. 'Fore anyone else gets there." He tugged Andy's coat sleeve.

"Thought we were going to Mesilla. Somewhere warm." Andy moved to his left, sidestepping to avoid collision with a man elbowing his way out of the throng. "Some place without cold!" Now he shouted to be heard.

"One month, Andrew. One month . . ." O'Malley followed Andy to the Buckhorn. "We'll be rich in no time. Then, by year's end, we'll go to this family of yers wealthy men." He stopped Andy at the saloon's doors. "Wouldnna tha' be gran'?"

It would. But he'd promised himself . . . and had already written and sent a letter home . . . he was coming back. And soon. But now, here he was thinking about changing his mind. Again. He hated that about himself.

"I can tell by the look on yer face, Andrew, ye ain't goin' to the mountains. So, I'll be buyin' ye one more beer, then ye can head south, and I'll be headin' north." O'Malley fished around his neck, pulled a rawhide string until a bronze token popped out from under his shirt. "I'll be kissin' this Saint Christopher's medal and prayin' for ye, Andrew."

"A good word's always appreciated." Andy squinted at the oblong medal pinched between his friend's fingers. "What's that?"

"Ye ain't never seen a Saint Christopher before?" O'Malley tsked and held it closer to Andy. "Provides succor for weary travelers and protects them."

Andy peered in close. A face, which could've been anybody's, sat in the middle of smoothed metal, surrounded by what looked to be leaves or possibly a rope. This icon was obviously important to O'Malley, so he would respect it. O'Malley certainly did. "Where'd you get it at?"

O'Malley's eyes widened with his sad smile. "Me máthair. Ma. She gave it to me when I was to be leavin' home. Said it would protect me." He looked up at Andy. "And what a fine job it's done."

"Ma cried and made me sandwiches." Andy looked at his friend and shrugged. "I ate 'em all before the stage changed the first set of horses."

"Then here's to our máthairs." O'Malley nodded to Andy. O'Malley's voice, his downcast eyes, his slumped shoulders generated pity. He gazed at the pendant. "For my máthair, who raised me at her breast." He gave it one quick look and shoved it back under his shirt.

Andy thought about Ma's sandwiches as he stepped up to the bar, then turned his attention to his future. What would be another month or two? He had made no promises, had no wife to return to. Brother James was still in Kansas and last he'd written was thinking to stay there permanently. So, it was just brother Trace and his wife and daughter in Mesilla. Hell, why not head farther up into the Mogollon Mountains and make a million? The work wasn't any harder than the blacksmith work he'd been doing at Swenson's Livery in Mesilla. It was, however, harder than that of a deputy sheriff. But he'd known hard work all his life, growing up farming in Kansas with his three older brothers and his folks. So, this panning for gold wasn't real work. Wasn't really fun, either. He fisted one hand. But if he could strike it rich, or find a good-sized nugget, then he could work at something he enjoyed.

"Gonna stare a hole all the way through tha' glass, Andrew." O'Malley clinked his beer glass against Andy's. "Drink up."

"Been givin' it some thought." Andy studied his beer. Why was this so hard? "Guess a month up in those hills won't kill me. I'll write another letter to my brother, let him know not to set an extra plate at the table just yet. Then, let's see if there's a set of flannels at the mercantile. I could use a new pair of johnnies."

O'Malley's grin stretched side to side, parting his beard. "Knew ye'd be comin' to your senses, me boy! 'Tis a fine time we'll be havin', lad. A fine time!"

Andy stood at the mercantile's postal service counter and thought about what he'd say to older brother Trace; how he'd explain the change of mind. Would he understand? Andy licked the end of the pencil and wrote, marking his letters just so.

Dear Trace,
Despite my correspondence dated last week, I've chosen to

continue gold mining. Don't worry. The Indian depredations have diminished a bit and I am well and safe. My partner, Thomas O'Malley, is a good man and both of us will be fine. We'll be following a well-worn trail to the fledgling mining camp of Cooney, down by Silver Creek. Hopefully, by year's end, I'll be at your house a very wealthy man.

Please give a tight hug to Teresa and a kiss to tiny Faith.

Your brother,
Andrew Jackson Colton

He reread the letter, made a correction for spelling, then sealed and addressed the envelope. He handed it to a woman who ran the mercantile, laundry and postal services. Ten cents to send the letter was robbery, he thought, but the convenience was worth it. She promised the letter would make it down to Mesilla within two days. Might take a bit longer if the river flooded or the Indians attacked again. If everything went as planned, two days seemed about right.

The woman scanned the address. "Put the wrong town on here, you did."

"How's that?" Andy peered at the envelope. "I know where I am."

"Don't you know? Town's been changed." She drew a line through Andy's return address and scribbled *Pinos Altos*.

"Pinos Altos?" Andy drew back and frowned. "What kinda name is that?"

The woman snorted. " 'Parently that's what it was before ol' Birch came through and found gold."

Andy shrugged. "Guess one name's as good as another." He stepped back, not sure if he was dismissed or not. The postmistress studied the envelope again.

"Colton, huh?"

"Yes, ma'am, that's me." Andy tipped his hat.

"Seems to me you got yourself a letter. Come in last week."

She placed one hand on her hip, reread Andy's corrected address, and then pursed her lips. "Yep. Addressed to you. Wait here, I'll fetch it."

Andy considered who would've written him, hoping it was Trace with news of Mesilla. Could it be James in Kansas? Maybe it was—

"Knew it." The woman appeared from the back room, waving a letter. She hefted it.

"Couple pages or better, I'd say." She eyed him as she handed over the envelope. "Better read it right here. You might wanna change what's in your letter." She cocked her head toward the back room.

As much as he wanted to tear open the envelope and read it right there, he sure as hell wasn't going to read it in front of Miss Nosey. A glance at the return address revealed it was from oldest brother Trace, current sheriff of Mesilla. This letter was sure to hold tales of arrests and misdoings by the citizens. His stories were legendary. Andy would savor the letter over a beer at the Buckhorn.

"Thanks, anyway, ma'am," Andy said, tucking it inside his vest pocket. "I've got some provisions to buy first." He threaded his way through the store, turning his attention on buying long johns. Something warm. O'Malley stood on the far side of the store, a new pick in hand. Judging by the way he was handling it, Andy figured his friend would soon purchase a pick ax. Why would he need such a tool if they were only panning? Maybe O'Malley would try mining. Now that was work! The thought of swinging a pick in a deep, dark tunnel made Andy shiver. He'd never liked caves, never liked digging into the side of riverbanks like his brothers. Playing robbers and pirates and hiding out. No, he much preferred the open sky and fresh air.

So, if O'Malley wanted to spend his days in a dark, cold cave, that was his business. But Andy vowed to have no part of it. It was one thing dunking his hands in icy water, searching for color, but it was something entirely different spending days in the dark.

Long rays of sunlight played in the street as Andy and O'Malley stepped out of the mercantile, a wrapped pair of *unmentionables* tucked under Andy's arm. Like providence, the clouds had disappeared, and the hills radiated a rose-gold. Tents in the valley glowed purple while tops of the aspens fired gold. Andy stopped and took it all in. Was this a sign? Perhaps he would, indeed, find the proverbial fortune. Maybe his luck had changed.

O'Malley thumped Andy's back. " 'Tis a fine evenin', it's bein'. The good Lord, indeed, is smilin' down on us."

Certainly looked like it from where Andy stood. "Tell you what, friend." Andy patted his pocket and heard coins jingle. "How about I buy you a steak tonight. It'll be back to beans and bacon tomorrow."

O'Malley's face reflected the glow. "I'll just let ye do that, lad." He patted his stomach. "This ol' belly's thinkin' breakfast was last week."

The Old Goat restaurant, next to the Buckhorn, was crowded by the time they pushed the door open and walked in. They took seats at the single vacant table against the far wall. While they waited on steaks, Andy opened the envelope, scanned the two pages and then took his time reading.

He chuckled at the antics of newspaper editor Tom Littleton. Trace detailed Littleton's run-in with a drunken cowboy. All the editor wanted, Trace said, was a quote about rustlers, a recent problem. Apparently, the cowboy wouldn't cooperate, so Littleton poured the cowboy's beer on the man's head. Wake him up, he'd claimed. All hell, as they say, broke loose and Trace almost arrested the newspaperman. Tom Littleton had been a good friend to the Colton boys, and Trace owed him. Andy assumed that's why Littleton hadn't landed in jail.

Andy read through the first page again and then moved on to the second. The news brought his shoulders back and air stuck in his chest. Quantrill's Raiders had attacked his hometown of Lawrence, Kansas. Over a hundred men died. But, Trace wrote, no one in the family was hurt. Ma, Pa, Luke, his wife, Sally, their two children were fine. Brother James and his wife, Morningstar, survived as well. However, Pa's barn had burned to the ground, his house was gutted and singed, and Luke's house had burned. At that time, they were all staying with Sally's folks, the Reverend and Missus Burroughs. One side of Andy's mouth curled up at the news—must be interesting with this diverse collection of people under one roof.

Would James and Morningstar return to Mesilla?

O'Malley tapped Andy's arm. "Eat up, lad." He pointed his fork at the steak in front of Andy. "Cools down enough, it'll start to moo again."

Pulled out of his thoughts of home, Andy shared the news with O'Malley while he ate. "Happened in August, Trace said." He spoke over a mouthful of potato. "How come we didn't know about it? I mean, a killer like that, like Quantrill, burns down a town and we don't hear about it? What if my Pa, Ma . . . hell, my brothers had been killed? And I'm just *now* finding out?"

"Simmer down, Andrew." O'Malley put down his fork and patted Andy's shoulder. "Yer family's unscathed, and for that, ye should be toastin', ye should." He picked up his beer glass and raised it.

Andy's gaze trailed from O'Malley's glass to the table. Even if he'd found out sooner, what could he have done? If he'd left with James last spring, would the outcome have been different? If he'd been able to defend Pa's house—

"Pick up yer glass, lad." O'Malley's voice brought Andy back.

"Here's to yer family in Kansas. Here's that they may always have a clean shirt, a clean conscience and a guinea in their pockets." The men touched glass and sipped.

But Andy wasn't sure toasting his family would serve any good. Maybe he should give up this gold chasing and get the hell home. Where he was needed. But was he? What difference would he make?

Andy looked up as O'Malley scooted back his chair. Plate and glass empty, O'Malley drew a sleeve across his mouth. "Thanks for the grub, Andrew." He pointed at Andy's barely-touched steak and potatoes. "Ye gonna eat this?" He poked his stomach. "Feels like there's room in there fer a wee bit more steak."

Chapter Four

With O'Malley close behind, Andy picked his way down the trail. The sun stood overhead, its rays splattering the ground in random patches. Here and there, like dots and dashes to a treasure map, the sun lit leaves and pine needles. The trail directly ahead narrowed to nothing more than a deer path. He hadn't seen any other footprints in hours, not since this morning after dousing the campfire, ending its encouraging warmth. Then he and O'Malley had trudged on. Up one hill, down the other side, up another hill, around a stand of trees, through a creek, up another hill . . . Andy figured they should be in Canada by now.

A glance at the sun revealed they'd walked about four hours. How much farther? Surely Cooney's camp was over the next hill. A rumble in his stomach stopped him. They'd have to shoot game or satisfy their hunger with venison jerky. Again. Today's midday meal would look a lot like this morning's breakfast, which resembled last night's supper. It was only the promise of wealth, gold nuggets the size of his hat, that kept his boots slogging through half a foot of new-fallen snow, kept his body fighting through cold. What had he been thinking? Deciding to stray up into the mountains instead of going somewhere warm? He cursed yesterday's blinding snowstorm. Andy struggled to change his thinking. Grousing did nothing to warm him or feed his belly.

He peered ahead, eager to find the trail, any trail, any sign someone or something had been through there recently. Instead, he found no boot or hoof marks. No branches or twigs bent and broken.

Swallowing, he blinked, ran his gloved finger under his runny nose and then stopped. Behind him, boots pushed aside snow. There was comfort knowing O'Malley walked nearby.

"What say we stop?" Andy shrugged out of his backpack. "My stomach's pressing against my backbone."

O'Malley dropped his knapsack and sat on it. He blew out a frosty sigh. " 'Tis farther across this bloomin' mountain than we thought, eh, Andrew?"

"It's a piece, that's a fact." Andy uncorked his canteen, the sweet water swishing inside. He drank long.

O'Malley pulled out his canteen as well but stared into the forest. "This damn jumblegut lane is takin' us nowhere." He frowned at Andy. "It's sure ye are we're makin' our way toward Cooney?"

"Not for certain. But, hell, we've walked three days now. Can't be far." Andy pointed north and east, looked at the sky, studied the light filtering through the pine branches. He sighed. "I'll see if I can find something to eat."

"Ye do that, Andrew. But be sure it's an elephant ye bring. I'm peckish enough to eat one."

"I'll see what I can do." Andy checked his rifle. "But keep your grumblings in check. Might have to settle for rabbit." He took a long swallow from the canteen, recorked it and slung it over his shoulder.

"It'll be a roarin' fire and beans cookin' when ye return, lad." O'Malley groaned up to his feet. "Just don't be too long. I may eat the firewood."

Andy chuckled, turned and walked into the gloomy forest. He followed the trail for a quarter mile until it narrowed into nothing. He continued on, clambering over fallen tree trunks, pushing aside branches, plowing through shin-high snowdrifts. He stopped. Kneeling, he studied the leaves, the twigs, even the snow for any sign of passage. A bird—sounding not exactly like a bird—chirped. Another one answered, not far off.

Air caught in his lungs. Shivers ran down his back. Had to be Apaches. He was out here alone. He licked his dry lips.

Heart pounding, he gripped his rifle and inched around, scanning the forest as he turned. Something wasn't right. He felt it. No birds called to each other, leaves didn't rustle in the slight breeze, and he sure as hell couldn't see where he'd been. Too many trees and not enough light.

"Need to get back. Right now." Was he crazy? Talking out loud? No, he decided. He needed to hear a voice. Rifle gripped, he picked his way back, cautious step by cautious step. He hoped. Wind had blown snow over his boot prints, and he had to search to find his prints.

As he walked, he watched for signs of deer, elk or anything on four legs. Bent twigs, branches, droppings were sure indications, but he found nothing.

Movement to his left. There and gone. A flash more than definite movement. Deer? He froze, afraid to breathe. Peering into the forest, he spied only leaves falling. Was it his imagination? His eyes playing tricks? Heart thudding, he let out a quiet stream of air, then consciously willed his feet to move forward, each step growing easier, quicker back toward his partner.

How far had he traveled? Had to be close now. "O'Malley!" he shouted. The hell with silence. The hell with male bravado. He needed to hear his friend holler back.

Silence. Unnerving silence.

Then sudden rustling in the trees to his right, someone running, branches snapping. Andy turned in time to catch an Apache hurtling toward him. The Indian pounced on Andy, wrapping him in strong arms. Both men crashed to the ground, rolling over and over, crushing leaves and plowing through snow.

Andy muscled the Indian onto his back. With Andy on top, he pummeled the Apache's face, but the Indian bucked, toppling Andy, who fell free and fumbled for his revolver tucked in his waistband. Andy scrambled to his knees, pulled out the Colt, cocked it and fired.

Gripping his side, the Apache groaned, his agony filling the forest. Andy straightened his shoulders, refusing to consider his taking of a life. He rubbed the side of his head hoping to stop the ringing. His rifle. He'd dropped it during the attack.

A quick scan to his left. There! A few yards away, stuck halfway under a snow-laden branch brushing the ground. Sure more Indians lurked nearby, Andy dove for it, but before grabbing it, a second Apache kicked him. Andy's revolver flew out of his clutches. Moccasins crashed into his ribs, his back, his head. Andy fended off the blows with flailing arms that did little to stop the assault.

Andy rolled onto his back in time to see a foot thrust toward his chest. He grabbed the moccasin and pulled. The Indian thudded to the ground, his knee landing on Andy's chest. They fought until Andy scrambled to his feet. He grabbed the rifle and swung. It connected. The Apache grunted, then jerked the rifle away from Andy. Using the rifle as a ram, the Apache smashed it into Andy's stomach.

Before Andy regained his breath, the Apache dropped the rifle and thrust a hunting knife at Andy's face. Andy jumped aside, but fire raced across his upper arm. He kicked, connecting with the Apache's leg. From behind, whoops and hollers pierced the air. An arrow thwacked into the tree next to him.

He hollered again. "O'Malley!"

Apache taunts and cheers replied.

Andy turned, hoping to run into the forest and hide. Could he run far enough to find the miners' camp? Three long steps before a third Apache stepped in front of him, aimed a bow and released the string. The arrow imbedded itself into Andy's right shoulder. Blinding streaks of pain. Not sure if he was still standing or lying in the snow, he grabbed at the implanted arrow. The shaft stuck straight out.

Someone headbutted his lower back. He flew forward, slid on snow and plowed into a tree. Andy spiraled into the ground. Blurry images, black and white, now red, circled him. Moccasins plowed into his ribs, his face. He pushed up to his knees. Arm burning and shoulder throbbing, the pain exploded into excruciating.

Without a sound, the images all glanced to their right, froze, then vanished into the forest.

Andy's world turned dark. He dug at the arrow head, the shaft broken in his fall. But it held fast. Screaming. Someone screamed. Was it him? As he contemplated the noise, a black tunnel opened. He sank to the ground and pulled a foggy blanket over his freezing body.

CHAPTER FIVE

November 1863

Mesilla, New Mexico Territory

Sheriff Trace Colton sighed, craned his neck to peer down the dusty street, pulled out his pocket watch, flicked the top open and checked the time. An hour late. No surprise there. He returned to leaning against the wall waiting for the El Paso–Santa Fe Overland Express, the stageline that never ran on schedule. Trace tipped his hat to two women who walked in front of him as he lingered against the north-facing wall of Sam and Roy Bean's Saloon. From this vantage point, he had an easy view of the dirt plaza where most events were held. Fandangos, baptisms, quinceañeras, weddings, funerals and everything in between were celebrated in this square. He'd spent many a good time here and looked forward to many more.

Good times with his brother, James. And sister-in-law, Morningstar. If they ever got here. Trace pushed off from the building and paced. Up and down the thin boards, his boots thudding, kicking up puffs of dust. He pulled his coat tighter against the morning breeze. Although the sun did its darndest to heat up the town, the effort wasn't making much of a dent in the cold. Gloves would feel good, too, but he resisted the urge to pull them on.

As soon as James and Morningstar arrived, he'd take them back to his house, where Teresa and year-old daughter Faith were waiting breakfast. As late as it was, it would now become an early dinner. And if they didn't arrive soon, he'd have to return to the office, check in with his deputy, Sammy Estrada, and take care of business. And continue waiting.

Rattling of a springboard wagon turned his attention to the "Royal Road" running south from Santa Fe and passing on the east side of the plaza on its way to El Paso. The road was supposedly made by the Spaniard explorer Oñate. Trace chuckled. A dirt trail through the desert, with snakes on one side and Apaches on the other, had nothing to do with being "royal." But, it connected Mexico City with Santa Fe, and people still used it. They could call it whatever they wanted as long as that damned stagecoach got here.

He pulled out his pocket watch again. The hands hadn't moved. He shoved it back into his vest and paced from Sam's Saloon down the boardwalk past a small mercantile specializing in Mexican produce. Next to it stood a recently-opened dram shop rivaling Sam's place. Last store at the end was the newspaper office. Trace sighed to a stop in front. The usual citizens were already out and about, bundled against the cold, scurrying from church to store to home. Horses clip-clopped, and wagons, loaded with assorted goods, jangled as they rolled by.

Trace snorted into his mustache and turned. He startled at the man standing within a foot of him.

The Mesilla Times editor, Tommy Littleton, frowned. "Wearing a hole in our boardwalk, Sheriff." One side of his mouth curved up. "Better slow down. This town sure as hell can't afford a new one."

Trace hid a grin behind clearing his throat. While Thomas Littleton was grumpy and snappish at times, he was also a good friend to the Colton brothers. "What're you doing out this early, Tommy? Figured you for operating on bankers' hours."

"I do. But people have a damnable habit of wanting their paper on time." He cocked his head toward his office. "Those no-good inkers don't have the common sense to start 'fore the sun comes up. I gotta give 'em a nudge or two to get 'em going."

"I guess the weary never rests, eh, Tommy?" Trace reached for his watch but stopped. *That damned stage will arrive when it damn well pleases.* Maybe he should go back to the office and do something useful. He'd know when the stage arrived. Such a fanfare—the squeaking of brakes, the driver yelling to the stock, people on the boardwalk waving and calling out to the passengers—general mayhem. Always a time of high spirits.

"You gonna stand out here all day checkin' your watch, wearin' out our walk," Littleton said, "or you gonna tell me what the hell you're doin' out here?"

"Thought you knew." A familiar flutter of excitement exploded in Trace's chest. He'd missed his brother, even though there had been terse words exchanged before James and Morningstar had boarded that east-bound stage bound for Kansas. "James comes back today. Any minute now."

"He's bringing that sweet wife of his, isn't he?"

"Both coming, as far as I know. Teresa's counting on it." Trace peered around an overloaded wagon navigating the dusty street. No stagecoach hiding behind it. "Got a letter last week."

Littleton pulled the pencil from behind his ear and fished out a small notebook from his vest pocket. He scribbled as he spoke. "So, you're back on speakin' terms with him, I take it? I'm surprised he's settin' foot in town. He's about as welcome as a tax collector."

"Now wait a minute, Tommy." Trace worked to keep his temper in check. "After the riot he . . . started, he did his time in jail. *My* jail." He faced the editor. "And that was damn hard to do. Lock him up."

"Didn't appear so at the time."

Pulling in air and straightening his shoulders, Trace had to agree. He'd been more than angry at James, but the army had pulled out of town, rescinded martial law and the citizens now had food—what was left that the soldiers didn't take. James had been right. The army had no business in town. Trace saw it now.

Trace glared at Littleton. "I'm not—"

"Whoa, now." Littleton raised his hand, pencil between his fingers. "Didn't mean an insult by it. Just saying what I hear." He used the pencil to point west. "What say I buy you a cup of coffee while we wait? I've missed your brother, too."

Anger popping like a cheap balloon, Trace nodded. "Might as well. Let's stop by the post office on the way. Haven't heard from Andy for a while."

The men sauntered across the frosty plaza dirt, sprigs of dried grass breaking under their boots. Trace held the post office door for Littleton.

"No mail, today, gentlemen," the postman said. He turned his palms up and shrugged. "Don't know what the matter is. Nothing's come in for days now. Especially mail from up north, around Santa Rita."

A cold knot slammed into Trace's chest. He blinked at Littleton, who frowned. "Ain't that where Andy went?" Littleton pointed over his shoulder. "Up in those mountains?"

Trace nodded, words refusing to form. Maybe it was nothing. But he'd heard too many stories of Apaches attacking settlements. Was that what had happened?

"Lost a peck o' color there." Littleton nodded at Trace's face and touched his shoulder. "I'm sure he's fine. You Colton boys have the damnedest knack for finding trouble, then finding a way out."

The postal clerk offered a shrug. "Some times the mail's late 'cause of flooding or a broken wagon." He turned his back, speaking over his shoulder. "Happens a lot."

Littleton opened the door and stepped outside. "He's right. Probably come clattering in later today."

Trace mumbled thanks to the man, then followed the newspaper editor into the cold air. At least by now the sun was making a slight improvement on the temperature. Trace no longer saw his breath as he spoke.

The men took a table at Maria's Café, just off the plaza. From there, Trace could meet the stage within a minute or two if and when it showed up. Littleton and Trace sipped coffee passing a half hour in pleasant conversation. Trace enjoyed chatting with his friend, who had endless stories. As Trace finished his second cup, the unmistakable sounds of squeaking wheels, horses trotting and driver hollering signaled a stagecoach's arrival. Finally!

Trace flipped two coins onto the table, tugged down his hat and sprinted out of the café. Littleton ran to keep up.

Across the plaza sat the Santa Fe Lines stagecoach, its passengers climbing out of the dusty coach. The driver scrambled up top to toss down luggage. Trace hurried behind the stage, came around, and spotted his brother and sister-in-law standing on the boardwalk. Morningstar straightened her hat and brushed her skirt, while James ran his hand over his face and spit into the dirt.

Trace didn't try to hide the grin he knew stretched wide, the famous Colton family smile. Damn, it was good seeing his brother again. They'd always been close, but, despite the latest set to, other events of the past few years sealed a bond he knew could never be broken.

James turned at the tap on his shoulder. Trace pulled him into a bear hug, then released him. A hug to Morningstar proved just as pleasant. Would they stay here in Mesilla or move on? Trace had considered it often but hadn't come to a conclusion. Not that James always did what Trace suggested, but surely at some point, they'd discuss it.

"Damn fine having you back, little brother." Trace refrained from giving another hug and instead shook hands with James. "And Morningstar. Looks like Kansas agreed with you!"

"Things got quieter'n a hole in the ground with you both gone." Littleton shook hands with James and tipped his hat to Morningstar. "Hell, it's been as peaceful as a church. In fact, I had to change my daily paper to a weekly—just 'cause you were out of town. But that'll change directly, I reckon."

James raised both eyebrows. "Missed me, did ya?"

Trace crossed his long legs and then uncrossed them. He sat forward and then back. The sofa cushion under his rear had turned into a brick, and the coffee cup Teresa had insisted on using today . . . well, his finger got stuck in the tiny handle twice. Teresa and Morningstar were busy sharing gossip and news, playing with baby Faith, while he and James sat across from them on the living room sofa, unable to add much to the ladies' conversation. He'd given up asking questions or interjecting news. He'd let the women talk. Besides, there was no way to stop them.

Trace regarded the cup in his hand. Done with trying to jerk his thick finger out of the handle, he resorted to holding it with two fingers, his pinky up in the air like an east coast sissy. Little pink roses paraded around the cup's sides and all around the saucer. A saucer? Good grief, give him a bigger mug without a saucer. Pinky down, he wedged a finger into the handle, hoping not to slosh the contents down his shirt again. He finished off the coffee, glad to be done.

James glanced at his cup perched on a side table, then met Trace's gaze. The brothers gave a furtive nod to each other, and then, like they'd planned it, both stretched and stood. James stretched again.

"Sorry, ladies." Trace rubbed his lower back. "Need to check in at the office. Besides, Mesilla can't possibly run without me."

Before the women protested, James grabbed his coat from a chair. "I'll get us a room at the Casino Hotel and then help big brother here." James thumped Trace's shoulder. "Don't know how you got along all these months without me."

"It was a struggle." Trace shrugged into his coat, bent down and kissed Teresa, swept Faith into his arms, set her down. "Got enough wood for the stove?"

Teresa rose from the rocking chair and gave Trace a second kiss.

Somewhat embarrassed by the affection, Trace muttered, "We'll be back before dark."

"Morningstar wants a warm bath, and we'll do that here," Teresa said. "No need to use the bath house in town." She turned her warm eyes on James. "Any time you want to wash off that trail dust, you're welcome to here."

"Is that a hint?" James leaned down and kissed Morningstar's cheek. "I'll be back after a while."

"Take your time." Holding James's extended hand, Morningstar stood from the other rocker a little slower than usual, her dark eyes trailing over the toddler. "Maybe you should check on a room at the boarding house too."

"That mean you'll be staying for a while?" Teresa picked up the baby.

Like a wool blanket, pressing silence settled over the room. James glanced at Trace and then his wife. Trace cocked his head at James while Teresa jogged Faith on her hip.

Morningstar shrugged.

James's gaze traveled the room landing on Teresa. "Not sure yet. Mister Bergstrom's offered me my old job back, but I'm not sure we're staying."

Morningstar's mouth curved up at one end. "I'm thinking of

going to medical school. In California." She turned to James. "I'd like to apply, but James isn't sure."

The regulator on the wall banged twice. Silence again strained conversation until Teresa stepped in. "That's exciting news, but, staying or no, Star would still enjoy a warm bath." She pointed her chin toward the door. "Give us a couple of hours."

Morningstar nodded. "Soon as Faith is down for her nap, and I'm clean again, I'll help Teresa with supper." She smiled. "Might even get to spend some time with the baby."

Had to be hard, Trace thought. According to Teresa, Morningstar wanted nothing more than to be a mother. But something was wrong. James and Star had been married well over a year, and all James had ever said, after much coaxing and three beers, was he still couldn't be the man, the lover, he wanted to be. Those damn Apaches. While Trace and James had spent two months as captives, James got worse treatment and remained in camp two weeks longer than Trace. It had taken a couple of years for Trace to recover, mentally and emotionally. But James? Physically healed, emotionally broken.

Maybe things had changed for James while they were in Kansas. Trace would wheedle it out of his brother eventually. But not today. Today they'd relax.

Following James, Trace stepped into the chilly afternoon air, shut the door behind them and sighed. "Time for some quiet, eh? My ears are ringing."

"What?" James cupped his ear. "Can't hear you. It's too quiet." He wagged his head and strolled toward the plaza.

The Casino Hotel, directly behind the old Butterfield stage offices south of the plaza, contained eight guest rooms, along with a billiards room and dram shop.

"Might get loud tonight," Trace told James as they pushed open the door. "The Corn Exchange might be better. Quieter." But he knew it wasn't. The Casino was the fanciest hotel in town and, as a lawman, it met with his approval. He hadn't broken up any fights in here, no drunken cowboys slamming each other with pool sticks. No complaints of thievery or misconduct by the patrons. A quiet place—after the dram shop closed at midnight.

"As tired as I am, I'll sleep through anything." James handed the clerk two dollars. "And I know Star's exhausted."

"Room eight," the clerk said as he handed James the key. "Last available room, sir. You were fortunate to check in when you did."

"Guess I'm lucky," James said with a hint of sarcasm only Trace could pick up.

The brothers wandered down a narrow hall and located the room. What Trace had heard about the accommodations was right. Flowered wallpaper offered comfort and relaxation. Trace sat heavily on the wool-stuffed mattress, springing up and down. He grinned. "This's better'n my bed. Maybe I'll move in here with you." Trace lay back on it, fingers interlaced under his head.

"Not a chance," James said. "I plan to be sleeping with my wife in here, not my brother." He glanced at the washstand against the far wall. "This'll do for a couple days." James snapped his fingers and pointed to the door. "Get up. Go."

"No need for being rude. It was just a suggestion." Why had his brother turned cold, almost mean, and so suddenly? Tired. Of course. Both James and Star must be exhausted, traveling day and night from Kansas. Trace knew to choose his words carefully. Occasionally, James exploded, even if not provoked. A result from his captivity days.

Out in the hall while James locked the door, Trace offered a distraction. "What say I buy you a beer? Over at Sam's?" He slid an arm around his brother's tense shoulder. "Supper won't be ready for a while yet."

45

"Thought you had to get back to work." James shrugged off the arm. Without waiting for a response, he marched through the hotel lobby and out into the street; Trace hastened to catch up.

Cold. It was damn cold out here. Almost as cold as his brother's disposition. A beer would certainly warm them both. "Listen, James. Sammy's got things under control. Let's go get that beer." He cocked his head toward Sam Bean's Saloon. "Besides, he knows where to find me."

James slapped his brother on the back. "Hell, why not? Sammy's the best deputy you've ever had, right? Only one you need. Right? Stinkin' Town Council's first choice."

Tugging on James's arm, the brothers skidded to a stop in front of the saloon. Trace jerked his brother around until they stood nearly nose to nose. "What the hell's eating you? First, you're rude to Littleton, snap at me, and now this? Figured you'd be glad to be back."

"Glad? Glad?" James's words escalated. "Christ, Trace. Don't you remember? Hell, I spent two lousy months in *your* jail! Then I got run out of this damn town. You can't expect the good citizens of this hellhole to welcome me back. Not ever. I'm waiting for the first one to spit at me, like before. To push me off the street, like—"

"It's different now."

"Is it?"

Trace's shoulders rose and fell. He gazed right and then left. What could he say, do, to explain the fighting was over. Especially between them?

James lowered his voice to a harsh whisper. "Only reason we're here is Star. She missed you and Teresa, especially. And Faith . . . well, you know how she loves babies." His gaze fell to the ground. His silence lingered. "Truthfully, I've missed you, too." He turned one hand palm up. "But we can't stay."

There was much truth in James's words. Trace wanted his brother to be wrong, dead wrong. But he was right. Most people were glad when James left, run out like a common rabble rouser. And he was. But that was in the past. Everyone had learned from mistakes. Trace would work hard to ensure the townspeople knew James had changed. He wasn't the crazy troublemaker from months' past. It would start with a beer.

Trace pointed to the sign. "Sam's hasn't changed. I'd still like to buy you a beer."

His brother's eyes flicked to the sign, then down the street.

"All right." One corner of James's mouth rose, most of it hidden under a sparse mustache. "I haven't had a good beer in a long time. Pa doesn't drink any more, so it was up to me and Luke to support the taverns."

"And did you?" Trace opened the door to Sam's Saloon, James on his heels.

"Let's just say they're all thriving."

Blue smoke lowered the ceiling and swirled around Trace's head as he peered into the dim room. Odors of whiskey and tobacco mingling with stale beer assaulted his nose as he made his way to the one empty table back in the corner. Using thumb and forefinger, he rubbed his stinging eyes, which threatened tears.

He blinked, swiped at a drop on his cheek and then settled into the hard chair. Trace ordered two beers. The brothers swapped stories, catching up on the past several months. Trace drained the last vestiges of beer, then pushed back. "Another one?"

"You buying?"

Trace shrugged.

James fished coins from his pocket. "Since I'm buyin', I want mine *extra* cold."

Trace took the money along with the two glasses and

threaded his way to the bar. Waiting for the barkeep to refill the glasses, he leaned against the counter surveying the room, wondering if any of the men would start a fight. He hoped not. And especially not James.

"Here you go, Sheriff." The bartender pushed two filled mugs toward him.

Before he returned to the table, a boy, one Trace had seen around town, peeked into the saloon, then made his way over to Trace's table. He held out two envelopes.

"Mister Ramos said to bring these to you, Sheriff. Right away. He said you'd want them."

A quick scan of the return address read *Andy*. Youngest brother of the four "Colton boys," as they were known around Lawrence. Trace sat as he nodded to James. "From Andy." He looked at the youngster, back to James, back to the boy and then to James. "Well, pay the man, James."

Tossing a frown toward his brother, James dug into his pocket, produced two pennies and then handed them over. The boy's eyes grew wide. "Thanks, mister."

Trace didn't watch him leave, more interested in the letters from Andy. He handed one to James, who tore open the end. Trace opened his and scanned the familiar handwriting. James moved his lips as he read.

The message was two paragraphs, Trace noted. He read a second time, then glanced over at James. "He's coming back."

"He's staying there," James said.

"What?" Both said in unison.

"No, he's staying up there. Going over to Cooney's camp, by Silver Creek." James pointed to the writing. "It says right here."

"He's coming back, he says." Trace leaned over and looked at the other letter. "I'll be damned." He frowned. "What's the date on yours?"

"Almost three weeks ago."

"Mine's four." Trace blew out a sigh. "Guess he's staying."

James played with his untouched beer glass. "That's too bad. I was hoping to see him before—"

"Ah, hell, James. That little brother of yours will show up one of these days, gold nuggets in his pockets, gold toothpick in his mouth. He'll be so damn rich he won't even speak to us." Trace nodded toward the beer. "Drink up. We should be getting back; it's almost dark."

"Dark? Already? Sure as hell don't wanna be late for supper." One corner of James's mouth turned up. "Ma packed us some sandwiches, but they ran out the second day. And you remember the food at the way stations." He grimaced. "Don't think I'll ever get filled up again."

"Know the feeling." Trace leaned back, stretched, then pushed up to his feet. Taller than most men, such an advantage came in handy when breaking up fights or settling quarrels peacefully. All four brothers were tall and about equal height. Andy might have half an inch on the others, but they all had Pa's contagious wide smile.

Trace and James threaded their way through the men and few women gathered around tables and people elbow to elbow at the bar. Swinging the door open, both men shivered in the cold breeze. They buttoned their coats and flipped up the collars. Shoving hands into pockets, the brothers headed for home.

"Trace, there you are!"

Both Coltons whirled around at the shout several yards behind them. They waited for the man sporting a long coat and shiny badge to catch up.

"What's wrong, Sammy?" Trace studied the shadowed face of his deputy.

"Knew you'd both want to hear right away." Sammy Estrada glanced at James and nodded. Taking a deep breath, he swung his gaze back to Trace. "Just got word the Apaches raided that little mining camp up in the Mogollon Mountains. Birchville."

Fighting to make sense of the news, Trace focused on the panicked face of his younger brother. "Good Lord." He ran his hand over his mouth. "Survivors?"

Sammy wagged his head. "Some. Not sure how many. Sorry to have to tell you. I know that's where your brother was last you heard."

James furrowed his forehead. "Dead? How can Andy be dead?" He clutched Trace's coat sleeve. "Hell, he's just a kid."

Trace stared into darkness.

"One more thing." Sammy looked over his shoulder toward the jail and hesitated. "There's talk the Apaches are heading north, toward Cooney's camp."

"Ah, hell!" James whipped off his hat, ran his hand through his hair. "That's where Andy was heading."

Sammy let out a long sigh. "I'm sorry. You going tonight or waiting 'til morning?"

"Morning," Trace said. "We'll pack, get our gear and supplies ready tonight, head out at first light." He turned to Sammy. "Mind things while I'm gone."

"You bet. Want me to hire an extra deputy?"

Trace nodded.

Sammy patted Trace on the upper arm. "Andy'll be all right. You gotta believe."

"Let's go, James." Trace took two long steps then turned around to his deputy. "I'll be back soon as I can. Check in on Teresa and Faith for me. Morningstar's there, too. Make sure they're all right."

"You got it," Sammy said.

Trace loped toward home, James at his side.

CHAPTER SIX

"Andrew, it's breath rattlin' in yer body, it 'tis." O'Malley's words spiraled around Andy's head.

From out of the gray mist, which had cocooned him, Andy surfaced into the world of the living, the hurting world. Tendrils wrapped around him, encouraging his eyes open, thrusting him into consciousness.

White light. Screaming, blinding white light pierced his eyes. Squeezing them shut offered no refuge. The brightness sunk into his stomach, mixing, stirring, churning. He curled into a question mark while any semblance of food surged into his throat, then out into the world.

Andy coughed, rolled up and onto his knees. Forehead against the ground, spasms continued long after the last strands of bile-encrusted jerky ribboned the snow. Sweat pasted his shirt to his back, his pants to his legs. Heat spread across his neck. He trembled.

What could have been hours passed before the spasms stopped, before he could sit back on his knees and open his eyes. When he did, he found a world not too much older than before the attack. Before he'd been shot, before he'd killed the Indian. The man lying under a bush. Andy closed his eyes and offered a short prayer for the life he'd taken. It was only fitting, and what Ma and Pa would have expected.

As if still in the other world of the welcoming mist, Andy took his time examining the arrow stuck through his coat and into his shoulder. Part of the shaft had broken off, what remained now about the length of his thumb. No telling how much arrow tip was jammed into his flesh and muscle. If the front of his shirt was any indication, he'd lost a lot of blood. Streams of it had run down his shirt, caked on his coat. But, oddly, his shoulder didn't hurt.

"Get up, Andrew. 'Tis time to go. Find help."

"Pull it out, O'Malley." Andy raised his eyes to his friend, his partner standing over him. "Get that arrow outta there."

"I canna do it, ol' friend. It's sorry I am." O'Malley pointed over his shoulder. "Down near Cooney's is a cabin. Less'n a mile away. Someone there can help."

It didn't make sense. Nothing made sense right now. Andy draped his good arm over his eyes. The sun was too much. The world too much. He considered. How could O'Malley know there was a cabin? And why wouldn't he help yank the arrow out? Andy's shoulder came to life. Gentle throbbing awakened the nerves. Sharper now. Pulsating pain roared down his right arm. His hand burned.

Get up. Find help. Andy repeated the mantra over and over until he said it aloud. Tired. So tired. He struggled to his feet, blurry trees pulling themselves into focus. To his right lay the Indian, lifeless as before. To his left, nothing but trees, bushes and snow. Where was O'Malley? Hadn't he been right here? Right beside him?

Andy stumbled in circles until his stomach threatened to bring up whatever remained. "O'Malley?" His word croaked over his dry throat. He tried again, louder this time. "O'Malley?"

Must have gone back to camp. Get the horses. How far away? Could he make it?

Wind stirred the branches, whipping up light snow at his feet. It swirled around his boots. He shivered. Despite the warmth his coat provided, freezing jolts wracked his body. *Move,* he told himself. *One foot in front of the other.* Like that. A step toward Cooney's camp. O'Malley will bring the horses and catch up. Another step.

Could there really be a cabin? Only a mile away? Andy rolled O'Malley's words around in his mind. Yet, nothing made sense. Questions refused answers. Shadows lengthened. He willed his legs to hold him upright. As he pushed, he hummed a song Ma sang when she lived in Ireland as a young girl.

"So fittin' today, it 'tis, Andrew." O'Malley traipsed beside Andy who jumped at his partner's words. O'Malley continued. "When I was a wee lad, me own máthair sang that song, she did." He sighed, his mouth rising in a soft grin. "I hope to be seein' her soon, I do."

Andy regarded his partner. "You planning on going back to Ireland?"

"Some day, Andrew. Maybe some day soon."

Wasn't his ma dead? Several years back? Andy opened his mouth, but the gray haze threatened his sanity. With no answers he understood, Andy pushed it away and plunged through the snow. "Where've you been? You all right?" A longer look behind him. No horses. "Didn't get—?"

"Indians took 'em, I'm afraid." O'Malley shrugged. "We'll have to use our own hooves."

If he didn't get to a cabin, or help by nightfall, Andy knew he'd die. His family would never know what happened to him. They'd spend their lives wondering where he'd disappeared. He couldn't do that to them. He couldn't. *One foot in front of the other.*

Dull, lifeless colors filled the heavens. Thin, gold clouds striped the sky across the western horizon, promising a sunset worth remembering. Andy didn't care. One more hill, then he should be in sight of Cooney's. Or somebody. What if it was Indians? More Apaches to capture him, torture him like they had his brothers. Apaches who would roast him alive. Turn his life into a living hell.

He shook. Tears clouded the top of the hill. He wiped them away, sniffed and struggled farther. Another step, the last one he knew he could take, put him up among trees and bushes and deeper snow. But below, far below, smoke—wisps of chalky black spiraled toward the sky. Andy squinted. He rubbed his eyes and again squinted. A cabin, yellow light through the single window pane, stood like a beacon. He was safe now. He'd live. He and O'Malley.

Snow mounding well past the tops of his boots, Andy wound around trees. Without much caution, he descended the hill. He slid twice, plowed into a boulder. Silver stars danced before him. A lusty snowflake glided inches from his face.

"Almost there, we are." O'Malley's words filled Andy's ears. "Few more steps."

CHAPTER SEVEN

Damn horse, James thought. Damn, slow horse. She refused to gallop anymore, no matter how often or hard he spurred her. Even now, her trotting was slow going. The hills he navigated, their spruce trees hiding deer and Indians, tired his horse more than he liked. The two of them, Trace and him, had ridden like the devil was on their tails. James had taken little notice of his surroundings as he charged by. Mile by mile, sandy mesas, cactus and mesquite transformed into low hills, then steeper hills dotted with stands of ash and juniper. Hawks swirled overhead while woodpeckers knocked out a meal.

At least he was faster than Trace. James glanced over his shoulder, his brother slumped in his saddle. Two days of hard riding, over a hundred miles, and two days thinking of Star's concerned good-bye, proved hard on man and beast. Yet, there wasn't time to rest, stop and eat, water the horses. Andy was out there in the forest somewhere. Somewhere all alone.

James knew that feeling and knew it well. Memories of months spent in Cochise's camp pressed on his heart. The moment Trace had left sat on his chest like a boulder. At Cochise's insistence, Trace was ordered to insist the army retreat and release Cochise's brother. James had never known being truly alone before, and the fear circled him like a horrifying dark hole, ready to suck him back in. James swore Andy would never know such kind of terror. Ever.

"Santa Rita's not far, James." Trace hollered against the icy wind. "Gotta stop there tonight. Horses are worn out."

A shake of his head was all James would give his brother. Was he crazy? They couldn't stop now. Not this close to Birchville, half a day's ride away. From there, they'd have to ask directions to Cooney's Camp, but if they rode hard all night, by sunrise, they should have Andy in their grasp.

Then he would be safe.

The closer to town they rode, the more people they met riding toward them. Families with wagons packed, trudged up one hill and down the next. Single men, walking, riding, their saddlebags full, flicked warning frowns at the Coltons.

One man held up a hand and stepped into James's path. As much as he hated to stop, James pulled back on his reins.

"You don't wanna be goin' that way, fella." He jerked a gloved thumb over his shoulder. "Best turn right around and hightail it outta here, fast as you can."

Trace leaned down closer to the man's bearded face. "Indians?"

"Cochise. Victorio," the man said. "Bad hombres."

"Cochise?" A cold knot in James's throat pushed out the word. Rawhide string cut into his wrists. His back throbbed from the beatings. His eyes narrowed, his jaw clenched. No. No more memories.

"That Apache leader's nobody to fool with," Trace said. He pointed to James. "We've had enough experience with that man to last a lifetime. Almost cost us our lives."

"Yeah. Nobody to mess with." The man adjusted the pack on his back.

Studying the man's weathered face, James detected fear with a tinge of defeat. He had to know. "How's Santa Rita? Anybody still there?"

"Not the smart ones." The man again shifted the pack on his shoulders and put one foot in front of the other. "Better git 'fore that crazy man killer comes after your hair."

James held his brother's gaze. "Can't. Gotta find our brother first."

Shrugs and grunts trailed behind the man as he marched south. "Suit yourself. Your funeral."

More wagons and people in the distance. Some running, most at a good clip.

Throat like desert sand, James pushed down panic before speaking. "Can't think of another way to go. Got mountains on both sides, Indians in between." He uncorked his canteen and handed it to Trace, who swigged then passed it back.

Trace reset his hat, shifted in his saddle. "I want you to turn back. I mean, no need three brothers dying."

"What?" James couldn't believe his brother had even considered such a crazy notion. But there were the words he'd thought himself earlier, spread out like a splayed hand of cards. No way in hell he'd turn his back on Andy. What the hell was Trace thinking? To save Ma and Pa the agony of losing three-fourths of their sons? To save Morningstar and Teresa the pain of burying their men? Of toddler Faith growing up without a pa? James pulled his hat lower on his forehead. "If anybody goes back, it oughta be you. You should live. Hell, you got a job, wife, child and a town depending on you."

Trace blew a stream of frost. "Not without Andy." He set his heels into the sides of his horse.

At least if he died, James thought, he wouldn't leave behind any children. What he had left behind, however, was a wife who wanted what he couldn't provide. Although they hadn't cut him, not like he'd seen happen to other captives, Cochise and his torturous henchmen had emotionally damaged him. James couldn't decide whether to hate Cochise or himself. Sometimes he hated both.

They rode into town under a late afternoon sky turning

snowy. Santa Rita didn't look the worse for wear. No black smoke roiling from Apache attacks. No people screaming and running for their lives. No Indians whooping and hollering up and down the streets. In fact, it was quiet. Too damn quiet.

"We're stopping here tonight." Trace pulled back on the reins allowing his mount to walk. "We'll kill these horses if we keep going."

"Dammit!" James said. "We can get fresh ones here and go on."

"Not tonight." Trace glared at James. "We're both exhausted and hungry. Won't do any good riding in the dark. Use your head. We gotta stop. Here. Now."

James and Trace rode down the center of town and pulled up in front of the Glory Hole Hotel. After dismounting, the men entered the lobby expecting to find people hurriedly packing and scurrying about. As they'd found outside, it was empty.

Trace dinged the bell on the counter waiting for a harried man to come barreling in ready to assign them a room. They waited. Nobody. Trace dinged a second time. Again, nobody.

"Hello? Anybody here?" Trace leaned over the counter then wandered the lobby. James paced the other way.

Empty. Deserted.

James leaned on the counter noting the room keys lying helter skelter on top. "This don't feel right. Us being in here, warm, Andy out there. The man's right. We gotta get the hell outta town. Grab fresh horses and just keep riding."

Trace grabbed James's coat sleeve. "Stop. Just leave it be. We're staying here tonight then leave at first light." He narrowed his eyes. "That's final."

James hated when his brother's words rang cold . . . and right. He wrenched out of the grip, marched end to end of the lobby, breathing deeply as he paced. He struggled to control his feelings. Not doing that had gotten him into trouble plenty other times.

"Think he's already captured?" Had he said it aloud? Apaches. Icy cold leather wrapped around his throat, strangling him as it dried. Drums pounded in rhythm to his beating heart. Chanting Indians circled his body, snared against a saguaro cactus. No. Not again. James fought back into reality. *Not again.* Damn those images. No longer would he allow his memories to overwhelm him, to push him, to cloud what judgment he had left.

He rubbed his eyes, as if rubbing away the past. Two deep breaths, and he opened them. He jumped at Trace's face inches away.

"You all right?"

James blew out a long stream of air and nodded.

Trace gripped James's shoulder, giving it a slight rock. "It's a helluva thing."

Of all the people in the world, in his life, James knew the only man who truly understood what he was enduring was his brother.

Trace glanced around the lobby, then swiped his gloved hand across his face. "Feel kinda like a sitting duck in here. But it's a helluva lot warmer than outside."

"Let's get a room on the bottom floor. Be easier to jump out the window if we have to," James said.

"How about room three?" Trace held up a key.

CHAPTER EIGHT

November, 1863
Lawrence, Kansas

Luke Colton gave a final squeeze to two-year-old Adam, wrapped in his arms. "Be a good boy for Mama."

"Yes, sir." Adam's words lisped, but Luke knew what his son had whispered.

One more hug, then Luke handed him to Ma standing on the boardwalk. Were those tears in her eyes? Torn. He was so torn about traveling to Mesilla. Here he was, the last of the four brothers to leave. Ma and Pa needed him. And hell, he had his own family, all right here in Lawrence. However, he needed to see his brothers. Have long talks with them. Get the hell out of Kansas. But for how long?

It all depended on Sally. Would she find room in her heart to forgive him? The lying about not riding with Quantrill when, in fact, he'd ridden alongside the feared Confederate Raider for months. Hell, he'd been one of the leading henchmen. The deceit. All of that was bad enough, but thankfully, she didn't know about his passes at James's wife. Morningstar needed a man, a whole man, and if she hadn't been married to his brother . . .

But at present, not only was it darn cold outside, it was downright frigid in his house. Only the children were glad to be around him.

After the burning of Lawrence in August, Luke vowed to

change his thinking. To amend his rowdy ways. He would become the man he should have been and make his family proud. Especially Ma and Sally. What about Pa? Even rebuilding their house together hadn't shored up the shaky relationship.

So, he needed his brothers' advice. Their words of wisdom.

"All aboard!" The stagecoach driver hollered at the people gathered on the boardwalk. He leaned over from his perch on the seat and pointed to Luke's tapestry carpetbag. "If that's goin', toss 'er on up here."

Luke hollered at the driver. "I'm keeping it with me."

Luke's Pa picked up the bag and handed it to him. Their eyes met. "Have a good trip, son." He extended a hand.

Pa's grip was firm. Luke pulled his coat tight around his chest and buttoned the top. Even with little Adam in her arms, Ma hugged Luke as hard as when he was a child and had picked wildflowers for her.

"Take good care of yourself," Ma whispered. "You have your sandwiches?"

Luke nodded.

A tear strayed down Ma's cheek. "Give everyone a big hug and kiss for us. Tell them we'll see them all soon. And we love them."

Nodding, Luke turned his attention to beautiful Sally, baby Hannah in her arms. He loved his wife now more than ever, but probably it was too late. She'd been the one to encourage—no, insist—he visit his brothers. He wanted to hold her one more time. Tell her how sorry he was—again—but she kept her distance. An icy distance. Luke leaned in close and kissed his daughter's cheek. At almost one, she sure looked like her ma. Blue-green eyes, blond hair.

"Gotta go!" the driver bellowed down at Luke.

This was it. What he'd lost sleep over for the last several

nights. His gaze traveled from face to face, then he stepped up into the coach. It rocked with his weight. Three other passengers, two men and one woman, scooted their feet for him to step over. The door banged shut. His heart rose into his throat.

A "Step up now," a hearty lurch, and they were off. Luke leaned out the window and waved until the coach turned the corner. His family grew into dots then faded into memory as he rode away.

Dusty prairie miles were swallowed under the stagecoach wheels while Luke thought. The past two days had given him plenty of time to consider his life and his brothers. He couldn't wait to see Trace and Andy. They hadn't been able to come to Lawrence this past summer with James and Morningstar. Trace was sheriff of Mesilla and Andy about to become deputy since he'd turned eighteen this month. Powerful jobs. Had it gone to their heads? Were they swaggering around town showing off their badges and harassing people? No, not his brothers. No doubt they were busy fixing a broken wheel or helping old ladies across the plaza.

He squirmed on the hard wooden seat. Stagecoaches were efficient forms of transportation, some even called them "luxurious," but after riding in one for a day or two, they sure challenged a man's sanity. Being cooped in a wooden cage with strangers, knees dovetailed with his or knees in his back from the passengers behind him, tested his patience.

The last stop had been to change teams and take a quick stretch. No food at the way station, but the driver had promised grub within a couple of hours. Luke's stomach grumbled at the thought of Ma's delicious sandwiches, long gone. Since daylight faded early this time of year, they'd stop soon in Council Grove at a home station that provided a home-cooked meal. If yesterday's food was typical, the fare would be onions, venison stew, biscuits and coffee. Strong coffee.

He looked forward to stopping, even though everyone would sleep there. Something about lying in a room full of strangers set him on edge; still he couldn't complain too much. For a dollar, in addition to the fare, he received food and a cot. Not a bad deal.

Luke stared out the window, watching rolling hills dotted with patches of snow. Soon, as the temperature dipped, they'd have to roll down the canvas curtains blocking out the cold, which also blocked out the light. But, for now, he took in everything he could—tall prairie grass, forests in the distance, streams meandering through the hills.

What he spotted chilled him worse than the snow. Just ahead to the left, a dozen Indians, mounted on pintos, sat motionless. Close enough to notice their hands gripping lances, feathers adorning the tops, Luke reached for his .44 Walker-Colt in the bag at his feet. Hoping he wouldn't have to use it, he knew he could—and would—if necessary.

"Whoa, boys!" The driver shouted to the team, and Luke stuck his head out the window for a better look. The stagecoach slid to a smooth stop.

Luke turned to the other passengers. "Looks like some Indians are wanting to talk, is all." He regarded the woman next to him, her eyes wide, hands clutched to her chest. She had more to lose than he did if those Indians attacked. Luke dug around in his carpetbag and extracted a loaded gun. He shoved it into his waistband beneath his vest.

"Should we get out and help?" One of the passengers, a scrawny man with an umbrella mustache and bowler hat, produced a pocket pistol. The single shot could kill at close range but was useless at distances.

"Not yet," Luke said. "We'll know soon enough."

The driver leaned down, speaking to an Indian who had ridden up to the coach. Luke strained to hear the conversation.

"Allegawaho," the driver said. "Good to see you again. You look well."

The man, obviously the leader, nodded. He grunted at the driver, shook his lance back toward his men, then thumped his own chest, turned back to the driver and pointed toward Council Grove.

The driver pointed also. "Got some dresses for your wives, food for your men. Up ahead."

"No." The Indian shook the lance harder. "Now."

Surprised at his English, Luke wondered how much the Indian knew. But were they demanding food and clothing? Sure looked that way.

"We're stopping later," the driver said. "Follow us, and you'll get it."

"Now." The leader raised his lance. Before Luke could suck in a lungful of air, the other Indians surrounded the coach. One yanked the door open, grabbed Luke's arm and pulled him out. Next out was the woman, who stood shoulder to shoulder with Luke. He slid his arm around her.

The other passengers followed. Lined up against the coach, Luke felt the gun warm against his side. Choosing not to draw right now and possibly get everyone killed, he waited with the rest. Watched and waited. Luke struggled to understand what was being said between the driver and the leader. He caught a couple words, but together they didn't make sense.

"I know him." The slim passenger stepped out of line and pointed. "That's Allegawaho, leader of the Kaws. I've dealt with him before." He turned to Luke. "He won't hurt us. Their tribe is hungry, is all."

No guarantees, thought Luke. But he knew about the Kaw tribe and how they'd sold over half their property to have some place to call their own. The government had made promises and gave them land now occupied by settlers. They called it

Council Grove. So much for government help. Nowadays, the Kaws didn't hunt like they had done for generations but instead, relied on the government for assistance. Luke wanted to spit at the idea of the government helping, especially now with this stinking war between the states still raging. The Indians were at the bottom of the concerns of the government. In a way, he felt sorry for these men, these "savages" they were called.

Before many more thoughts hit him, Luke found himself helping unload the coach's boot. In there he discovered brown-wrapped packages. The driver pointed, and Luke pulled them out. The Kaws accepted the parcels, nodded, then turned their horses and rode away, laden with packages under their arms and cloth draped across their pintos' backs.

Once again inside the stagecoach, Luke leaned back and thought about those Indians. How would it have been different if they had been Apaches?

CHAPTER NINE

Snow past his knees, Andy pulled one boot out, stomped it into the fresh powder in front of him, then pulled the other boot. Stomp. Pull. Stomp. Pull. Stomp. He glanced over his shoulder at the impressions he'd left, a string of prints meandering through the forest. Maybe it was slow, but damn, he was making progress.

"Wee bit farther now, Andrew." O'Malley's encouraging words pushed Andy forward. "That's me boy. It's bein' saved, we are."

O'Malley marched beside Andy, whose good arm flailed with each step. He was frantic to remain upright. Andy eyed his friend. "Suppose those Indians're still around? Haven't seen a sign, but that doesn't mean anything."

O'Malley shrugged. "Back there at our camp, where I met our native brethren, I thought I was done for, I was. But that young buck didn't find enough o' my hair to take." He shrugged again. "Let 'em come. My Saint Christopher will protect us." O'Malley pulled out the medal from under his shirt, held it up and then kissed it before shoving it back under his jacket.

"Hope that thing works." Andy pulled in cold mountain air and thought about the Apaches, how they had treated his brothers. What would he do if he got captured? Thoughts turning to his brothers, he sent a thanks heavenward that Trace was home in Mesilla safe and James and Luke safe in Kansas.

Focused on a thin wisp of smoke, there and then gone, Andy

mentally crossed his fingers he was getting close to the cabin—
the sanctuary that would save him. Another boot in the snow
brought him to a ridge edge, sharp boulders jutting above the
snow. Below, a narrow valley rolled out at least a mile long, a
stream running through it. Should be Silver Creek, if he
remembered right. He squinted. At the far end—a cabin,
jammed back against the hill.

The cabin, closer than he'd last seen it—he could pick out
the wooden sides, the snow-draped trees, smoke from the stove
pipe. All he had to do was get down there. They'd be saved, for
sure. Andy's arm throbbed; his chest, which had been cut, stung
like fire and now . . . his stomach growled, remembering Ma's
Sunday chicken suppers were a thing of the past.

Cold. Damn it was cold. So why did he have to wipe sweat
off his forehead? Hot. He was damn hot. Unbuttoning his coat
brought relief and then chills. Fingers near frozen, he fumbled
to re-button his coat, then took a deep breath and pulled out a
boot from the snow.

But where was O'Malley? That man had a habit of disappearing and then reappearing at odd times. He'd quit hollering for
him an hour or so before. No need. He'd show up or not. When
Andy got to the bottom of the valley, he decided, he'd hike on
to the cabin. O'Malley knew where to find him.

Gathering all the energy he could pull together, all his will to
live, everything he had, he took another step, the last leg of this
ordeal. Maybe by tomorrow, he'd be warm, dry, recovering. No,
not *maybe*, he thought as he tested a tree branch for support; *for
sure* he'd be warm. Dry. Patched up.

He slid, gripped, stepped, fell, clambered through the snow,
around rocks and trees, crashed through bushes until he landed
at the bottom. Flat land. He shaded his eyes as he gazed up to
the top of the ridge. Hell, he'd come quite a ways! And still on
his feet, more or less.

Water trickled along the creek bed, ice thrusting its jagged fingers into the stream. A bit colder, Andy thought, and this creek will freeze over. But for now, the water would quench his thirst, clean off his face, and. with a little bit of reinforcement, he'd make it to the cabin. Using his good arm, he pulled off his hat, set it on the bank, splashed his face with frigid water, drank what he could.

A quick wind gust sent his hat into a bush and then rolled along the snow bank. "Damn wind!" Andy hollered, knowing it did no good.

O'Malley stood at Andy's side. "If we don't get to that cabin, Andrew, it's dyin' ye're gonna be doin', I'm fearin'."

Andy jumped. "Where've you been?"

"Behind ye." O'Malley pointed over his shoulder. "Always behind ye."

"Gotta get my hat, first." Andy pushed up, his knees trembling, threatening not to hold his weight, his shoulder throbbing. One step and Andy collapsed. Lying on his side, snow clogging his nose, he knew he couldn't spend the time looking for his damn hat. He'd come back for it in a couple of days.

O'Malley's voice in his ear. "Get up, Andrew. Almost there."

"Gotta rest. Sleep."

"Get up."

"One minute."

"Now." O'Malley knelt beside Andy. "Gonna give up so easy? That's not the Andrew Colton I know."

"Just a minute or two. I'll get up and walk to the cabin. I'll be warm. Find somebody to take this arrow outta my shoulder. Sew up this cut." Andy closed his eyes.

"What'd ye be sayin', Andrew?" O'Malley leaned closer. "Ye're mumbling."

★ ★ ★ ★ ★

Andy grabbed for his head. The brass band marching through it thumped and thundered, a cacophony of mismatched screeches. Prying one eye open, he slammed it shut and grimaced at the light assaulting his face. Soft, pathetic moans sank into wooden walls.

"Mornin'." A voice from obscurity sung deep, melodic tones. It wafted through the stillness. A soft chuckle followed.

A hand slid under Andy's throbbing head and cradled it. Rough metal rubbed against his bottom lip.

"Sip of water'll get dem eyes open."

Something wet dribbled down Andy's chin. He opened his mouth. Nothing but pain. His lips moved, but his jaws held tight. Roaring ache stretched across his face, even into his ears. Thirsty beyond thirst, he clutched at the canteen. Sweet water flowed down his throat.

"That's 'nuf for now. Best not drink too much all to once."

"Ummmbbb . . ." Andy struggled for words, one arm flailing for the water.

"Ain't gonna get much said. Face of yours don't look too good. All streaky black and blue." The man cocked his head. "Jaw's probably broke."

Nothing made sense. Broke? Who was this man?

From under half-raised lids, Andy stared into an ebony face offset with jaundiced eyes. Chocolate brown irises glistened. With each blink, the face took on a little more form. Several blinks later, thick, curly black hair perched on top a lean face, weathered, but not ancient. Crinkles gathered around the eyes. A broad, flat nose pointed down toward lips rising on either end. The rounded chin sported a sparse beard, one that hadn't seen a razor in weeks.

"Name's Dawson." The face, connected to a body, sat on Andy's bed, the canvas sagging close to the plank flooring.

Andy squeezed his eyes shut and rubbed his throbbing temples with his left hand. His entire right arm refused to move.

"Dug that arrowhead outta your shoulder. In deep. Thought that cussed critter'd never let go."

Andy heard most of the words, felt the man's body next to him, a hand on his forehead. Convincing his eyes to open once more, he stared at the face inches from his.

"Damnation." Dawson wagged his head. "Your fever's high 'nuf t'heat this here cabin. Don't need no firewood."

He patted Andy's bare shoulder, then held the canteen just out of Andy's reach. "You'll get strength back soon enough. Then you can work like the rest of us." Dawson frowned into Andy's face. "Yeah, work and sweat, sweat and work. They say that's all we's good for, just like mules." He snorted. "Nah sir, we gonna show 'em different."

CHAPTER TEN

Mesilla

Morningstar peered at the overcast sky and pulled her woven shawl closer around her shoulders. A walk to the post office and maybe then around the plaza would be a pleasant distraction from her worry about the men. A slight breeze tugged at her skirt.

As she walked, she thought about Andy. The first time she met him was well over a year ago when he'd ridden into Tucson with James. One corner of her mouth lifted as she remembered Andy asking her for a dinner date. She turned him down in hopes the older brother would ask. It took a few more days and all the courage she knew James could muster.

Morningstar nodded at two Mexican women walking past, their gray shawls wrapped over their heads protecting them from winter's chill. The bundled women nodded back. Her thoughts turned to James. If he could just be the man, the lover he wanted to be, maybe the torment—the nightmares—would end. Then they'd have children. Lots of children. But what *was* the problem? Was she not woman enough? She shook her head. No, James had assured her it wasn't her. It was him. But there was something else. Or was it some*one* else?

The boardwalk creaked as Morningstar stepped up on it. Her eyes cast right and left as she located the post office tucked in the back of the mercantile on a side street. Would there be a letter waiting for her? From Kansas, she'd written to Pa several months back asking about his doctor friend. She knew Pa, who lived in Tucson, couldn't teach her, but his friend might. So, would Pa's letter tell her the doctor in California would accept her as a student? After a few years of study, she would become a full-fledged doctor, like her pa, and she, too, could help people. If she couldn't be a mother, she'd be a doctor. And best of all, James agreed.

A bell dinged as she opened the door and stepped in.

"*Un momento!*" A voice rang out from the back room.

"Take your time," Morningstar replied. The small potbelly stove, perched in one corner, radiated a welcome heat. She held her hands over it, relaxing at the warmth.

A woman, dark brown hair tied back, round face set off by rosy cheeks, bustled into the room. Hesitating for a moment as she stared at Morningstar, she then produced a wide smile matching her outstretch arms. "Missus Colton! You are back!"

"*Hola, Señora Ramos.*" Morningstar hoped her Spanish hadn't deteriorated. "Just got in a week ago."

After a brief hug, the postmistress stepped back. "*Muy bonita,* as usual." She beamed. "Always pretty."

"Thank you." Morningstar's cheeks warmed.

Señora Ramos turned her backside to the stove. "Ahhh. Feels good, no?"

Morningstar couldn't help but like this woman. "Sure does."

"Have you any word from your men? Did they find Andy?" The postmistress turned, holding her hands over the stove. "I pray for them."

"We all do," Morningstar said. "Nothing yet. But we should hear any day." And then she remembered why she'd made the trip to the post office. "Teresa's not feeling well today and asked me to pick up the mail. And maybe you have a letter for me?"

"Your sister-in-law is expecting, no?"

Morningstar nodded.

"Aye," Señora Ramos said. "With my third one . . . no, fourth, aye, I was so sick. All I could eat was tortillas. And tired! Aye, so tired all the time!" She patted Morningstar's arm. "Just wait, your turn will come. Then you'll have stories." She winked, tossed a smile at Morningstar and disappeared into the back room.

Morningstar raised her voice, hoping the postmistress would hear. "How many children do you have?"

"Cinco."

"That's a lot. How do you manage five?"

Señora Ramos appeared, letters in hand. "You just love them. But . . ." her face blossomed into a smile, "I made my husband sleep in the barn for two years, or we would have *siete.*"

Both women laughed. There was truth in there somewhere, Morningstar was sure. Señora Ramos handed three envelopes to Morningstar, who scanned them. One from Teresa's aunt in Santa Fe, one could be a bill or sheriffing notice for Trace, but the last one caught her attention. She drew in a sharp breath. Luke Colton.

"Are you all right, Señora?" The postmistress touched her shoulder. "You look troubled."

She read the return address again, but her gaze still rested on the text. "I'm fine, thank you." She slid the three envelopes into her coat pocket. "I really should be getting back. Teresa's probably needing me to watch Faith."

She opened the door, then turned back. "Thank you, Señora Ramos. I'll see you again soon."

CHAPTER ELEVEN

"Let's go, James." Trace banged on the privy's closed door. "I'm freezin' out here."

"Hold your britches." James's sharp words softened as they shot out over the snow-laden yard in back of the hotel. Usually at this time of early morning, people would be either waiting in line to use this two-seat outhouse, or they'd be bustling down the main street ready to begin a new day. But now, the entire town stood empty, deserted. Spooky.

Trace, his horse's reins in hand, rechecked the cinch and tightened one more notch. "How long does it take?" He hollered over the saddle. "Aren't you cold?"

"Damn cold." James pushed the door open and stepped out, buttoning his coat. "You gonna just stand around all day?" He tossed a half smile at Trace. "Let's go."

Trace swung up into the saddle and then looked at his brother. "We'll find him."

A nod and James climbed into his saddle. Setting his boots into his stirrups, he pulled in biting mountain air. "Wonder what we'll find in Birchville?"

"Wondering the same thing." Trace gigged his horse. "Let's go see."

Once Santa Rita was behind them, the Colton brothers spurred their horses into a gallop. Snowdrifts kept the strides short, but the strong animals managed to plow through.

Would they ever get out of this cold? Ever get to Birchville?

74

Trace considered. They were still a few hours away, but the horses' heads were drooping, and their breathing was labored. Slowed through the growing drifts and ice patches, the horses picked their way toward Birchville. Galloping had been reduced to a trot and further reduced to a walk.

Steep hills closed in on both sides of the trail. Trace surveyed the area. Ponderosa pines towered over the aspen. The forest, dense and thick with chokecherry and juniper bushes, was a convenient hiding places for Indians. Trace gripped his reins harder than necessary. He'd been inspecting every bush, tree and movement as they rode, but the Apaches cloaked themselves well. Sleet pellets stung his face. "Damn snow! Way it's picking up, it's gonna be full dark before we get to town." He grumbled into his coat and stuck one hand under his armpit.

"Couple more hours should do it." James rode next to Trace. "Hope somebody knows about Andy."

Trace leaned over and ran his hand down his horse's neck. He gave a quick pat. "Gonna have to rest these horses soon. And, don't know about you, but I'm ready for some grub." Snow fell harder, coating Trace's hat. "You bring extra biscuits?"

"Ayyeee!" Apaches materialized from behind trees and bushes. An arrow whistled past Trace's head.

Ducking, Trace swung left then right. Apaches on both sides of the trail. War cries, threats and whooping reverberated throughout the hills. Like enraged hornets, the Indians swarmed toward the Colton brothers.

"Head for those boulders!" Trace spurred his horse, hoping she would dredge up enough energy to run, and aimed for an outcropping farther north. James rode full out.

Trace glanced left then right. He counted four, maybe five Apaches bearing down fast. Red and blue war paint striped across faces, Trace recognized the markings of Cochise's tribe.

Images of his captivity flashed through his mind. He vowed, *not this time.*

Trace leaned over his horse's neck as he rode and yelled at James. "Follow the trail left. Turn here!" Left rein in hand, he yanked it straight down.

Turn too sharp and ice too slippery, Trace's horse slid. Both rider and animal crashed against a snow-covered boulder. *Whump.* They hit the ground. Trace lay under the eight-hundred-pound horse, flailing on top of him. Leg pinned firmly under the animal, Trace strained to dislodge his body. Stuck.

Alongside, James jumped from his horse and ran to his brother. "All right?" He knelt by Trace, scooped his shoulders off the ground and pulled.

Apache whoops, closer, louder, Trace groaned and struggled. He pushed against James and the frozen ground, but his horse's thrashing kept his body pegged. Trace mumbled a string of oaths. He twisted.

"Leg could be broken." James looked up at an Apache running toward him. He aimed his Colt and fired. The man stumbled back, crumpling to the ground. The acrid odor of gunpowder sank with the heavy snowflakes.

"Get me out." Trace grimaced, his left leg scraping between the saddle and ice-encrusted earth.

James slid his arms under Trace, yanked and then wrenched. One final powerful pull and Trace broke free. James sat back hard, then scrambled to his knees while Trace lay on his side, rubbing his leg. James hunkered behind the fallen horse, an arrow at full attention in its neck. "Stay right there." James spoke low, between clenched teeth. "Keep down."

Would this be enough cover? Knowing it wasn't, Trace hoped it would be over soon. One way or the other.

James knelt with his back to Trace. "If they capture me—"

"What?" Trace pushed up onto his elbow. An Apache, black

hair tied down with a leather band, sprinted toward him. Trace fumbled with the gun still in his holster. Pulling it out, he fired. His shot splintered a tree branch. Another shot pinged into dirt at the Indian's feet. He sank down behind his fallen horse. James's shot hit the Indian.

"If I'm taken prisoner," James said, "promise you'll kill me. Right then."

"They won't—" He fired twice. Both times missing his targets.

"Promise. On Grandpa's grave, Trace. *Swear it."* James shot a third time.

As much as he hated, Trace knew he would do it. "I promise. Same for me?" he shouted above the war cries. Two more shots at the Apaches, their leggings showing behind trees.

"Promise."

Would it really come to that? Trace sat up. If he was going to die, at least he'd take a few with him. He took aim.

Click.

He pulled the trigger again.

Click.

"I'm out!" Trace's words turned shrill.

James scrambled to his feet, crouched low and bolted into the forest. He knelt behind a juniper and fired.

Bang! Blood blossomed on the Apache's chest as he hit the ground. James sprinted to another bush, coming almost face to face with an Indian, his horse-jaw tomahawk raised overhead.

Leg throbbing, Trace pushed against his mount. He wobbled to his feet. A weapon . . . Something. Anything. He'd never hobble to his brother in time. Trace threw his gun, barrel first, at the Apache. Spiraling, it hit the upraised arm, giving James enough time to fire.

Bang! The Indian clutched his chest and staggered into the woods.

Silence. Trace's rasping breaths filled the forest. His eyes searched the trees, bushes, boulders, even the sky for signs of the attackers. Nothing. Again, they'd melted into the forest, disappearing like the deer and elk that roamed this area. One second there, the next one, gone. His gaze landed on his brother, the color in his face draining to pasty white. Did he dare hope for an end? Another search and he counted three dying or dead Indians. Four, if he added the one who got away. That left maybe one unscathed.

James let out a long, quiet breath. "Damn! Where'd they come from?" He rubbed one hand down his pants leg. "Think they're gone?"

"Maybe." Leg still throbbing but pain not as sharp as earlier, Trace knew it wasn't broken. But there would be one helluva bruise come morning. He slumped against a pine, then slid to the ground. James sat next to him.

"Let's reload, then get out of here. Don't much like the company."

"Powder and caps in my coat pocket." Trace patted his side and relaxed as he felt the bulge of the powder sack. But now, his left arm stiffened, shoulder ached. He fisted his hand. Like a hungry rat, pain gnawed its way from his fingers up through his shoulder and into his neck. In addition to his leg, his arm would be bruised. At least, nothing was broken.

James retrieved Trace's gun, chuckling as he picked it up. "Glad you throw better'n you shoot."

Side by side, the brothers sat, reloading their Colts. Clouds scuttled past, pushed by cold air. Blue jays squawked, fussing at the men. James's horse tugged at the reins snarled in a tree branch.

Fully reloaded, James doubled-checked the filled cylinder, sighted down the barrel, then slid the weapon into the holster. He stared into the forest. "Think they'll be back?"

A blast of anticipation and dread whirled inside Trace. "Think we'll hit town before dark?"

James ran a gloved hand across his eyes. "Riding two up's gonna take extra time." He scanned the sky. "Maybe."

His horse whinnied. Both brothers snapped around, searching for whatever alerted Sophie. Returning Apaches? Trace winced as he rolled to his knees, struggling to stand. James launched himself upright, gun ready. And then there it was. Clip clops mucking through mud, saddles creaking, tree branches moving. Horses plodding from the north, down the trail, aimed right their way.

Trace ducked behind a tree, the juniper bush next to it providing acceptable cover. James scurried across the road, planting himself behind a boulder. Within moments, three men on horseback pulled up by Trace's dead mount.

"Lookit here." A man, small eyes peering over a tangle of red beard covering his face nose to chin, turned in his saddle. He scanned the forest.

"Gotta be Apaches." A second man, larger than the other two, swung off his horse, placed his hand on Trace's dead animal. "Not too long back."

Dismounting, the third man, who looked younger than shaving age, stared down at the dead horse. "We gonna take time to bury bodies, if we find any?"

" 'Course we are," the second man said. "It's only Christian."

Gun in hand, Trace stepped from the bush. The three men whipped around, all drawing guns. James rattled the bush he was near. Two of the men whipped toward James.

"No need to shoot." Trace held out a hand, palm up. "Apaches ambushed us. Killed my horse."

"Reckon they did." The red bearded man took his revolver off cock, then nodded. "You two all right?"

"Right enough, I suppose." Trace holstered his gun, then stuck out his hand. "Trace Colton. Sheriff of Mesilla." He tilted his head toward James. "This's my brother, James."

Holstering his gun, the man then shook with Trace. "Folks call me 'Red.' My brother back there calls me . . . well, can't repeat what he calls me." He pointed to the youngest of the group. "That's Jack. My boy."

James moved in close as the other three holstered their guns. "You just come from Birchville?"

Red eyed James. "Aye, that we did. Glad to be rid of the place, too."

"Maybe you've seen our brother. We're looking for him." Trace glanced at James.

"Maybe." Red shrugged. "Lots of fellas up there."

"His name's Andy. Andy Colton. Looks like us." James waggled his finger between Trace and him. "Only younger. Eighteen this month."

Rubbing his arm, Trace dared a glimmer of hope these men had seen Andy. "Last letter we got was from Birchville. Dated a couple weeks back." His head throbbed along with his leg and arm.

Red's brother retrieved a canteen from his saddle horn, handed it to Trace. "Lookin' mighty peaked there, Sheriff. This should help."

Trace drank and squirmed under the men's scrutinizing gaze. Red squinted, his brother shrugged; Jack turned, glancing over his shoulder.

A second, long drink and Trace's world turned brighter. James stood shoulder to shoulder with him.

"Look, Red," James said. "You sure you haven't seen him?"

"I might've," Red's brother rubbed his bearded chin. "Saw a fella like what you're describin' down at the assay office. Some Irishman was with him." He brightened. "You find that Mick, probably find your brother."

"But you're gonna wanta wait." Red held up a hand, pried

off his hat and ran a meaty hand through his hair, the color matching his beard. "Not a good idea to be headin' that way right now. I'm thinking you best turn around and head back to Mesilla."

"Why?" Trace asked. He sure as hell wasn't turning tail, but they should know what they were riding into.

"Indians. Thieving, murdering savages." The second man jerked his thumb over his shoulder. "Pretty near run everyone outta Birchville."

Red's son took a sip from the canteen then added, "I hear they run over Cooney's Camp and a camp near there. Mogollon, I think it's called."

Sudden coldness hit Trace. He was numb. James's hand on his arm jerked him back into thought. "That's where he was headed."

"Survivors?" James's voice turned soft, shaky.

Red glared at his son, then turned sad eyes to Trace, then James. "Happened a few days back. Those sumabitches been raiding non-stop."

"Were there survivors?" James grabbed Red's coat front and shook him. "Anyone left alive?"

Red blinked. "Well," his voice, deep, tobacco-roughened, "just us and a couple others." He wagged his head. "Most don't survive Apache attack."

"We did!" James snapped, heeled around and stomped toward his horse.

Trace scanned the ground for any glimmer of hope.

"Tell you what," Red said. "We just left our cabin right off the main street in Birchville. You'll find it directly behind the Buckhorn Saloon. If you're fool enough to head on up there, you can sure bunk down at our place tonight. Don't have an extra horse for you, though."

"We appreciate the shelter." Trace shook with the man. "How far to Birchville?"

CHAPTER TWELVE

Mogollon, New Mexico Territory

Andy rolled onto his side. A blinding wave of pain scuttled down his shoulder, along his arm, then planted itself in his hand. His body burned, like being pricked by a million cactus needles. Nausea bolted to his throat, like the quick, hot touch of the devil shooting through him. He swallowed panic. His eyes blinked open into a room, the surroundings unfamiliar. Under him, a lumpy mattress; over him, a wool blanket. The room—wooden ceiling, rough-hewn walls, dirt floor. In the corner, a stove, wood stacked next to it, a table close to the stove. Soft light flooded through the single window, bathing the room in rose and gold.

"Soup's 'bout ready. Want some?"

Andy recoiled. He gripped the blanket to his chest and searched the room for the source of the voice. A stocky man, arms loaded with firewood, stood at the foot of his bed.

The man ambled to the stove, stacked the sticks next to it, and turned to Andy. "I said 'soup's 'bout ready.' It's damn tasty, even if I do say so myself."

Images of another life, another time danced through Andy's mind. Somewhere he'd seen this man before. Mesilla? Birchville? Inch by inch, he rolled onto his back and thought. Shadowed figures rippled across his memory.

"Here. Water'll help." The man offered a canteen.

Andy propped himself up with one elbow and drank as if

water would heal his shoulder, save his life. He gulped until the man tugged the canteen away. A longer, less fuzzy look at the man revealed a wide, black face. Wrinkles or scars made figuring his age almost impossible. His hands—gnarled, thick, strong. Andy stared.

"What's wrong?" His eyes narrowed into cold slits. "Ain't never seen a man o' color before?"

Words refused to form, much less gather into a sentence. Andy nodded. Sure, he'd seen plenty. He and James had spent time playing poker with buffalo soldiers over in Tucson when they were in the army. If memory served, he'd lost close to two weeks' pay to one mighty large, black soldier. "Who . . . ? Where . . . ?"

"Don't gawk. Don't like gawkers." Dawson pulled back Andy's blanket, allowing his eyes to roam over Andy's body. "Name's Dawson." His gaze landed on Andy's face. "Uh huh. You're a strong one all right. You'll do fine."

None of this made sense, but the beefy aroma of stew caught Andy's attention. Ravenous, suddenly ravenous, he sat up and scooted around until his legs hung over the side of the bed. His bare feet touched rough hewn wood. He held out his good hand. "An—" Damn, he couldn't get his jaw to work or his lips. He ran a tongue over them and tasted blood. Cracked, split, swollen. He worked his jaw around until he thought he made sense, then managed to put sound with it. "An . . . dy."

Dawson gripped the extended hand. "Nice meetin' you, Andy. My cookin' ain't t'best, but it's all we got. Me and the jerky hid while them A-pach' was busy. Dried old meat makes pretty tasty soup. I'll get ya some."

"Thanks." With Dawson's help, Andy shuffled to the table and sank into the single chair. From there, the room took form. Larger than he first thought, the cabin had been built sturdy enough for these cold mountain winters. Besides the bed, a trunk took up one corner, and in the other, near the table, a blanket was spread on the floor.

Dawson slid a bowl in front of Andy, then sat on the bed, a bowl in his hand. Andy nodded a thanks, then picked up the spoon. His hand shook, but most of the stew made it into his mouth. Delicious warmth rolled down his throat. After a few bites took the edge off his hunger, he scooped out a piece of meat. He couldn't identify it, but it sure was tasty. Probably rabbit. Or deer.

His bowl empty, he looked forward to a well-deserved rest. Maybe by this time tomorrow, he'd feel good. If not *good*, better, anyway. Fighting heavy eyes, he pushed up from the table, glad to know he could stand without the room spinning.

Dawson stood and pointed his spoon at the blanket on the floor. "You gonna sleep there from here on out." He put the bowl on the table. "Only got one bed, and this one's mine. You'll be fine there."

Fair was fair. But as hurt as Andy was, the bed, lumps and all, would heal him faster than outside on the ground. At least he was out of the cold. For that he was grateful.

Fire in his arm. Andy's eyes shot open. Light from the lantern warmed the room. He winced. While the pounding in his head had lessened, jolts of pain shot from his shoulder radiating throughout his body. He lifted the red-stained cotton binding encasing his injuries and stared at the jagged wound in his upper chest, black stitches lacing the swollen skin together. Eyes trying to focus, he searched the tiny room for the man who'd saved him. The room stood empty except for Andy and his throbbing arm.

The cabin door squeaked open. A blast of frozen air exploded into the room. Behind that, in stepped Dawson, arms loaded with sticks. Snow blew into the room. He shoved the door shut with his foot.

"Damn! Colder than a witch's tit." Dawson looked at Andy as he laid the wood side by side. Neatly stacked from largest on the bottom to smallest on top, the pile would last several days. "Ain't used to this kinda cold. Back where I come from, snows only onest in a while. Every other year if we be lucky."

The room stifling, Andy kicked off the wool blanket covering him. Sweat plastered his heavy cotton pants to his legs. He knew he'd pass out from the heat if he didn't get some cool air. Now. Pushing up to his elbows, he struggled to his hands and knees, and then to his feet.

A rough-hewn sawbuck table, the stack of firewood, and Dawson tilted as Andy swayed. Long seconds passed before objects quit moving. He aimed his pointed finger toward the door and stumbled across the room.

Icy air assaulted his lungs and shirtless chest as he lurched into the night air. The half moon cast enough light, its soft silver reflecting on the snow, allowing him to see. All around, snow whitewashed the landscape. Rough boulders smoothed under the crystalline canopy. Layers of ice glistened on top of the stream curling down the valley.

Andy gulped gallons of cold air, and within moments, his mind cleared. O'Malley. Where the hell was his friend? Hadn't they come in together? Yet, Dawson hadn't mentioned a second person. He rubbed his eyes, brought his sore shoulders back, and noticed an odd-shaped snow bank. Curious, he limped around to the other side. An arm protruded from the white.

Shivering, he plowed through a knee-deep snowdrift and squatted by the arm. He swept off snow and ice until most of the man was visible. O'Malley? Please, no.

Andy hung his head. Not his friend, but someone's husband, son, brother wouldn't be coming home. Not tomorrow. Not ever.

CHAPTER THIRTEEN

November, 1863
Mesilla

Leaving the postal office, Morningstar stepped into Mesilla's chilly air and scanned the return address on one of the three letters. Luke Colton. Third brother of the Colton dynasty. Father of two children. Why did he and Trace have children but not James? She gripped the letters until her fingers turned white. Andy probably had some, too. She scolded herself for her bitter feelings; it wasn't polite to think like that about unmarried Andy. He was a responsible man.

Her feet thudded across the plaza, down a block, turned right another block. By the time she reached Teresa's house, Morningstar had worked herself into something close to anger. She blamed Cochise, Butterfield Stage Lines, James's former fiancée, even Trace for James's inability to produce children. What if they *never* had a family? Would she be able to live with that? But . . . what if she found someone who could . . . Luke, for example? Since the brothers looked alike, the baby undoubtedly would look like James. She pushed such thoughts out of her mind when she opened the door and stepped into the warmth of the house. Baking bread smells filled the room. She breathed in comfort.

"Back so soon?" Teresa called from the kitchen.

Morningstar swallowed then answered. "Missus Ramos sends her regards." She pulled off her shawl, draped it over the back of the rocking chair, shoved more thoughts of Luke further away, and fought to subdue her bad mood and lusty ideas. "How does she work all day and take care of those kids?"

"She's gotta be a saint." A soft chuckle sailed out of the kitchen followed by a child's laugh. "Any mail?"

Morningstar clutched the letters and followed the giggles. Relaxing, she ruffled Faith's hair. Seated in a high chair, the baby munched on a fresh tortilla. Crumbs decorated the wooden floor, the baby's lap, and her face. Morningstar brushed white flakes out of Faith's curls.

"You and Trace got a letter from Luke. Sorry, I peeked." She offered the short stack to Teresa, who held up floury hands.

"Would you open it and read?" Teresa glanced at the bowl of flour and water waiting on the counter. "He's your brother-in-law, too. It's all right. Plus, you've met him. I haven't." She plunged her hands into the doughy mixture.

Morningstar opened the letter and read out loud.

Dear Trace and Teresa,

Ma and Pa send you their love and wish they could hold little Faith. They're hoping to visit you next year if you can't get home first.

We're doing well, considering the house burned earlier this year, but I have much to talk about, too much for this missive.

Therefore, if you have no objections, I will be coming for a visit the twenty-ninth of November. I wanted to be there for Andy's birthday, November 1, but affairs at home wouldn't permit travel then.

I will be alone, as Sally will stay with the children who are still too young to travel such a distance.

Until then.

-Luke

Teresa stopped kneading and looked at Morningstar. "Visit,

huh? Trace'll love it.'"

"The twenty-ninth." Morningstar folded the letter and shoved it into the envelope. "That's next week."

"Correction," Teresa said. "Four days from now. We'll never be able to get word to him that Trace isn't here."

"He's already on his way." Morningstar tapped the letter against her palm, lusty thoughts returning. "Guess we'll have to keep him busy until the men return."

"Plenty of chores to do," Teresa nodded to a dwindling stack of firewood.

"And soon as they find Andy, all four brothers will be reunited." Images of Luke paraded through her head. What were the chances he'd be coming now? Maybe it was fate.

Teresa Colton jumped at the sharp knock on the front door. "Wonder who it is?"

"I'll get it." Morningstar ruffled Faith's hair, brushing more crumbs from the pink cheeks.

More knocking—louder the second time.

"Who's there?" Morningstar leaned against the door.

"Sammy Estrada. Sorry to bother you, Missus Colton."

She tugged the door open and produced a smile for Trace's deputy. "Please come in. It's too cold to be standing outside."

"Thanks, ma'am." Sammy wiped dirt from his boots before stepping in, then jerked off his hat and gripped it with gloved hands.

She closed the door behind him. "Can I offer you something hot? Coffee?" Morningstar studied the deputy's face. Eyes narrowed, mouth set tight. Something wasn't right. He wouldn't stop by just for a visit. He'd already checked in earlier today. She pointed. "We're in the kitchen."

"Smells great. Coffee'd be fine, ma'am. Just half a cup." Sammy followed Morningstar. He greeted Teresa and waited while Morningstar poured coffee. Steam snaked upward like a seductive apparition.

Morningstar poured coffee for herself and then motioned for the deputy to sit. She sat across the table from him. She sipped. He sipped. The baby jabbered. Teresa wiped her hands on her apron, tortillas forgotten for the moment.

Sammy took a long second drink, then lowered it to the table. "Missus Colton, both of you, I have two reasons for stopping by." He glanced from woman to woman. "First, to check that you're all right."

Teresa smiled. "That's sweet of you. We're fine. Appreciate your concern."

Sammy regarded Faith, then the insides of his empty cup.

Teresa straightened her shoulders. "Something else?"

Sammy raised his gaze to Teresa. He sighed. "I'm sorry. A fella come into the office a few minutes ago . . . Seems Santa Rita was hoorawed by the Apaches. Couple days ago." He shifted his eyes to Morningstar. "A few houses burned to the ground, but a snowstorm kept the damage to a minimum."

"Santa Rita's between here and Birchville, right?" Teresa leaned against the sink. "They were thinking they may have to stop in Santa Rita overnight."

Morningstar's hand flew to her mouth. "James? Were he and Trace there? Have you heard?"

Sammy's tired eyes traveled from Morningstar to Teresa. "No word about your husbands, but the fella said none of the men killed looked like yours." A shrug. "I asked."

Morningstar's calmed nerves flared as she realized he had more to say. Was it more news about her man? A familiar knot of worry grew in her stomach.

Sammy's shoulders straightened. "He also said after the Indians hit Santa Rita and Birchville, they rode northeast to Cooney's Camp." Sammy eased to his feet and handed the cup to Teresa.

Teresa's trembling hand touched Sammy's arm. "And?"

Sammy pursed his lips. "No word."

Edging through the living room toward the doorway, he pulled his coat tighter around his chest. "I'm afraid those men of yours rode right into a swarm of trouble. 'Tween the Apaches and snow, they'll be lucky to get back anytime soon." Sammy turned around to the women. "Sorry for the news, but wanted you to know first off. If there's anything I can do to help, please just ask. I'll be right here."

CHAPTER FOURTEEN

Birchville, New Mexico Territory

James's eyes snapped open. A deep, throaty growl rattled to his left. He fought to identify the sound—or even where he was. Another rumble—deep, more menacing. Close.

He sat up, squinting through the darkness. A sliver of moonlight wedged itself past a narrow window, throwing a shred of light into the room. James reached for the Hawken shotgun always nestled beside him but instead grabbed a handful of his brother's leg. He slumped, realizing where he was—inside Red's cabin. It was Trace, deep asleep, snoring next to him. Filling his lungs, then letting out a frosted breath, James shivered.

Easing back down, he pulled his blanket tighter around his shoulders. He cursed the fireplace's gray smoldering ashes, which last night had been a toasty fire, a fire they'd built before lying down. The wool blanket warmed him, then, noticing his frozen nose, James hid his face under the covers. Squeezing his eyes closed, knowing he should get as much sleep as possible, he willed himself to drift off. He twisted onto his side, but Trace's heavy breathing, intermingled with deep snoring, kept him awake. His eyes closed then opened. He willed them shut.

Sleep, that elusive commodity, just out of reach, tantalized and toyed with his consciousness. Was he asleep and dreaming or awake and wishing he was sleeping?

Lying there deciding which it was, his thoughts turned to hours earlier. At twilight, he and Trace, riding into Birchville had followed small bonfires lighting a few houses along the road. Several families huddled around the fires and nodded as the Coltons rode past.

Surprisingly, the cabin was intact. Indians had raided, ransacking the place, but it was still in one piece, nothing even burned. He and Trace had righted the bed, put the tick mattress back on and found enough blankets to settle down for a much-deserved night's rest.

The graying room took form as Trace mumbled something and sat up. He ran his hand through his tangled hair, words now developing into complete sentences. "Knew if we waited long enough, hell'd freeze over." He rubbed his eyes and peered at James. "Just didn't think it'd be this soon." He yawned.

James thumped his brother's leg, careful not to thump too hard. "I'll get wood. Think you can hobble well enough to stoke the fire? Gotta cook breakfast before we try to buy you a horse. *And* more bullets."

"Bullets. Yeah. Brought plenty, but more is always better." Trace groaned to a stand. He stared out the single-pane window. "He's out there. Alive. I can feel it."

James nodded, opened the door, and stepped into cold and snow. He found several branches cut and stacked near the cabin. In no time, Trace had a roaring blaze in the fireplace. But even the heat did nothing to warm James. Nothing would until they found Andy.

After scavenging through the cabin's meager supplies, the men ate beans and jerky while toasting their backsides near the fire. Meal finished and tin cup in hand, James turned and stared into the flames, which danced and licked the bottom of the frying pan. One Wing's flame-face crackled and sneered at James. The lips rose on one end, snarling, exposing sharpened teeth. Popping whips, crackling rawhide as it dried around his head, chanting Apaches filled his memory, all crammed into the room.

Coffee sloshed over the cup's edges. James sucked in air, afraid to let it out. If they heard him, the Apaches would attack again. Hurt him again. Torture him again.

A hand on his arm. James jerked away, his hot coffee splashing over his hand, across the floor.

"It's all right. Just me." Trace's words turned soft. "You're all right."

Tears clouded James's vision. He blinked back more tears as the room pulled itself together. His brother stood at his shoulder.

"You're safe," Trace said.

Why did he still react like that? Why did he still see the Indian's face? He'd fought for months to be well. Hands trembling, he gulped the last of his coffee, then tossed the tin cup into a corner. He straightened his shoulders, took a deep breath, let it out a little at a time. "Let's go. Gotta find Andy."

Trace's hand on his chest stopped him. "One Wing again?"

A couple quick nods, and James leaned back.

But Trace wouldn't drop the topic. "You killed him. He's dead. Remember?"

"Tell *him* that! Tell the bastard he's dead! He won't go away. He won't die." He ran shaking hands through his hair, then across his face. "He . . . won't . . . go . . . away!"

Trace's gaze traveled across James's face, then dropped to the floor. Only the hissing and popping of the fire split the room's silence. James brought deep breaths into his lungs, fisted and flexed his hands. His arms and shoulders relaxed. In control again, One Wing gone for the moment, James raised one shoulder. "It's hard to kill an enemy living in your head."

Trace stopped, studied his hands, the ceiling, then nodded.

Folding blankets and repacking the saddlebags in silence, James mulled over the Apaches from yesterday's attack. "Think those Indians were Cochise's?"

Trace tilted his head. "More'n likely."

Glancing out the window, James crossed his arms. "Think Standing Pony's anywhere close by?"

Trace stopped shoving socks into the saddlebag. He brought his gaze up to James. "More'n likely."

"What if he's waitin' outside of town? He knows we're here! Why didn't he kill us last night?" James scratched his chest. Standing Pony had taken One Wing's place at the whipping post more than once. Several of the knife scars on James's side were thanks to Standing Pony. That Apache was vicious. Ruthless. And ever since James killed One Wing, Standing Pony had been hell-bent on killing James. But with Standing Pony, it wouldn't be a fair fight to the death.

Trace stood, tucking in the saddlebag's flap. "If he's Cochise's henchman, and he probably is, he's gonna be fighting mad we killed a couple of his warriors."

James pressed the rolled saddle blanket to his chest. "Damn, Trace."

"Yeah."

CHAPTER FIFTEEN

Andy Colton regarded the black man sitting across from him at the table. What was Dawson's story? And where the hell was O'Malley? He hadn't been around much. Usually about the time Andy was falling asleep, the Irishman would appear, telling Andy about his day. He'd been all over camp, talking to other miners, discussing the gold they'd found, especially a few miles over the ridge at Cooney's Camp. The recent Indian raid and the possibility of more to come was a major topic as well. Andy guessed from what O'Malley said, this camp, Mogollon it was called, avoided the brunt of Apache attack. Only a few people were killed. Good news for the miners.

While O'Malley had talked almost non-stop—when he was around—Dawson sure as hell hadn't said much. Maybe he'd open up when Andy felt better. He spooned more soup into his sore mouth and spoke over the broth laden with meat chunks. "How long you gonna stay here in Mogollon, Mister Dawson?" The words difficult to form, he took his time aligning his jaw for each syllable.

Dawson shrugged, his eyes meeting Andy's gaze. "Whilst longer, I suspect. With dem miners gone now, I got this place alst t'myself. Plenty t'do. An' the weather's cooperatin', so guess I'll be hangin' around."

"Miners? Gone? But O'Malley said—"

"Who's this damned O'Malley you keep rattlin' about?" Dawson made a show of glancing around the cabin. "Ain't nobody here but us childrens."

Whatever. That was the third time Dawson had refused to acknowledge O'Malley. So be it. Andy knew no more words would be forthcoming today, his jaw still too swollen, too out of place, too sore to continue.

"Only other children we gots to be worried about is Indians." Dawson's cackle split the stillness. "But Indians ain't gonna bother me. See, I'm on their side." He leaned over the table, inches from Andy's face. "See, we both hate you white people. Us and them Indians. You white folk take and take, whip and whip. And why? So's you can have more—more land, more money, more . . . things."

Andy lowered his spoon and pushed the bowl away. He shivered. He pulled both sides of his ripped shirt close, only two buttons keeping the fabric together. The rest must've been torn off when Dawson sewed him up. He shivered harder.

And something else wasn't right. Dawson's lips pulled back like a rabid wolf while his eyes grew round, then narrowed into slits. He swiped at Andy's bowl, knocking it off the table, stew remnants and bowl clattering to the floor. Like a ribbon of smoke, Dawson rose, his body rigid, fists clenched.

"Gotten by the sweat of our backs." Dawson leaned across the table, nose to nose with Andy.

"Yeah, *our* sweat and blood so you white people can go to your parties, your teas. We . . . we don't get no parties, no fancy doin's. We just work."

Dawson edged around the table. He grabbed a skinning knife from the shelf behind him, then threw his arm around Andy's neck. The curved blade slid against exposed flesh. Andy's throat burned.

"White boy, now it's *my* turn to play. *You're* gonna work. Work 'til you can't stand up. Work 'til your muscles won't lift your hands. Work 'til you pass out. I wanna see sweat and blood on your back. I wanna see you work 'til you die."

Andy gritted his teeth, trusting Dawson wouldn't push the blade any farther. Sticky wet inched down his neck. Mashed back against Dawson's warm chest, Andy knew in his weakened condition, he was no match for this irrational man.

What seemed like an hour dragged by. Sighing, Dawson relaxed his hold. With surprising strength, he yanked Andy to his feet and threw him. Andy sailed across the room, thudded against the bed, and slid to the floor. Knife wound throbbing, arm on fire, jaw ready to explode, Andy stared at the man stalking him like a hungry cougar.

He hovered above Andy. Their eyes locked. Dawson bent, then shoved the knife tip against Andy's bare stomach. "Now you gonna be *my* slave." He poked harder. "One wrong move, boy, and guts'll spill. Before you die, you'll mop 'em up."

Andy flinched at the burning. Any man this crazy should be obeyed.

Dawson snorted, withdrawing the knife. He shoved it under his waistband, then reached into his vest pocket and pulled out two lengths of rope. "Gonna tie you tight. You struggle, this knife's the last thing you'll ever feel. Understand, boy?"

Andy nodded.

"Now, hold out dem hands." Dawson leaned in close. "Don't try no funny bidness."

He couldn't do any "funny business" if he wanted to. Dawson was safe from Andy, for the moment. He winced as Dawson wound the rope around his wrists, binding them together. Tight.

A snarl warped across Dawson's face as he roped Andy's ankles. "Yeah, ol' Dawson ain't no fool. Not no more." He wagged his head. "Left first chance he got."

Andy twisted his hands, managing to regain some feeling.

"Yeah, ol' Dawson made short work of dat owner. Mas'er Johnson ain't never gonna beat 'im no more. No more whippin's." He swung his gaze to Andy. "Hell, he ain't never even gonna breathe no more."

"You a runaway?" Andy pushed out the words.

"Runaway?" Dawson's shoulders jiggled. " 'Course I'm a runaway—unless Old Man Lincoln set us free. That ain't never gonna happen." He re-tightened the ropes around Andy's wrists. "I run 'cause nothin's keepin' me there. Woman, kids all sold—or *dead*. Friends, family died off. Nothin' left for me."

"Sorry." Andy, surprised he could speak, stared into Dawson's fiery eyes. "But not my fault."

Dawson clutched both pieces of Andy's shirtfront and hauled him up within inches of his face. "Not your fault?"

Spit hit Andy's cheek.

"Hell, you white, ain't you? That's fault enough."

Heart in his throat, Andy stuttered, "Color's not important."

"What the hell you know, white boy? All your life you been free. Free t'do what you want, free t'learn numbers and letters, free t'go anywheres you want."

Dawson shook Andy until his teeth rattled. As if in a fog, Andy realized the sound belonged to him. Dawson's eyes bore into him with each shake.

Dawson released Andy, shoving him back. He crashed onto the bed, certain every joint in his body was loosened. Objects spun around his head before he focused on one—a fist hurtling toward his face.

CHAPTER SIXTEEN

Standing Pony nocked the arrow, pulled the string taught near his cheek. He focused on a juniper bush to his right. It rustled, just enough to reveal the rabbit's hiding hole. Fur colored the same as the gray/brown undergrowth, the rabbit hid well. The Apache leader squinted into the sun. He stood still. No need scaring the animal by over-shooting and missing, and no need taking a chance of losing the arrow. No, he'd wait. Wait and watch. Until he was certain he could kill.

Relaxing his grip, he crouched on his haunches, signaling to his friend behind him and to his left that he'd spotted food. A slight crunch of leaves told Standing Pony that Dancing Hawk had also crouched. They'd both wait until the time was right. His stomach grumbled. Now would be a good time to kill a rabbit, roast it and eat. Stave off the hunger gnawing since morning. But, he'd use patience learned as a small boy.

From this position, he enjoyed an unobstructed view of peaks to his left and many feet below him, a narrow road. This road, he knew, ran north to Birchville and south to Santa Rita. Two towns he'd already raided. As long as he'd been in this area today, he'd not seen nor heard a person pass on the road. His chest swelled knowing he and the other Apaches had run out or killed every white man. Wind sighed through the pines, reminding him of his mother's songs when he was young. Standing Pony closed his eyes, basking in the glow of victory.

A blue jay squawked from a nearby pine, answered within

seconds by another one. They chattered back and forth like the women around the cook fires. Back in camp, when he wasn't leading his men in battle, he'd listen to the women and then soon grow tired of their talk. How did they find so much to discuss?

Standing Pony snorted, quietly. Women.

His gaze trailed from the juniper bush up into the forest, which marched up a hill, covered with low berry bushes and acorn trees. Behind the hill stood the Mogollon Mountains, his tribe's sacred hunting ground. It had been filled—no, *crawling*— with white men, Americans, crazy men digging in the dirt, swishing pans in the cold streams. All of that for metals Mother Earth had spent an eternity making.

Leg muscles cramping, Standing Pony pulled in a deep breath, ready to stand when the juniper shook. From underneath the lowest branch, a rabbit appeared. Its ears lay back and the nose twitched, probably listening for any sign of attack. Inch by agonizing inch, the Apache straightened his shoulders, gripped the arrow, pulled back the string, took another breath, and let go.

The arrow sliced the air, hitting the rabbit. It bounded off, running in a short circle and then collapsing. Both Standing Pony and Dancing Hawk sprung up, knowing a meal would be forthcoming.

"I can taste it now," Dancing Hawk said. "Skin crackling, meat dripping in its juices. Mesquite rubbed all over." He picked up the rabbit and pulled out the arrow.

"This one will feed us well." Standing Pony dipped his head and then raised his eyes to the sky. "This life gives us life."

The clopping of horse hooves on the muddy trail spun Standing Pony toward the road. He stood still, knowing he blended in with the forest. Soon, two Americans emerged from behind a tree, their horses unable to gallop in the muck. Instead, they had to pick their way up the road. The men—Standing Pony recognized them. The brothers Cochise had captured and tortured not so long ago.

He glanced at Dancing Hawk, also watching the men ride past. How easy would it be for the two of them to jump from this cliff, plunge knives into the enemies' backs? Too easy.

Too easy for a warrior of his status.

Dancing Hawk pulled back on his string, the arrow in line with the men's backs.

"Wait!" Standing Pony held up a hand. "Not yet."

The two riders rounded a bend, disappearing into the forest. Dancing Hawk eased next to Standing Pony. "But, wasn't that the brothers we captured, taken to Cochise's camp?"

Anger pushed on Standing Pony's chest. He grunted. "The white-eyed brothers. The ones who cry at the whip."

Dancing Hawk turned to Standing Pony. "And aren't they brother to the man who killed Tantoo from Lone Wolf's tribe only days ago?"

"The same." Anger turning to rage drew his lips into a snarl. "The one in the black coat killed my brother."

"Why do you let them live?" Dancing Hawk released the bow's tension, returned the arrow to the quiver on his back.

Standing Pony wagged his head. "I told Cochise to kill them. But he wouldn't listen."

Dancing Hawk nodded. "I remember. The one your brother hated the most, the younger one . . . almost tortured to death."

"It wasn't enough. He should have been stripped of his skin for what he and the other white men do." Standing Pony tightened his jaw and fist at the same time. "Keeping the brothers alive served no purpose. They could not keep the army from our tribe. I questioned Cochise then and question him now." He glared at his friend. "I have not forgotten. The young white eyes even lay with the Pima captive promised to me. My woman.

He stole *my* woman."

"But, Cochise himself gave—"

"Hear my words, friend. That young Colton killed my brother. Took my woman. If Cochise had allowed One Wing to do what was necessary, show the Americans this is our land, my brother would live today, and those two white eyes would have been food for coyotes long ago."

Dancing Hawk raised his eyebrows. "But . . . why did you let them live this time?"

How could he make Dancing Hawk understand? He lowered his gaze to the dead rabbit, then shifted it to include his most trusted warrior. "Killing them now? It will be too easy. We are not squaws. We are warriors. We follow them, track them like this rabbit. Hunt them at every turn. I want them to fear. To know fear. But we will not harm them . . . yet." He pulled a skinning knife from a sheath. "*That,* I will do myself."

CHAPTER SEVENTEEN

"Next stop's Mesilla." The stage driver shut the door and peeked through the window. "Should be there in a couple hours." He nodded, smacked the coach's side, and climbed up onto his seat. The coach rocked with his weight.

Luke smiled at the good news. The snap of the whip and the "Step up, mules!" command of the driver propelled him along the final leg of his journey. He touched his hat's brim and nodded to the two ladies arranging themselves on the hard seats. Could be mother, daughter.

One was younger, much prettier than the other. Her elongated brown eyes sparkled as they met his a time or two, then she'd turn her head away as if embarrassed to be caught.

Enchanting. Her light brown complexion set off by those stunning eyes and hair . . . Luke thought of his own wife nine hundred miles behind, then wondered what lay ahead. The driver's words thundered across his brain. *Mesilla.* Two hours more and he'd be with two of his brothers again. Three, if James hadn't moved on yet. And lovely Morningstar. He still wondered about her. Back in Kansas, he'd felt as if she needed his warm arms around her. But she'd backed off every time he got close. Maybe by now, she and James were already in Tucson or way over in California, for Christ's sake. He'd never see her again.

Luke turned his attention back to the woman across from him—too young. Instead, he concentrated on the journey and his impending arrival. He couldn't wait to see the look on everyone's faces—Trace, Teresa, and Andy—as they hugged on the boardwalk. As when James and Morningstar came to Lawrence this past spring. Would there be happy tears?

Coach rocking front to back, Luke regarded the various shades of brown out his window. Ever since the last stop at a way station fifteen miles north of Mesilla, beige desert sand dunes flecked with dark-brown brush stretched in every direction. The turquoise sky, the only other color, created a breathtaking backdrop, like it was painted with a broad brush. A few miles to the west, a row of finger-like tree branches silhouetted against the blue. Ancient cottonwoods ran along the Rio Grande, the area's lifeblood. To the east, the Organ Mountains stood tall, rugged, defining the Mesilla valley.

Adobe houses, some coated with flaking whitewash plaster, became more frequent nearer to Mesilla. He'd read about the Southwestern-style houses, the small, boxy dwellings of mud and straw mixed together, how they provided warmth in the winter and respite from the summer's paralyzing heat.

Leaning out the window as the stage turned the last corner on this portion of the route, Luke knew Mesilla was home. Something about brown on brown, even the brown-skinned people on his journey, appealed to him. No wonder Trace and Andy loved it here.

The stage slowed as they entered the bustling plaza. Wagons rattled past, and people stopped to wave. Shops and signs advertised items from nails to shawls. Luke searched the people as he rode. Nobody looked familiar. Where were those brothers of his? More than likely already at the stage stop waiting. Luke hung out the window and gawked.

The coach jerked to a skidding stop, dust billowing up under the wooden wheels. It settled in front of the El Paso–Santa Fe Overland Express office. The shotgun guard jumped down from his high seat, and opened the door. Luke helped the two female passengers navigate the cramped quarters and waited for them to climb down. After they alighted, he grabbed his hat and the empty sack of sandwiches his mother had packed.

Last one out, Luke stepped from the stagecoach. Twisting and turning, he wanted to rub his numb rear end but instead settled for popping his back into place. He nodded to the driver, who, still on top of the coach, dropped the last of the carpetbags to the shotgun guard on the boardwalk. Luke shielded his eyes against the sun. "Great trip, sir."

The driver scooted across his seat, set his foot on the wheel, then jumped to the ground. He dusted his gloved hands. "Yup. Any trip without broken wheels or red-devil Injuns's a good one." He disappeared into the stage line office.

Luke reached back inside the coach for his red and black carpet bag and nodded to the dust-encrusted shotgun guard. "Thanks again for the ride. I enjoyed it."

"Slow and steady. Just the way we like it." Running his hand across his mouth, the man pointed down the street. "Gotta find something to slake my thirst, friend. Wanna join me?"

Luke glanced in the direction of the pointed hand. "Thanks, anyway. Supposed to meet my family here. Guess I'm early or they're late." He searched the street, hoping for a familiar face. A pound of disappointment pressed on his chest. This wasn't the greeting he'd envisioned. Sheriffing duty at the last minute had probably come up. Or maybe they hadn't received his letter.

"All right, suit yourself." The guard nodded to Luke and marched off.

"Must be Luke Colton."

Booming words behind him spun Luke around. Locating the owner of the voice, he stared into a face he didn't recognize. "Why's that?"

"Look just like your three brothers." The man extended a

hand and a lopsided grin. "Sammy Estrada, Mister Colton. I'm your brother's deputy, right hand man so to speak. Pleased to finally meet you."

"And you, sir. He's mentioned you in his letters." Luke returned the genuine smile.

"All good, I hope." Sammy picked up Luke's bag.

The third Colton brother scanned the crowd. "Where's Trace?" Too long of a pause from the deputy melted Luke's smile. "Something wrong?"

Sammy touched Luke's arm, nudging him toward the plaza. "Walk with me . . ."

Three long blocks and Sammy filled Luke in on the current situation. Luke frowned at times, chuckled once, but worry filled his thoughts. Were his brothers safe? He and Sammy stopped in front of Trace's white-plastered adobe, its porch running the width of the house.

A brown-haired woman flew out the front door, across the wooden porch and down the stone walk. The grin was wide. "Luke Colton!" They met halfway where she hugged him and then held him at arms' length. "I'd know you anywhere. I'm so glad to finally meet you." She turned to the deputy. "Now the family's complete."

Luke took in a woman taller than most, her ginger colored eyes lighting up an oval face, rather delicate. Pinked cheeks glowed. "Gotta be Teresa. You're exactly what that lucky brother of mine described." He nodded toward the deputy. "Sammy tells me I couldn't have come at a better time. Not only do I get a long visit with you and your new daughter, but I also get to see Morningstar again. And visit with all three brothers when they get back."

"So glad you're here!" Teresa beamed at Luke.

Luke glanced over her shoulder, expecting to see Morningstar and the toddler. "So, where *are* the other two?"

Hand flying to her mouth, Teresa shook her head. "Forgot my manners, I'm so excited. Please, both of you, come in." She nodded to Sammy and then Luke. "We baked a pie today and have a pot of mutton stew waiting for you. Star's feeding the baby."

Teresa opened the thick wooden door, ushering the chilled men into her warm living room. "Star," she called. "They're finally here."

Sammy pushed the door shut, set Luke's bag next to it, and stood just inside the room. He shifted his weight from one foot to the other.

Morningstar dashed into the living room, baby on her hip, and grinned at Sammy, then Luke. "So good to see you again!" After hugging Luke, she handed Faith into his outstretched arms. "Meet Faith Brigid Colton."

"Brigid, huh?" Cradling the squirming youngster, Luke patted her back. "Like Ma?"

Teresa nodded. "Trace and I agreed that after four boys, your ma deserves to have the first girl in the family named after her!"

Luke grinned at the toddler and stroked her brown hair. Hair reminding him of his own kids'—both auburn brown; Faith's had hints of curls hanging at her shoulders. He handed her back to Star. "And Faith?"

Teresa glanced at Morningstar. "We had faith all along that Trace and James would come home some day, safe." Her eyes misted. "And we still have faith that *all* the brothers will be home soon."

Luke studied the baby while Teresa fought to compose herself. A heavy silence stung the room. Sammy squirmed by the front door; Morningstar's gaze hit the floor.

Pointing over his shoulder, Sammy opened the door. "I best be going. Just wanted to make sure your visitor found his way." He tossed a quick nod toward Luke. "Would hate to lose you before we even met. I'll be back later and take you over to the Corn Exchange Hotel, Mister Colton."

"Thanks, Sammy. But, please, just call me Luke." He knew why Trace liked this man. Honesty and sincerity exuded from him. Probably made a helluva deputy.

Teresa pointed toward the kitchen. "Stay for coffee, at least."

"Thanks, no," Sammy said. "With Trace away, I gotta be two men. Some other time." Sammy tipped his hat and stepped into the afternoon.

Luke shook hands with Sammy and then shut the door. When he turned, he met Teresa's friendly gaze and arched eyebrows.

"Can't get over how much you look like James," she said. "More than the other two. You could be twins." She pointed to the sofa. "Please make yourself at home. I'll pour some coffee."

Instead of sitting, Luke followed Teresa into the kitchen. He lowered his voice. "I have a question."

"Sounds serious." Teresa handed a steaming cup to Luke, then one to Morningstar and took one for herself. She pointed over Luke's shoulder toward the living room. "We can talk more comfortably in there."

He eased to the couch, enjoying its softness. So different from the stagecoach. He waited for the women to take their seats. A start then stop. How could he put this politely? "I'm wondering . . . why didn't Andy become a deputy? James says he'd worked with Trace for months, and now . . ." He held up both hands, palms up. "What's going on with him? I mean, *prospecting*? That's a foolhardy thing to be doing. He could get himself killed. Crazy kid."

"You sound just like your brothers." Morningstar's mouth curved upward, holding promise of more to come.

Even her lips . . . Luke fought for control. He gripped his cup. "How long's he been gone? I didn't realize he'd left until Sammy told me. Did he write home? Tell Ma and Pa? Because he sure as hell—. Excuse me. He certainly didn't tell me."

Teresa blew on her coffee, took a sip, then set the cup down. Faith crawled up on the couch and nestled next to Teresa. "I remember him sitting there at the table," she pointed toward the kitchen, "writing to your folks. Back in late July, first of August. He'd run into some men who'd come from Birchville, up in the Mogollon Mountains, and said they'd found gold. He sure was excited. Like an overgrown puppy."

"August." Luke leaned back. Now it made sense. "That's when Quantrill attacked Lawrence. Nothing got in or out for weeks." He glanced at Morningstar, who studied the inside of her cup. She was there. She knew. "I'd heard the mail burned with the rest of town. Guess that rumor was true."

Teresa swiped at a hank of hair hanging across her daughter's face. "As much as Andy wanted to be a deputy, he told us he'd come back after striking it rich, and he'd buy the town!" She chuckled, her warm eyes glowing at the remembrance. "Said he could be a deputy any time, soon as he turned eighteen, but gold wouldn't wait."

"Sounds like my baby brother." Luke relaxed. That much of the puzzle solved. Now for the hard part. "Tell me about the Indian attacks. Are my brothers really in danger?"

CHAPTER EIGHTEEN

Mogollon

Late afternoon sun glistened off snow mounds, intensifying the sparkling light covering the crystal landscape. James squinted, despite the shade his hat afforded. The brothers rode into the narrow valley once housing the mining camp at the base of the Mogollon rim. Muddy canvas sheets sprawled against rocks as reminders of life run amok.

"Dammit, James. Look here." Trace reined up, foot hitting the snow before James realized Trace had stopped. Brushing aside crusty snow, Trace uncovered a man, face down, an arrow stiff in his back.

James slid off his horse, then knelt beside his brother, the frozen specter at their knees. "Please don't let it be Andy."

Trace pushed the man over. "It's not him."

James brushed snow off the man's face.

"Can't do this." Trace's breath hung in frosty puffs.

"Do what?"

"Turn over every dead body expecting to find Andy." He met James's stare. "What if we never find him?"

"We will. If he's not here, then we'll look some place else. Hell, he's probably already in Santa Rita or even Mesilla by now having a beer and wondering where *we* are." James walked back to his horse and picked up the reins, hoping his own doubts didn't show. "Let's just take this one step at a time."

Trace blew out another long stream of crystals. A slow nod.

As the Coltons led their horses down the mile-long canyon, James spotted a lone cabin, one side and part of the roof visible through the trees. Maybe they'd get lucky. Maybe somebody was there who would know something. On the way, they studied every body, lump, and torn tent along Silver Creek. No Andy.

Long shadows deepened as the men approached the cabin near the end of the shattered encampment. A thin column of smoke spiraled from the rusty iron chimney. James knew they'd found Andy. Had to be. "Looks like someone's home."

James flew out of his saddle and tied his horse to a large bush near the front of the cabin. Trace dismounted and pointed to a lump on the other side of the bush. A leg stuck out. The brothers brushed snow off the face. Again, not Andy.

James pushed down rising nausea. "Hello the cabin!" He rapped on the door, then glanced at Trace. Worry had aged his brother's drawn face. Panic dissolved into apprehension. A second knock. Shuffling inside.

"Come on in, it's open."

Not Andy's voice. James's shoulders slumped as he pushed on the door. It scraped against the rough, wooden floor. Glancing behind him at Trace, James stood straighter and stepped into the one-room cabin. Warmth from the tiny stove sent waves of security radiating up and down his body. The aroma of stew wafting through the room made James's stomach rumble. He grinned.

Hand extended, James introduced himself and his brother.

The black man nodded. "Dawson's the name, Mister Colton. Good t'know ya." One hand gripped a spoon while the other shook with the brothers. "Want some stew? It's just ready."

James unbuttoned his coat and surveyed the room. A bed, potbelly stove, rough-hewn saw table, and one chair crowded the space. "Only if you've got enough to spare. It does smell inviting."

Dawson plucked bowls from a shelf and ladled stew into the tin containers. "Plenty where this come from. Lots of fresh meat. All kinds of game 'round here. Plenty t'pick and choose from. Still got vegetables I found back in an old mine I use for cold storage." He aimed the spoon over his shoulder.

James shrugged out of his coat and sat at the table. "Nice cabin you built."

Dawson spoke into the stew pot. "Thanks, but ain't mine, leastways official like. Belonged to a white gentleman named Treolo, but he skedaddled 'bout the time those Apache come. Ain't been back since, so figured it's mine."

Trace eased down onto the bed. "You were here during the Apache attack?"

Dawson set a steaming bowl in front of James, then handed the other to Trace. He held out a spoon and pointed it at Trace. "Eat afore it gets cold."

"Were you?" Trace blew on the stew.

Unable to decide if he was more hungry for news of Andy or grub, James figured they were almost equal and wolfed it down. Something in there whetted his appetite for more. A special seasoning or kind of meat he'd never before tasted? Whatever it was, he liked it.

The black man nodded. "I was here. We all was." He pointed the spoon toward the front door. "Came on us quick like. Nobody had time ta escape."

"Found a fella about a mile back up in the woods," James said. "Red hair, about our age and height. You know him?"

Dawson wagged his head.

"Interesting. We think," Trace nodded at James, "that man was alone. Or maybe he wasn't, but we didn't see any more bodies."

"Might be he was tryin' to escape dem Apache." Dawson shoved stew into his mouth and spoke over it. "That's 'bout as far as he got."

"Maybe." James lowered his spoon, stew now gurgling like a happy beast in his guts. "You know our brother, Andy? We're looking for him, and last we heard he was here. He's eighteen, our height, brown eyes, straight brown hair hits the collar."

"Looks a lot like us." Trace waved his spoon between himself and James. "We're real worried."

Dawson studied each face and then stared into the distance. A long silence. He rubbed his stubbled chin. "Yeah, thinkin' on it, I do remember a fella like that."

"Where's he at now? Was he here during the attack?" James hesitated to ask the question but had to know. "Is Andy alive?"

Trace stood, the empty bowl clattering to the floor. He grabbed Dawson by the shirt sleeve and leaned into him. "Tell us. Tell us what you know. Is Andy alive?"

"Let me go." Dawson wrenched his sleeve from the frantic grasp. "Don't cotton to people pawin' at me."

"Sorry." Trace stepped back. "Whatta you know?"

"Not much. Played cards with him down at Frenchy's tent awhile back. Saw him once or twice after that but ain't seen him since."

"Damn." James slumped against the chair.

"Heard he moved on down toward Santa Rita." Dawson gazed from face to face.

"When?" Trace asked.

"Afore the attack."

"So he's alive." The rock on James's chest crumbled. His shoulders rose and fell with the breath he pulled in and then let out. James frowned at Trace. "Doesn't make sense. Should've seen him or at least signs on our way here." His relief turned cold as he cocked his head at Dawson. "You sure?"

Dawson scratched his head and gazed into the cabin, his dark eyes roaming from bed to brother to the window. Head bobbing up and down, he mumbled. "Sure, I'm sure. It snowed real good few days back, so maybe them tracks are hid. And I'm the only onest 'round here now, excepting 'ol Henry."

"Who?" Trace's eyebrows knitted.

"Henry. Real nice fella. Didn't know him too good 'fore the attack, but we've 'come real close now. We eat together regular like."

"Where's he at? Maybe he'll know where Andy is." Trace swung his gaze around the cabin.

"Just right outside. Must've passed him on the way in."

James pushed his bowl back and eased to his feet. "You mean that dead fella over by the bush?" He pointed toward the door.

"Dat's the one. Don't talk much any more, but when he do, it's mighty interestin'." Dawson scooped up the bowls and tossed them into a tub.

"I'll bet it is." Trace buttoned his coat and fingered the revolver on his hip. He cut his eyes sideways at his brother. James caught Trace's down-turned mouth, pulled-together eyebrows. Tugging on his coat and gloves, James backed toward the door. "Thanks for the grub, Dawson. We gotta move on before it's dark."

"You can sleep in here if'n you'd like. This floor's drier'n that forest out there." Dawson pointed at the wooden planks.

"Thanks, anyway. Best be headin' out." Trace pulled his hat down tighter.

"I'll keep my eye peeled for dat brother of yours. Ol' Henry'll sing out first, I reckon." Dawson's grin split his face. "He talks mostly at night, but if Andy comes dis way durin' the day, I 'magine he'll call out then, too."

"That'd be a real help, Mister Dawson." Trace gripped the door handle and yanked. "Thanks again for the grub."

Both Coltons bolted into the crisp evening air and pulled the wooden door shut. Without saying a word, they swung up onto the horses and galloped away.

Half a mile later, James reined up, turned to Trace. "I'll bet he actually hears Henry talk to him." He shrugged. "Grub was good, though."

"Yeah." Trace met James' stare. "Real good. You know what kind of meat that was?"

Quick as a lightning strike, it became obvious. James leaned over his horse as his stomach brought up everything. Several spasms later, his body drained, dry heaves lessened, he slid off his horse. Gulping mouthfuls of snow, he swished it around and around. He spit stew streams.

Trace flipped up his coat collar and pulled it close to cover his nose and mouth, then knelt next to his brother. Both men gulped more snow.

Stomach still knotting but empty, James wiped his mouth with a coat sleeve, the taste lingering. He sat back in the snow. "Wonder how much of ol' Henry we ate."

CHAPTER NINETEEN

"Top o' the mornin' to ye!" O'Malley's voice. Andy raised one eyelid, its puffy skin crashing against the eye socket. Wincing, he fought to raise the other lid. No such luck. He'd have to settle on squinting at his friend. And from this angle, lying on his left shoulder, back against something rock hard, he made out O'Malley, seated sideways, cross-legged.

"I was wrong, I was. 'Tis not truly mornin' now." O'Malley produced raised eyebrows and a tilted smile. "More like evenin' milkin' time."

A pinprick of light squeezed its way through the blackness, lighting nothing but air. Andy's head throbbed, mouth desert dry. "Where are we?"

O'Malley leaned closer. "Couldn't understand ye with that rag tied 'round your head." His pointed finger spun in a small circle. "Goes all 'round, even over yer mouth, it does. Slick as me pennywhistle."

Andy hollered louder, his mashed words echoing. O'Malley shrugged. Andy opened his mouth as far as possible, then stuck his tongue through a narrow opening between his lips. Cloth, he tasted cloth. That Irishman was right. Andy was gagged. He brought tied hands up to his face and with them, his ankles. For whatever reason, Dawson had tied his hands and feet together, a length of rope between them. No way would Andy walk away. He groaned. Hog-tied like a calf at branding. Without O'Mal-

117

ley's help, he wasn't going anywhere. But where was *here*, anyway?

And what the hell was wrong with his friend? Why didn't he untie him? O'Malley sure as hell wasn't tied. It would be easy enough for him to reach over and set him free.

"Help me!" Andy knew that's what he'd said, but did his friend understand? He rolled forward onto his hands and stomach, his injured shoulder sending electrifying jolts down his entire side. He wriggled, reminding him of those worms on fishing hooks before he cast the line into the stream. Now he knew how they felt. Dirt flew into his one open eye, bringing tears.

"Dammit, help me!" Andy hollered as loud as possible, his throat tree bark raw. He pushed against the ground, rolled over onto his back. That sliver of light glinted off of something above him. Andy sat, his one open eye focused on the spot above his head. Rock. Some kind of shiny rock. And then he knew. He was in a cave, not too far from the opening, but far enough.

O'Malley uncrossed his legs and pushed up. He had to stoop, the cave not high enough for him to stand upright. " 'Tis a wee bit drafty in here, Andrew. I'll see if I kin find ye a cover."

"Untie me!" Andy screamed, wriggling and rolling toward his friend. More dirt in his eye, he closed it. When the tears had washed it clean, he looked around the cave for his friend. Gone. Flat vanished. Just like before. Normally, Andy truly never hated anyone. He'd always find a reason to like them—or put up with them. But today was different. He never hated anyone as much as right now. Thomas O'Malley. He hated him for not helping, for not explaining, for everything.

Lying in the dark, energy spent, Andy feared today would be his last day on earth. He'd die here, buried in this cave for all eternity, and his brothers, his family, would never know what happened to him. If he ever . . . *ever* . . . got out of this alive, the first thing he'd do was go home. To Mesilla, then back to

Kansas. No more prospecting. No more running after a crazy dream. No more taking unnecessary chances. What the hell had he been thinking, anyway? What gave him the right to run off? Chase gold? Idiot. He was an idiot, and maybe this was the way he paid for it. But was his life the cost? Seemed a bit high.

Faint rustling of bushes near the cave's entrance. He listened hard, closed his eye, concentrating on what exactly he heard. A horse pulling on a bush, munching away. Must be Dawson's horse, tied nearby, waiting to be put up for the night. Andy strained to hear more. More munching and rustling. Had to be two horses. Two? Nothing made sense.

Distant conversation. Indistinct words. Men's deep voices. Andy sat up again. Two people were outside, talking. Two people, not just crazy Dawson. Maybe it was O'Malley come back with help!

"Please, please, please." He squirmed snake-like, scooting on his rear, toward the light. Twice he hit his head on jutting rock, twice he stopped to let the spinning stars slow. The light faded, and then someone or some thing blacked it out.

Andy stopped. His rescuers could help him the rest of the way. Saved! And not a moment too soon.

"Look at you! How'd you get yerself this far, Andrew?" Dawson's booming voice filled the cave. "Didn't tie you tight 'nough, I reckon."

Andy hung his head.

CHAPTER TWENTY

No matter how hard he jerked, squirmed, twisted, and cursed, those damn ropes remained tied—tight. Andy had lost feeling in his hands and feet early into this ordeal. After Dawson had come into the cave—how long ago, Andy didn't know—Dawson had tightened each knot, pulling the noose tighter around Andy's wrists and ankles. He'd even retied the gag around Andy's mouth. No way were words, much less his body, escaping. So, he sat. And shivered.

Shuffling sounds and a torchlight glow brought Andy's shoulders back. Dawson stopped at the cave's entrance. "On your knees, white boy," he said. "No lollygaggin' for you."

Strong hands clamped onto Andy's healing shoulder and yanked. On his knees, he peered into the cold, inky cave, then up into Dawson's glowing eyes. Dawson jerked the ropes around Andy's wrists. Braided horsehair dug into raw flesh. A groan rattled in his throat, the wide strip of material wound around his mouth stifling his screams.

"Be nice 'n quiet here, Andrew, an' I may let you live." Dawson loosened the rope around Andy's ankles, and pulled him to his feet. Like O'Malley and now Dawson, Andy stooped in the cave.

Andy looked down. Lifeless, useless feet held his attention. They weren't his anymore. He lifted one and shook it. It jiggled, precisely like a marionette he'd seen back in Kansas at a traveling medicine show promoting Hamlin's Wizard Oil. The marionette's wooden limbs were controlled by someone unseen. That made Andy a puppet—under the control of the man with the strings.

"You gonna dance, white boy?" Dawson clapped in time with Andy's foot. "Dance, white boy! Dance!"

Teetering on numb feet, Andy envisioned his hands around Dawson's neck, strangling life out of the man. But anger wouldn't do any good right now. No, he'd bide his time and then escape. Or kill him.

Dawson grabbed Andy's arms, rocking him side to side. Dawson mimicked Andy's movements as he pushed him back and forth. "Mama sure gonna be proud now! Ooo eee! Here I is, dancin'. I is free! I is free, white boy, and nobody . . . *nobody* gonna take it away!"

They danced a couple more steps, and then, winded, Dawson released Andy's shoulders. "Don't that feel good?" He wiped sweat running into his eyes. "No wonder you white people always goes to them dances. That's fun for certain."

In a different circumstance, Andy would agree with Dawson. Dancing was fun if it was with a pretty young lady. *This* was not fun.

A quick jerk on his healing arm brought a silent cry. Dawson towed Andy through the abandoned mine, the men navigating around crates of vegetables. Andy stumbled into frigid night air, darkness giving way to starlight.

Shivering, Andy shuffled next to Dawson, the vise-like grip on his arm like the time back home he and older brother Luke took turns puffing on a cigar behind the schoolyard outhouse. And then . . . caught! That old marm's clamp around his arm had left bruises for days.

They stopped halfway between the mine entrance and the cabin. Dawson smiled into the forest. "I had me an idea. I's gonna be a real dancer. Like those fellas up on stage." He leaned in close to Andy's face. "You gonna teach me to dance, white boy. Real dancin'."

Play along. Say—do—whatever the man who pulled the strings wanted. Andy nodded and tried to do a jig, but his feet, now waking up, turned to clumps of bone and muscle at the end of his legs. They plowed through snow and mud.

"Like that, white boy! Just like that, only better!" Dawson shoved Andy. "Let's go." Andy stumbled through the door and into the warm cabin, exuding a strange sort of comfort. If he could just regain feeling in his bound hands . . . and his body quit trembling . . . and find a weapon . . . then he'd be all right.

Dawson shut the door, moved in close, and glared. Lips drew into a sneer.

Close enough to feel Dawson's breath on his face, Andy questioned his chances for survival, despite his now becoming a dance instructor. Gnarled hands pushed on Andy's chest. Powerless to stop the motion, Andy flew backwards, crashing against the bed, sprawling over a wooden box, and landing in a corner. His head smacked into the wall, more silver dots pulsating around the room.

Slumping back against the wall, Andy stared into orbs, white eyes glowing like ice against bronze horsehide. Those eyes turned colder as they zeroed in on him. Like a demon, Dawson's face materialized inches from his. Lips moved before he understood the words.

"I'll take off that gag, but one sound, an' that's the last dance you've ever had." He untied the old bandana. Andy spit lint and dirt. He worked his mouth side to side, licking his lips, the movement tingling to his face.

"Two men rode in this evenin', lookin' for you."

"Trace and James?" Andy worked his mouth. Even *he* couldn't understand what he'd just said.

"Sent their white asses on their way. Headed them back to

Santa Rita looking for a fella who's drinkin' hisself a time."
Dawson chuckled, reached over the crate, then yanked Andy to
his feet. "Yeah, they ain't gonna be comin' back no time soon."

"No. Please, no!" A sour taste coated his mouth. Was this
another of Dawson's crazy games? Something he'd conjured up
just to see him suffer? On the other hand, Dawson had said *two*.
Did that mean James was back from Kansas? Last he'd heard,
James was considering moving back. Either way, Trace and
somebody would come to his rescue. Was it his brothers he'd
heard this afternoon? Maybe they were camped out of sight.
Out of reach.

Dawson grabbed Andy hands. "I'll untie you, but try to use
these on me, and your family ain't never gonna find you. Won't
be enough left *to* find." He stared at Andy. "Got it?"

He nodded. *Family.* Dawson had said "family." Maybe it *was*
James with Trace. Did he dare hope?

Dawson pushed Andy into the chair. "Sit." He plopped a
bowl of cold stew in front of him. "Eat. Need strength for
tomorrow."

His right shoulder, fire radiating down his arm, throbbed,
close to useless. Nevertheless, Andy used his other arm to work
a spoon into his mouth. He managed to swallow the lump, bits
of carrots and turnips clinging to meat. Several gulps of water
washed it down.

Scraping the last half spoonful of glop, then pushing it into
his mouth, he studied the man who controlled his life. The puppet master stood at the stove, his back to Andy.

Now or never. Andy searched the cabin for any type of
weapon. Nothing. He sprung to his feet, bolted for the door,
yanked it open, and raced into the night.

"Trace! James!" Andy hoped against hope the sounds were
intelligible. "Help!" His words echoed throughout the narrow
canyon. Rumbles bounced off boulders.

Somewhere behind him a door screeched across wood.

He ran.

Ice crunched. Footfalls behind him.

He ran harder.

Hot breath on his neck. Powerful arms wrapped around his chest.

Andy screamed. Wrestled to the ground, he slammed into rocks of ice. His face plowed through a snowdrift, then lodged against a boulder. The pain, the excruciating agony of a jaw broken, spiraled his world into a black void, a space filled with hurt.

Dawson flipped him over onto his back like a turtle, grabbed his feet, and pulled. Rocks and sticks poked Andy's body as he slid over frozen ground. His numb hands refused to fend off the attack. Cabin in sight, Andy knew crazy Dawson wouldn't let him live.

Dawson yanked with the strength of ten men. Screaming, Andy clawed at the doorframe, but his body scraped over the rough flooring, then stopped near the stove. Somewhere behind and above him the wooden door slammed shut. The bolt clicked into the frame. Andy stared up into a boiling mad face.

James turned on the hard ground and pulled the blanket tighter under his chin. Still, he shivered. His eyes fluttered open. What had awakened him? A noise of some kind? Trace? He checked his brother. Still asleep, rolled up inside his blanket on the other side of the fire.

James sat and reached for the rifle at his side. Running his hand down the barrel, he wondered if Indians would attack at night. Was that Apache or animal? Sounded more animal than human. Stars peeked back as James thought about the creatures in this frozen mountain valley. Mountain lion? Black bear?

Trembling, James leaned closer to the glowing embers of the

fire. He blew. Small flames danced as frosted air fanned the fire. James added small sticks, then nodded at the welcomed heat. His hands, extended over the crackling flames, warmed.

Bang!

James jumped. Frowning, he cocked his head and listened. Somewhere down the valley, something like a door slamming—wood on wood. Someone stirred. Probably that crazy Dawson visiting Henry.

Trace mumbled, rubbed his eyes.

"It's all right. Just noises." James glanced over his shoulder, then back to his brother. "Go back to sleep."

Trace pulled his blanket closer, nodded, and within seconds snored.

CHAPTER TWENTY-ONE

Mesilla

Luke wiped his mouth, suppressed a low-key belch, folded the cotton napkin, and pushed back from the supper table. "Mighty fine cookin', ladies. Best stew I've had in ages. You put some special seasoning in there?" While he cooked only when there were no other choices so he wouldn't starve, usually around a campfire, he appreciated the special care given this stew.

Morningstar grinned and picked up their bowls. "Yes, there's special seasoning, and, no, I'm not telling." After placing the dishes in the washtub she then returned for Teresa's.

While Morningstar poured coffee into three cups, Luke leaned over and ruffled Faith's hair. "Hey, Cupcake, you want your old Uncle Luke to take you and your mom and aunt for a buggy ride tomorrow?"

Faith wiggled and held out her arms. Luke freed her from the wooden highchair, holding her close against him, enjoying the softness only a small child brings. An empty space opened in his chest—his children. He missed them more than he'd realized.

Teresa gathered the spoons and napkins and pushed back her chair. "That'd be fun. You haven't seen the rest of the area; it's beautiful this time of year."

"Been doing all the heavy work this past week, and we appreciate it." Morningstar handed a cup to Luke and flashed a breath-grabbing grin. "It's about time we give you the day off and do some sightseeing."

"Good." Luke bounced the baby while his heart beat a bit faster. He returned the grin. "I'm looking forward to it."

Lupe's Café stood next to The Corn Exchange Hotel, which faced the plaza, the center of town. From there Luke watched the world go about its business. People scurried past, as if the sun would melt them. He glanced up. Not a cloud around—the earth would soon warm. Perfect for his planned outing.

A cool morning breeze greeted Luke while he lingered at the restaurant's doorway. Following breakfast and two cups of coffee consumed at Lupe's, he had time to kill before his outing. Extra time afforded him opportunity to take an early-morning stroll around town. Maybe a walk would work off some of the *frijoles* he'd enjoyed, and maybe he could even bring some gossip back to Star and Teresa.

After a yawn and stretch, Luke sauntered past the newspaper office and glanced in. Editor Tom Littleton sat arguing, rather vehemently, with a man in a black duster, standing in front of Tom's desk. The man's high-crown Texas hat, pulled down low, reminded Luke of the pictures he'd seen of gunfighters, outlaws.

Curious as hell, but deciding not to interfere, Luke sauntered west up the wooden plank sidewalk past the former Butterfield Stage office. He peered in the window and was surprised to find a dram shop. He stepped back and looked up over the door. *Sam Bean's Saloon* the freshly-painted sign professed. He ran his hand over his mouth, then promised himself a beer later. Or maybe something with more kick to it. Luke wandered farther toward the southwest corner of the plaza.

Several yards from the intersection, an old gnarled cottonwood stood guard over the *acequia madre*, the main irrigation ditch. His throat tightened remembering stories James had written about his near miss of hanging, what . . . three years ago? Must've been that tree right there. He pulled his coat around

his body but shivered, despite the fleece lining. James sure had been through a mighty lot for someone just twenty-two. Almost hanged, then captured and nearly killed by Apaches, stage shotgun guard for a year, Army private, and now?

Luke counted his accomplishments on one hand. Two children, wife, and a farm. Sure as hell paled in comparison. On the other hand, four months ago he *had* warned the people of Lawrence, Kansas, that Confederate William Quantrill and his Raiders were about to attack. Luke's riding with Quantrill had given him a chance to know the leader's plans. Although Luke's warnings hadn't saved Lawrence, he sure as hell had tried. That had to count for *something*.

A raspy voice broke Luke's reverie, its Spanish lilt as warm as the day. "Morning, Señor Colton. Beautiful day, no?"

Luke spun and nearly plowed into postmaster Ramos. "Sorry, didn't see you behind me." Luke stuck out a hand and pumped the man's. "Yeah, it's a great day."

"It's a small bit cold, but what do you expect? It's December."

"December?"

"*Sí*. Eighth." Ramos pocketed his right hand while one knitted eyebrow lifted. "Don't know what happened to the rest of the year."

Luke agreed. Had it already been two weeks since he'd stepped off that stage?

Señor Ramos produced a key and stepped toward the post office. Luke followed. Since he was here, might as well pick up the mail for Teresa. Once inside, both men unbuttoned coats, and Ramos hung his behind the counter. Luke pushed firewood into the potbelly stove in the corner and lit the kindling. Within seconds, the small room warmed.

Backside to the heat, Luke surveyed the office. Stacks of letters and packages sat in neat piles around the room. A narrow counter ran its width.

"How do you like Mesilla, Señor Colton?" Ramos spoke over his shoulder.

"Like it fine. But I'd like it better if you called me Luke."

Ramos disappeared as he bent over behind the counter then reappeared with a handful of mail. He held up one letter. "Ahhh . . . *sí*. For you." He offered it to Luke. "From Sally Colton. *Tu madre?*"

Luke snatched the envelope out of Ramos's tight grasp and stuck it inside his coat pocket. Why would his wife write him so soon? Must've written the day he left. Good news? Bad news? The possibilities soared around his head, flying round and round like vultures over carrion.

He needed some place alone to read. Sam Bean's Saloon beckoned. A beer and a shot of whiskey over Sally's letter would surely take the sting out of the message. Luke hurried out of the post office. Fresh, chilly air hit his face. He waved a backwards *adios* over his shoulder while his long legs carried him up the boardwalk to Sam's saloon. He yanked on the door. Closed.

Closed? He yanked again. Not only closed, but locked. He stepped back, re-reading the sign over the door. Yep, correct saloon. One more rattle, yank on the doorknob, and it held tight. A sigh escaped his chest. He'd have to settle on reading it over a cup of coffee . . . or not at all. Maybe he'd ignore it. Probably not. Maybe it was from his children. No, both too young to write. Why would Sally write so soon? It was obvious—she missed him already. Yep, had to be.

Or maybe not.

The letter burned like a branding iron against his shirt.

Instead of a drink or two, or if all else failed, another cup of coffee, Luke ambled toward Bergstrom's Stable around the corner and a couple blocks down the street. He'd rent a buggy, couple of horses, and arrive at Trace's house earlier than expected. Maybe he would help out with some more chores. Or read the letter.

He stepped into the barn, where manure and axle grease smells collided, bringing a half-smile to his face. Just like home. His pa's barn smelled the same. There was something comforting in such feral odor. Horses he understood. Women, not so much.

A clanging, metal against metal, caught his attention. In the far corner stood a man, back to Luke, hammer gripped in a gloved hand raised over his shoulder. The man brought the hammer down heavy on the anvil. *Clang.* The hammer bounced, then another *clang*. Twice more before the man appeared happy with his work. He used long tongs to pick up a horseshoe. He poked it into a fire, then wiped his forehead and turned around.

The man stopped, squinting into the daylight surrounding Luke. The ferrier pulled off a glove and walked toward Luke. "James? Good to see you!" He slid to a halt mere feet away. "James? You're not James." He pronounced the last sentence like a proclamation.

Luke chuckled and held out a hand. "No, sir, been called a lot worse, though." He shook with the man. "I'm Luke, James's younger brother."

A relieved guffaw filled the barn. "Swede Bergstrom. I own this place. Heard you were in town. And now look at ye, lookin' just like that brother of yours." He smacked Luke's upper arm. "Could be twins."

"Heard that before."

"Thought maybe James had changed his mind and was ready to come work for me again." The man pointed behind him. "Could use him, now with Andy and his muscles gone."

While he'd never thought of his little brother with muscles, Luke had to admit Andy was strong. After all, he'd written that in addition to helping Trace with sheriffing duties, he still worked full time with Swede Bergstrom, mainly as a ferrier.

Horseshoes must be in the blood, Luke decided.

Luke couldn't help but like this man. According to James, after he returned from Cochise's capture, Bergstrom had been the only person willing to take a chance on hiring him. James, by his own reckoning, had been suicidal, drunk, belligerent, prone to crying jags, restless, and would fight for any little reason. People had said he would try to kill with no provocation. And that was on good days. But still, Bergstrom saw something in his brother that others hadn't—his fight for survival. James had deserved a second chance. Trace had, too.

Luke brought his focus back to the man standing directly in front of him. His blond hair, mashed down by sweat, matched bushy eyebrows and thick mustache. Blue eyes danced.

"You must've come by for a reason, Luke. Although, it's good to meet ya, I gotta get back to my shoeing." He shrugged.

"Fact is, I'd like to rent a buggy, couple horses. But before we do that, I'd like to . . ." Luke studied the ground. Why was this so hard to say? "To tell you how much I appreciate you looking out for James when he got back—"

"He's a good worker, your brother. Both of 'em, in fact." Bergstrom gazed over Luke's shoulder. "I understand James. He had a hard time putting his feet under him. When he and Andy returned from the army last year, James had changed. For the better."

"James didn't want to join the army, but Andy liked it, from what he said." Luke eyed a big roan tied nearby. It looked to be waiting for new shoes. "Until Andy took a Reb bullet in his side." He recalled his brother's letters describing the surprise and pain. "*That* changed his mind about the army."

"Guess it did." Bergstrom chuckled. "And walking all the way over to California and back didn't hurt. Wore out some boots, I reckon, but gave him muscles he didn't know he had."

"Andy's always been mule strong."

Bergstrom's friendly smile turned into a tight line. "You heard from Andy? Or your brothers?" He leaned in a bit close, like he was telling a secret. "I heard they went searching for him."

"They did."

"Crazy kid." Bergstrom swiped his hand across his forehead. "Got gold fever real bad. Tried to talk him out of going, quitting me. But said he had to try. Knew just where to strike it rich. Crazy kid."

"Haven't heard anything yet. Reckon it'll be soon, though." Luke glanced outside, the blue sky beckoning. "Been a couple of weeks now."

"You going, too?"

Bergstrom's steady gaze pierced Luke. Good question. A pound of concern sat on his chest. What the hell was he doing taking women on a picnic when he should be looking for Andy? What was he thinking? What kind of man was he, anyway?

Icy cold fingers squeezed Luke's heart.

CHAPTER TWENTY-TWO

Mogollon Mountains

Startled from fitful sleep, Trace rolled over in his wool blanket. Words, pleas shot into the awakening daylight. He glanced across the smoldering campfire to his brother, fighting his blanket.

"Please, no . . . don't make me . . . no!" James's arms flailed as if defending off attackers, his legs kicking under the cover. "No!"

Trace threw off his blanket, knelt next to his brother, gripped his shoulders. He shook him. "Dammit, wake up! You're dreaming . . . again."

James jerked against the hold, his knees drawing up toward his chest. "I'm sorry . . . Sorry . . . Don't hit . . ." He whimpered.

"No one here but you and me." And half the Apache nation in your head, Trace thought. "You're safe." How many times had he uttered those words? A thousand? Damn those Apaches. "It's all right, James. It'll be all right."

James froze, as if he'd vanquished his dreams. He blinked awake into Trace's face. Chest heaving like he'd just run ten miles, James pushed sweat-drenched hair off his face. He sat up, shoving Trace's hands away.

Trace stood, his fists tightened, eyes narrowed. His dreams were bad, too, vivid like his brother's. How many times had Teresa wakened him like he had done for James? Why couldn't those memories be over and done? Why did they continue to haunt dreams?

James struggled to his feet and kicked the blanket away. "Gotta find Andy. Maybe this'll stop when we find him."

Trace trained his thoughts elsewhere, squinted into early morning sun. "Help me get coffee on." He poured water into the enamel pot, then added spoonfuls of ground coffee beans.

Across the campfire, James snapped a few sticks in half, pushed them into the fire, and blew into growing flames. Trace perched the pot on rocks stacked inches from the center of the fire.

Trace regarded James. Lines of fatigue across his forehead, jutting from his eyes, aged him beyond his years. Maybe his brother's nightmare was triggered by the body they found yesterday. Maybe it was the way the man had died—at Apache hands. Cold, cruel, vicious. Exactly the way he'd seen before at Cochise's camp.

What could he do to help James? "Cold stream water on your face'll make you look like my brother again." Trace pointed to his right. "I'll watch the camp." He cocked his head. "Go."

"All right. Couldn't hurt." James dug through his saddlebag and pulled out a clean blue shirt, small towel. He held up a bar of soap, trembling in his grip. "Think I'll take a look around, then wash some of the trail off while I'm at it."

"Don't get too pretty, little brother. Might shoot you for some stranger."

"The way you shoot, I'll be plenty safe." James tossed a wave over his shoulder as he ambled through towering Ponderosa pines and scrub oak.

CHAPTER TWENTY-THREE

Mesilla

Luke reined the buggy to a slow walk. Leafless cottonwoods stood like sentinels on either side of the Rio Grande, providing an idyllic place to sit and relax. His three passengers had chatted the entire half-hour trip, pointing out interesting features of the area—the Organ Mountains and tales of stashed gold by Coronado's conquistadors, acres of dormant fruit trees, old Indian dwellings along the route. And, as only a child could do, Faith had jibber-jabbered along with them.

Teresa pointed to a low-hanging branch. "How about there?"

Luke nodded and pulled back on the reins. Teresa sprung from the buggy before he could get out and offer his hand.

"Perfect!" Morningstar handed Faith to Luke, and then she scrambled out without his assistance, either.

Faith darted under the blanket as the two women tried to spread it. Luke chased her around a tree, returning in time to help set out the food.

They passed an hour telling stories while filling their stomachs with ham sandwiches, cold buttermilk, and shortbread. Luke leaned against the tree watching the women play with Faith. The only thing to make this moment perfect would be a glass of whiskey . . . and a cigar. Maybe now would be the time to read Sally's letter. He fought the inclination. This was too nice of a day to spoil it.

"Think Faith and I'll play by the river for a bit." Teresa held out her hand to her daughter, then turned to Morningstar. "You want to come with us? Luke?" Her eyes darted from Luke to Morningstar. Luke squirmed, reading his sister-in-law's questioning gaze.

Morningstar pointed to the tree, part of the blanket spread under it, the other part now occupied by Luke. "Think I'll sit right there and enjoy the sun. But Luke, you go if you want. I'll be fine here by myself."

"I'm sure you would." Luke smiled up at Teresa. "But if you'll be all right by yourself, think I'll stay here, too." He patted his stomach. "Need to let dinner settle."

Another hard stare, those slightly narrowed eyes of Teresa's produced the warning Luke knew was intended for him. He made a quick mental check. Nope. Nothing he'd done wrong. Teresa's unspoken accusations were misplaced.

Teresa nodded. "We won't be long."

Morningstar and Luke waved as Faith toddled off with Teresa. Not knowing whether to stand or stay seated, Luke squinted at Morningstar. As if reading his thoughts, she sat next to him. "Beautiful out here, isn't it?" She leaned back, closed her eyes, and sighed.

"Certainly is." His gaze strayed over the woman. He took in her blue riding outfit, which accentuated her narrow waist. The hair, wound daintily on top of her head, set off her high cheekbones. His sister-in-law. His seductively beautiful sister-in-law. He looked away. He'd promised himself to stop chasing women other than his wife. Sally was everything he needed and more. But, did she need him?

The gurgling of water, harsh jabs of crows crying out for food, his heart beating. Luke willed his body to relax. But the sun only served to heat up his already-burning face. What was it about Morningstar that enchanted him? Her light brown skin? Her shiny black hair? Those haunting eyes? Whatever it is, he thought, leave it be.

"Penny for your thoughts." Morningstar cut her eyes sideways.

Luke scrambled for a topic. "Just wondering where those crazy brothers of mine scooted off to. Shouldn't they be back by now?"

"It's a ways up there and back. And if they can't find Andy, no telling how long it'll be." Morningstar's gaze met Luke's. "Let's hope it won't be much longer."

He picked up a rock and examined it. Should he mention he was leaving? Go find his brothers? No, he'd wait until supper.

A long silence, breathing stops and starts from Morningstar. "I hope you won't think I'm too bold, but I can't get over how much you remind me of James. You're easy to be around. Feel like I've known you for years."

"Months, anyway. So, how am I like my brother?"

"For one, you look like him. The way you turn your head a certain way, your mouth curling up at one end." Morningstar looked away. "And also, your eyes . . ."

"Yes?"

"Same as James's. They take in the whole world at once."

Luke laughed out loud. "What else would they see?"

Growing serious, Morningstar stared at the ground. "Some people never see what's right in front of them. They never enjoy the beauty of life. They hurry from one thing to the next and don't stop long enough to appreciate what they've got."

Luke shifted uneasily, not sure how to respond. Why was she so damn beautiful? "You always this philosophical?"

Morningstar ducked her head. "You bring it out in me."

Pushing away the awkward silence, Luke chose a neutral topic. "Think you're gonna stay in Mesilla?"

"Maybe. Probably not." She turned to Luke. "What I really want is to be a town doctor, like my pa, and they've already got a couple here."

"A doctor?" Luke's eyebrows shot up. "I had no idea."

"I'd been doing some doctoring here before we left. Mostly midwife. I've checked around. In most other towns, doctors don't know broken bones from bad biscuits, I'm afraid. So, they can use my services." Morningstar shook her head. "But James doesn't think they'll accept me into medical school. And even if they do, he doesn't want me to go."

Luke tossed the rock, watching it bounce along the riverbank. "Why?"

"Guess he's afraid of losing me." She wagged her head. "I can be a good wife *and* doctor." Her delicate grin lit her eyes. "I've written my pa in Tucson—he's the doctor there—to see if he can help find me some training."

"You'd be great at it." Besides, if she became the town doctor here, she'd be close enough to see every day. Another reason to stay in Mesilla. Or wherever she was.

Torn between wanting to know more about her or more about James, Luke settled for a combination. "Tell me how you and James met. I don't think he ever said."

Her eyes softened, and a tiny grin slid up one corner of her sensuous mouth. "I assisted my father in Tucson. Trace was a patient, and Andy discovered he was there. Then he brought in James." Morningstar chuckled. "Andy asked me out for supper, but I was waiting for James to ask. So, I told Andy no."

"Sounds like my baby brother. He's not shy."

"No, he's not." Morningstar shook her head. "It took James a while to ask, but he finally did. And the rest . . ."

Luke clutched a stick and scratched in the dirt.

Morningstar squinted as she glanced at Luke. "How about you and Sally?"

He didn't want to talk about her, about them, but his silence would say more than he'd want. Star was smart. She'd figure it out. Hell, she'd probably already realized Sally didn't want him back, no matter what the letter may say. He'd made a terrible husband despite his half-baked overtures of reconciliation. He studied one of his crude dirt drawings. "We've known each other for years. Went to school together. Our families been friends as long as I can remember."

"So, it was meant to be." Morningstar nodded.

"I suppose." Luke raised an eyebrow. "We . . . Sally and me . . . I took her to a dance one night." His stomach knotted. "Well, we got married a couple months later. Had our son a few months after that."

Cheeks reddened, Morningstar touched his arm. "It's nothing to be ashamed of. You've got a fine family now. You should be proud."

Luke took in her misty chocolate eyes. Knowing he shouldn't, but unable to stop himself, he asked anyway. "When are you and James gonna have kids?"

Morningstar picked up a pebble, tossed it toward the river.

Luke chided himself for his brass. "I'm sorry. Didn't mean to pry. I apologize."

"That's all right. You're family." She met his soft gaze. "We want children, more than anything, but James . . . he can't . . ."

"Is he all right? Did those Apache . . . ?"

"He says they didn't abuse him like that. But, Luke, something happened. Something he won't talk about." Fingers knotting the corner of the blanket, Morningstar stared into the wool material. "Something keeps him from . . . from . . ."

"Loving you like he should?"

Morningstar nodded. A tear trickled down her cheek.

Luke slid his arm around her soft shoulders pulling her against his chest. He looked up at Teresa standing yards away, arms folded, staring.

CHAPTER TWENTY-FOUR

Mogollon

Most of the coffee and a strip of beef jerky consumed, Trace paced from horse to campfire, pines to horse, back to campfire. He'd rolled both blankets, tied them on the back of the saddles, repacked his bag, fed the horses, cleaned then loaded his gun. Both rifles stood loaded, ready. He gazed toward the stream. How long does a dunk in the creek take?

Trace spun the cylinder on his revolver again, shoved it into his holster, pulled his coat tighter around his body, then pushed his way through the Ponderosa pines. He rubbed his leg, realizing his limp was gone.

He marched a couple hundred yards down the trail, then spotted his brother coming toward him dodging branches, carrying his dirty brown shirt, a towel, and . . . a hat. Was it Andy's hat?

Trace plucked it from James's tight grip. "Where'd you find it?" He studied it as if it held the answers to Andy's whereabouts.

"Near the stream." James jerked his thumb over his shoulder. "I walked down a ways, saw it poking up through snow."

"Lucky for us you did."

Hesitation from his brother made Trace stop. James shrugged. "Strange, though."

"How so?"

"Maybe just my imagination, but . . . well, sure felt like somebody was tugging on it. Like it was his and he didn't want me to have it." James kicked at the ground. "Fact is, it was jerked out of my hand—twice."

Was this another of his brother's odd visions? His nightmares during the day? A long look at James, and he wasn't shaking, or hell, even crying. No, he seemed rational, if having a hat pulled out of your grip is rational. Trace chose to change the topic. He braced himself. "You find any . . . *body*?"

"Just some prospecting tools. Might've belonged to the fella we found back yonder." James shrugged. "Nothing else for sure of Andy's." He used the hat to point behind him, then turned back to Trace. "He was still here when they attacked. Dammit, he was still here."

Trace studied the hat, and when it stayed in his hand, not tugged or pulled as James said, he spun on his heels, sprinting back to camp. James trotted behind him.

Kicking snow, mud, then dirt toward the fire, Trace tossed the remaining black coffee into the sputtering flames. He spoke over his shoulder. "We're talking to that strange black man again. He knows something."

"All *I* know is I'm not eating his stew." James tightened the saddle's cinch strap. "Got a bad feeling about this."

"Yeah." Trace untied the reins, swung up into his saddle, glanced over his shoulder at his brother. "A *real* bad feeling." He gigged his horse into a gallop.

Dawson's small house stood in view a few minutes later. Trace flew off his horse before James could rein his in. Mud danced around the horses' hooves as Trace tied the lead lines to a bush. He stared at the cabin in front of him. Had Dawson told the truth? Had any of it been true? He bolted toward the door.

Before reaching it, James grabbed his brother's coat sleeve and pulled him to a stop. "Easy." He lowered his voice. "We don't know anything right now. Just that he's crazy. And more 'n likely dangerous."

Trace massaged the Colt holstered on his hip. "Dammit, you're right. We'll let him explain, then I'll take his head off."

The Colton brothers approached the front door from both sides. Trace knocked on the wooden door, waiting for a voice to call out. Nothing but wind whispering through the tall pines. He knocked again, glanced at his brother.

James shrugged, pushed open the door. It screeched against the floor.

Not waiting for another sound, Trace bolted inside. To his left, a blanket askew at the foot of the sagging bed; to his right, the table held one dirty plate and a half cup of coffee.

James stuck his finger in it. "Cold." He held his hand over the stove. "Hasn't cooked in a few hours, either." Mouth set in a hard line, he stared down at the sticks of wood crisscrossed at haphazard angles. "Odd." James knelt by the woodpile.

"What?"

"The firewood here?" James pointed at the pile of sticks. "Knocked over. Remember yesterday they were stacked just so?" James peered out through the single window. "Suppose he's close by?"

"Well, one thing's for certain. He's not in *here*." Trace sighed long, stepped out of the cabin. Cold morning air brought goose bumps to his arms. Behind him sat nothing but a black void of questions, in front lay frozen dead men and no answers.

Trace ambled across the dirt path running down the bottom of the valley. He wandered alongside the stream, its water trickling through the ravaged camp. He joined James, who had finished circling the cabin, checking the nearby hill. They stood in the area between the cabin and the mine.

Removing his hat, Trace ran fingers through his tousled hair, then slapped his hat on his thigh. "Dammit! Where the hell is he?"

"Still lookin' for that brother of yours?"

Trace spun, his gun clearing leather. Hammer cocked, he aimed it toward the voice echoing from the dark mine. He squinted, then recognized the man as he stepped into the light. "Good Lord, Dawson. You about got yourself shot!" Trace eased down the hammer.

James moved beside Trace, stood shoulder to shoulder, James's gun also held waist high.

Dawson produced a yellow smile. "When I heard y'all talkin', I reckoned I best go see who's botherin' my peace and quiet. Never can tell when them Apache'll come back." Dawson held up carrots. "Next pot of stew."

Trace flicked his eyes toward James, a grimace crossing his face. Trace wanted to chuckle, but, instead, his stomach roiled.

Dawson shuffled toward the cabin. "If you put those pea shooters away, you're welcome t'stay. First meal'll be ready directly." He reached the door. "Yeah, ol' Henry and me get mighty lonely eatin' all t'ourselves."

Even if he was hungry, a meal with Dawson was out of the question. Trace pointed to the mine. "Our brother's around here somewhere. We're gonna look through this mine shaft."

"Suit yourself if you've a mind to. Ain't gonna stop ya." Dawson glanced over his shoulder. "Nothin' but vegetables and meat in there."

"What kinda meat?" The question escaped James's lips before he could reel it in.

Dawson shrugged. "Whatever's lucky enough to wander by." He turned his back and sauntered into the cabin, a chuckle shaking his shoulders.

Several feet into the mine, Trace stopped, grabbing his brother's coat sleeve. "Can't see a damn thing." He ran his hand along the chill rock wall. "Feels like they stopped drilling about here."

"Why?" James's voice pierced the dark.

Trace shrugged. "Maybe decided gold was someplace else. Colors didn't run right, or they hit water."

"Dark in here. My skin feels like it's crawling all over me," James said. "Should've brought a torch."

Determined not to lose another brother, Trace kept a firm grip on James's sleeve, tugging him back toward the entrance. "Seems to be all there is here. Let's go ask Dawson some more questions."

James balked at a second tug and called out. "Andy? Andy, you in here?"

Silence.

"Where the hell are you?"

Trace paused at the cabin's door, waiting for his brother to stand beside him. "We'll find him. He'll be all right. We'll find him."

"You're mumbling." James leaned closer. "What'd you say?"

"Nothing." A frosty cloud spurted from Trace as he spoke. He gripped the doorknob and turned it. The cabin's warmth did nothing to soothe Trace's frayed nerves as he stepped inside. He spoke to Dawson's back. "Got some questions for you." Trace struggled to keep his voice normal. What he wanted more than anything was to yell, demand answers. Instead, he flinched as James shut the door.

Dawson stoked the stove's fire while the brothers perched on the edge of the bed.

"Coffee'll be ready 'bout two shakes." Dawson blew into cups and set them on the table. "What kinds a questions?"

Trace surveyed the cabin again. No sign of Andy. He pulled in a drag of warm air. "We found our brother's hat by the stream. We know he was here when those Indians attacked."

"Maybe he lost it before." Dawson hoisted a knife overhead.

Whack. A carrot part shot off the end of the counter.

Both brothers jumped.

Recovering, Trace rubbed his forehead. "We don't think so. We've looked up and down the canyon. Nothing but the hat."

Knife still in hand, Dawson turned to the men. "You for sure it's his?"

What kind of game was crazy Dawson playing? Trace nodded. "Our pa gave him the hat band."

"And our other brother carved curly designs into it. He does things like that. Makes his marks on anything leather." James drew circles in the air. "This's one of a kind."

Trace shrugged. "Andy wouldn't be caught dead without it." He sucked in air. What the hell had he just said?

A chuckle rose from Dawson's chest, filling the cabin. "Looks like you mighta done spoke the truth without even knowin' it." Another chuckle.

Lurching to his feet, James smacked the table with an open hand. "He ain't dead, Dawson, just missing. We turned over every stiff body out there. Thank heaven Andy wasn't one of 'em."

"Ain't no need hollerin' at me. I hears just fine." Scratching his stubbled chin with the knife, Dawson wagged his head, shrugged, turned back to the counter, slammed the blade through another carrot. "Stew'll be ready soon . . . Plenty a fresh meat in it."

Trace stood so fast, the bed scooted back. "We gotta go. Come on, James."

"What abouts the stew?" Dawson poured water into a pan.

Trace backed to the door. He jerked it open, then bolted into the cool morning air.

"What's wrong?" James pulled the door closed. He untied his horse's reins. "He might've told—"

"I'm not eating Andy!"

"What?"

Trace swung up into his saddle, set boot heels to the horse's sides. "That crazy devil's not feeding me my brother." His words trailed behind him as he trotted off. "Gonna prove Andy's still alive. Gonna find him . . ."

James stuck his boot into a stirrup, then swung his leg over the saddle. He hollered at Trace's back. "That's disgusting." He spurred his horse. "We didn't! Did we?"

CHAPTER TWENTY-FIVE

Andy stretched his eyebrows high, hoping his eyelids would spring open. Then he could tell where he was. But they were stuck, glued together by . . . he wasn't exactly sure what, but certainly, dried blood and smeared snot were partly to blame. His face pulled and stung with each muscle twitch.

If he couldn't see, he'd listen. Sounds would tell him where he was. He concentrated. Heart pounding—that was his. Breathing—his, too. Then . . . off in the distance, faint. Horse hooves? He listened harder. Maybe horses, maybe not.

His nose itched. No matter how much he wiggled it, he couldn't scratch, his hands again tied to his ankles. Stretching out proved impossible, but he could roll. Which he did—right into a rock wall.

"Ow!" Andy's head throbbed, but his face was against the rock, where he wanted to be. Carefully, he rubbed his nose on the wall. The itching stopped, and his left eye opened. He let out a long sigh, gave a slow nod, and rolled onto his back. Using his one open eye, he scanned the area. Black dark. If he could put his hand in front of his face, he wouldn't be able to see it.

Where was he? No wind on his face, so he was inside. Rock wall, so it had to be the mine tunnel. How far back in there he had no way of telling. At least he knew where he was.

"Gotta get out of here. Gotta get home." Andy chuckled at his words as they bounced off the rocks. They didn't sound like his, anyway. But he renewed this vow to stay in one piece. He'd return to Mesilla and his family, or he'd die trying. No insane man—black or white or in between—would keep him slave. Not like his brothers had been. And certainly not like Dawson.

He scooted to the rock wall, rolled onto his side, wiggled around until able to sit against it. Maybe from here, he could see—or least hear—someone come in. As he sat, he thought. This was at least the second, maybe third time he'd been tossed in here. Starting to feel like home. He couldn't chuckle at that.

Minutes, maybe hours, ticked by as he sat there, waiting, hoping, listening, plotting an escape. Scraping sounds in the distance, and then a pinprick of light caught his eye. Was there something on the floor nearby he could use as a weapon? A few rocks, but he couldn't pick them up, not with his hands roped with his ankles.

Before he found something useful, torchlight filled the narrow room. He squinted at the brightness but used the chance to see where he was. About the area of the inside of a stagecoach, this "room" sat at the end of the tunnel. Based on the shadows, the tunnel made an abrupt right turn, and, if someone wasn't paying attention, he would miss that turn. A black prison wall of rock created a critical hiding place. Maybe Dawson hid from the Apaches here.

Did he dare hope someone other than his captor was at the end of the torchlight? Twice he'd hoped and twice was disappointed. No, this time he'd wait and see.

And then from behind the light, Dawson's form took shape. "Surprised to see me?" He chuckled. " 'Bout time to get outta here." He grabbed Andy's arm, yanking him toward the entrance. Like a branded calf, Andy flopped back and forth, eating too much dirt. By the time light boiled in, his pant's leg was ripped, and he was sure his shoulder was dislocated.

At the entrance, Andy lay on the sunlit ground, panting.

Dawson pulled out a knife, flashing it at Andy's face. "Gonna untie you now, but one move, one try to gets away . . ." He leaned in close. "I'll kill ya."

Andy choked down rising fear as Dawson sliced the ropes. Tingles flooded back into his body. Arms and legs prickled. Stretching, he struggled to his feet. He gulped lungfuls of sweet air, then rubbed his other eye. Flakes of dried blood and other goo peeled away. Andy opened the eye. Blurry and fuzzy . . . his world fought to put itself together. But here he was, on his feet. Life would be all right.

Dawson yanked Andy close to the cabin. "See those sticks right there, boy?"

Andy nodded. A mountain of limbs, branches, and sticks sat piled against the cabin's wall. Looked like an entire pine taken down, ready to be firewood.

"Stack 'em nice and neat." Dawson pointed with his knife. "I likes things nice and neat."

All right. His shoulder was healing; toting firewood wouldn't be so bad. While he worked, Andy could figure out a way to take out this deranged man, find a way to escape. A way to live.

He slogged through knee-deep snow, his boots keeping his feet dry but certainly not warm. A glance at the sky revealed it was getting on toward dark. How long had he been in the tunnel? Hours, if he guessed right.

"Get a move on!" Dawson shoved him hard. Andy flew forward, his feet scrambling to keep him upright.

"Sorry." Andy knew he mumbled, but his jaw still refused to open wide enough for many words.

"What'd you say?" Dawson grabbed the back of Andy's coat, spinning him around. "What?"

"Sorry?"

"Sorry what?"

Andy scrambled for another word. He thought back to his

recent stint in the army. "Sir?"

"Damn right, boy." Dawson spat as he spoke. "You address me as 'sir' or 'masser' from now on." He poked Andy's stomach, the knife tip resting on a button. "Got it?"

Andy nodded.

"What?" Dawson pushed the tip, brushing skin.

"Yes, *sir.*" Andy pulled in his stomach.

Dawson waggled the knife in Andy's face. "Don't you forget that now, white boy." He turned his back on Andy. "Well, what d'you know. I gots me a slave now. A sure-enough real white boy slave." He mumbled to himself and ambled toward the cabin. "You ever figure on ownin' your own slave, Dawson? No siree, you never did. You surely deserves one, though."

Andy listened at the man's ranting, one eye on the knife, the other on the pile of wood. One small limb would take Dawson down. Knock him out, if not kill him. Did Andy *want* to kill him if given the chance?

Now would be the chance. With Dawson turned away, still talking to himself, Andy knew he could clobber the man and escape. He'd even take the horse.

He kicked a small limb. Not too big or heavy, it would make a good club. Andy bent to pick it up. If he hid it as he turned around, maybe Dawson wouldn't notice. That was a big if, but a chance he'd take. Hefting the branch, he straightened and turned.

And ran right into Dawson. Why hadn't Andy heard the insane man behind him? What had he been thinking? Andy stammered. "I . . . I—"

Dawson grabbed Andy's coat front, throwing him into the outside wall of the cabin. The top of Andy's head slammed against the rough-hewn lumber. He crumpled to the ground. Snow filled his mouth, clogging his nose. Even through the blackness of closed eyes, silver stars pressed against his eyelids.

Thumping. Pounding. Afraid to move, he knew his head would explode.

Dawson's grating voice struck Andy's nerves. "I knows what you're doin', you ungrateful whelp! Thought you was smart, did you? I oughts to kill you right where you lie."

Pushing up on his elbows, Andy righted himself, wishing he could melt into the wall. Get away. He stuttered. "Sorry. Sorry . . . *sir.*"

Toes of Dawson's muddy boots crashed into Andy's sore ribs. He opened his mouth to scream, but nothing came out. Andy wasn't an especially religious man, but right now he prayed. Hard.

Mumbling, Dawson strutted in front of him. "That's right. I give him food, shelter. Hell, I even patches him up, and what do I gets in return? Nothing. I gets nothing but an ol' stick waved at my back." He chortled. "But that's awright with Dawson. Yes, siree. Just means ol' Andrew's gonna work double hard."

Dawson stopped, wheeled around to Andy. "Now you pick up them firewood sticks, like I told you. Cart 'em into the cabin. Stack 'em neat." He kicked Andy's foot. "Now!"

Firewood lay scattered around the cabin like oversized toothpicks. Lightning bolts of pain hammered his shoulder as Dawson yanked Andy to his feet, hauling his body upright, his legs taking the weight.

Dawson's sour breath pelted Andy's face. "I said pile 'em neat, slave!" He pointed at the wood. "Get it through that ugly head of yours. I want 'em stacked right!"

Andy willed his injured right arm to hold the bulky sticks. Picking them up one by one, he balanced the wood on his arms. He pushed aside pain. It would all be over soon. By the ninth branch, muscles trembled, and his strength faded. He pulled in air. As he bent over for the last stick, Dawson kicked the back of

Andy's knees. Both Andy and firewood crumpled like wooden blocks.

"Fool! Imbecile!" Dawson raved. "Should kill you!"

Boots slammed into Andy's ribs and lower back, striking again and again. Andy covered his head with his hands and rolled. Somersaulting through snow, he scrambled to his knees. Muscles not willing to stand him upright, he crawled.

Get away. Get away. The mantra repeated as he clawed his way through mud and snow.

Dawson snickered. "Go on, boy."

Andy clutched a thin shrub branch and pulled himself under it.

Dawson bent down, peering at Andy. "I see you." He chuckled. "There's 'nother bush over there you might try ta hide under." He pointed to his left. "Go on whenever you get tired to huggin' that one."

Lying on his side, Andy spotted two snow mounds in front of him. If he could just make it to the one by the stream, maybe—

"I like playin' hide 'n seek," Dawson said. "But I'll still find ya, though."

Andy curled into a trembling ball, wishing for a miracle.

"I'll always find ya. Anywheres you go, I'll find ya."

"Help!" Did anything come out? "Help!" A squeak.

"Ain't nobody 'round to hear ya, but you just keep on hollerin' all ya wants." Dawson clawed at the back of Andy's coat.

Arms wrapped around the branches, the wooden lifeline, Andy used dredged-up strength to hold on. "Trace—"

"Keep yellin', boy. Good for your lungs." Dawson yanked Andy out from the bush and onto his feet.

Andy wobbled, furious hands holding him upright. Dawson lowered his voice to a venomous whisper. "So, you wanna play rough? You ain't seen nothin' yet, white boy."

Dawson released his hold and dug into his pocket, bringing

out rope. "What you've been through so far's a picnic."

Andy refused to whimper as the rope sawed into his tender, raw flesh. He wouldn't give this more-than-crazy lunatic the pleasure of hearing him cry.

Dawson clutched the front of Andy's coat, then pulled. "Now—you're goin' to hell, boy. Straight to hell."

CHAPTER TWENTY-SIX

Mesilla

Mesilla Times editor Thomas Littleton took a second drag on his cigar and puffed out blue circles. He pointed the cigar at Luke. "You're different from your brothers, you know that?"

"I am? How?" Did Luke really want to know? It seemed lately everyone he met remarked on the similarities.

"Yeah, helluva difference. You're buying *me* a beer." One eyebrow raised. "Always it's the other way around." He nodded a thank-you and downed half his glass. "Since you're in the buying mode, a second one would taste good."

Luke chuckled and raised his full glass. "They warned me about you, Tommy."

"Don't call me Tommy." Littleton drained the beer and plunked the empty glass on the table. "Got my suspicions about you, though."

Here it comes, Luke thought. Did he want to know? "How's that?"

"Gotta be another reason you're buyin' me a drink. An 'ulterior motive' it's called."

Luke matched the editor's spirals with his own cigar and regarded his beer glass. The darkness of Sam Bean's Saloon soothed his soul. Relaxing in its shadowy cloak, he could lose himself or become someone else.

He reflected on Sally's letter he'd read this morning. Just as he'd expected, she didn't forgive him or want him back. Hell, she hadn't even ended with "I love you" or "Love." Or even an "I miss you." All she'd wanted was to remind him the minister in El Paso was a friend of her father's. She reminded him—again—to be sure to visit as soon as he got the chance. As usual, she was nagging—even this far west.

All right. He breathed heavily. She was doing what she thought was best, no matter how damn irritating it was. She wanted what was best for him. He had to believe that. Again, for at least the hundredth time, he vowed he'd win her back. There was no forgiving what he'd done, and he knew it. Maybe if he became someone different . . . someone . . .

Littleton cleared his throat—loudly. "Talkin' to you." He pointed to his glass. "Just like your brothers, you find something rattlin' around in that pointed head of yours, and there you go . . . riding off somewhere, leavin' the rest of us behind."

"What? Sorry." Luke turned his attention to the man sitting across the table. "My brothers think highly of you, and I thought we should get acquainted."

Littleton leaned back into the wooden seat, the cigar held in one hand. "Talk about me, do they? Better be good."

"Yes, sir. It's all good."

A flicker of a smile rose on his face, his mustache rising with it. "Yep, just like your brothers . . . you're a piss poor liar."

Did it show? Luke signaled the bartender for another beer. Part of this invitation was to meet the man his brothers counted as a friend, but the other part? He'd have to be honest. "I don't know what my brothers said about me, but I've changed."

"Have you now?"

"Yes. And I'm wondering how to get back into their good graces and . . . win back my wife." Luke stared into his glass, hoping the answers were in there. Without waiting for Littleton to speak, he continued. "This summer, I let everyone down. Rode with Quantrill. Did some burning, looting . . . killing.

155

Lied to James, my folks, Sally. Hell, Littleton, I even lied to myself."

"Sally?"

"My wife." Unable to meet the editor's eyes, Luke's gaze swept across the saloon. "Did things I'm not proud of." Swigging his beer, he drew in a long breath, brought his gaze back to Littleton. "How do I make them trust me again? You know my brothers better'n most. How do I make them see I've changed? Not the man I was."

There. It was said. His invisible poker hand splayed across the table for the entire world to see. To examine. His heart and soul lay exposed. Would Littleton laugh or . . . ?

The bartender appeared at their table, two full glasses in hand. He set them down, nodded when Luke produced coins.

The other question sat on Luke's chest, weighing it down like a sack of flour. He lowered his voice. "And Trace. Haven't seen him since he left home, back five, six years now. James says he's all right, considering his time with Cochise. But I've seen James's scars, seen how he behaves sometimes. Trace like that, too?"

Silence stretched into a minute. Littleton huffed into his mustache, blew smoky *O*'s, finished off his beer. "Yes and no. James is easier to figure out. He lets you know what's going on inside. Not Trace. Not as many scars outside, but if he lets his guard down, the inside demons come out."

"He fight and drink, too?"

Littleton blinked rapidly, as if something was stuck in his eyes. He rubbed them. "Not like James. No. Trace keeps it mainly inside. He's a hero around here. Proud and rock steady. But make no mistake, he'll crumble if he's overwhelmed." The editor spun his glass, suds splashing over the edge. "You say you've changed?"

"I have."

"Best way to prove it is respect James's wife. Respect Teresa. They haven't had an easy time, either. Hell, Luke. They're the ones who pick up the pieces when their husbands fall apart—and they do. Both of those gals have spunk." Littleton pointed his cigar at Luke. "I'd say if you want your brothers to have a good opinion of you again, do what you can to help your sisters-in-law. Ride on up there, find your brothers, bring Andy back."

Good ideas. All of them. Could he keep Morningstar out of his lusty thoughts? He'd try harder. "How do I win back my wife?"

Littleton sighed. "Looks like we'll be needin' another round or three."

CHAPTER TWENTY-SEVEN

"What are you thinking, Luke?" Teresa set a bowl of steaming potatoes on the kitchen table. "Traveling up to Santa Rita? Birchville? That's crazy. Suicide."

"Gotta find my brothers."

"There's Indians everywhere. You'll be killed, if not—"

"Captured. I know. I've thought about it." Was he crazy? While he didn't know much about staying out of Apache hands, he'd listened to James talk about his experiences. Stories of his brother's captivity brought a shiver. Maybe those conversations would come in handy. And, he vowed, he'd do whatever necessary to keep out of the Apaches' grasp. "If I can help my brothers, I will."

Should he tell her what he'd told Littleton? Might as well. She'd find out soon enough. "I'm trying to change. I'm sure James, probably Morningstar, told you what I did back home. Thought I was one real silver-plated curly wolf. Turns out a disappointment is all I was. A four-flusher. How I—"

"He mentioned you'd ridden with Quantrill, who tried to kill you himself. Said you were lucky." She handed him three plates. "Said he thought you'd finally figured out right from wrong."

Doubting that was all James had said, Luke arranged napkins and plates while Faith sat in her highchair playing with a spoon. He ruffled his niece's hair. "She reminds me of my son. Her hair, that is." He studied the back of Teresa standing at the stove. "You'd think differently if you'd seen me then."

158

Teresa half turned. "And you'll think differently when your brothers—all three—ride into town."

"I hope you're right." Luke caught Teresa's stare. "Still think I should ride up there, help out where I can."

Footsteps caught Luke's attention. Morningstar, pausing in the kitchen door, cocked her head. "You're leaving?"

"Yeah." One shoulder shrugged. "Thought it's time I find those brothers of mine. Drag 'em back. Probably holed up in some poker game and lost track of time."

Morningstar frowned. "I don't want you to go." She turned to Teresa. "*We* don't want him to go, do we?"

"I've told him no," Teresa said. "Too dangerous alone."

Morningstar touched Luke's arm. "We need you here. Please stay."

Stay? Go? Stay? Go? Same choice he'd recently faced before climbing into the stagecoach and leaving his family behind in Kansas. Had it been the right thing to do? Would it be the right thing to stay here in Mesilla, in the safety of town, and wait for his brothers to return? But in how many pieces? Or should he head out to help rescue Andy? He was damned if he did and damned if he didn't.

"Luke?" Teresa pointed to the table. "Luke? Have a seat. Please."

He focused on the present. Morningstar was already seated, tearing a tortilla for Faith.

Teresa pulled out her chair and sat. Luke eased into his seat, comfortable in the homey kitchen full of tantalizing smells. Tortillas and *posole* aromas mingled, swirling around his head. His mouth watered while his stomach rumbled.

He leaned back, one arm hung over the back of a chair. He missed this. Sitting with Sally and the children. The long talks they'd had over nothing important. The feel of her soft body curled next to his when they lay in bed after a long day of work—the children asleep, stars peeking through the window, Sally's arm over his chest.

He missed it. Craved for its return.

"Luke?" Morningstar's voice broke the images. They disappeared like a ghost. "Haven't touched your dinner. Something wrong?"

Two pairs of eyes looked at him. Time to be brutally honest—for once. He sucked in air, letting it out bit by bit. "Ladies, I need your help."

Morningstar put down her fork, wiped her mouth with the napkin. "How so?"

Suffocating sadness took Luke's breath. Would things ever be all right again? "My wife." He laid his fork on his plate. "Sally . . . kicked me out. Said I needed to get some 'perspective.' " He studied his hands. "Hoping you could tell me what to do." Luke's gaze trailed up to Teresa. "How do I win her back?"

Silence surrounded the table, Faith's kicking and munching on a tortilla the only noise. Morningstar broke the tension. "I've come to know Sally pretty well, Luke. Let me think on it. Give us some time and Teresa and I can come up with something."

"Only plan I've got is to try to find my brothers, get lost in the mountains, and never come back." Was he that despondent? That was a coward's way out. Did he really, truly mean it? Probably not.

Teresa reached across the table and patted his hand. "No need to go to extremes. We'll help. I've got some ideas already."

"I do, too." Morningstar beamed. "And it involves shopping."

Great, Luke thought. Just the way to spend a day.

CHAPTER TWENTY-EIGHT

Morningstar tied her bonnet under her chin. "I've gotta ma letter. Be right back."

Luke eased out of his chair and stretched, Teresa's noon n sitting heavy in his stomach. "I've got one, too. Mind if I along?" He thought about his letter to Sally. Would she bel what he had written? He missed her and the kids. More ever? Maybe it was too soon. Maybe too late.

"Pick up any mail we've got, if you don't mind." Teresa sp over her shoulder as she turned toward the bedroom. "1 your time."

Morningstar and Luke nodded.

Luke held the door for Morningstar, who stepped into the afternoon sun. His letter, Señor Ramos had promised, sh be in Sally's hands within ten days. Providing the mail wa wasn't attacked by Indians. Or Comancheros. Or Texicans too much rain. Or wind. Luke chuckled as the postmaster down the litany of possibilities.

Shrugging them off, he soaked in the warmth reflecting the white plaster of the Corn Exchange Hotel and the pee white of the sheriff's office across the dusty plaza. He could used to living here. Would Sally?

Morningstar held up her purse. "Listen, I've got to sto the grocer's and pick up a couple things for tonight's supp Her grin grew to a full-fledged smile. "I'm cooking!"

"What're you fixing?"

"Fried chicken, Mister Colton. With green beans and biscuits."

Luke licked his lips. "Maybe I'll just come on by. These restaurants 'round here probably don't make biscuits like you do."

"I'll take that as compliment, sir."

Luke caught a look in Morningstar's eyes reflecting the growing knot in his stomach. What exactly was it? Being so close? Guilt for his thoughts about James's wife? He pushed images aside, determined to stay faithful to Sally. "If you don't mind, I'd like to accompany you to this grocer's. But, please let me pay. I want to do my share."

Morningstar nodded. "That's an offer I won't turn down."

He dug in his vest pocket, extracting several coins. Counting, he shrugged. "Don't know how much I'll need, but I've got more money up in my room." Luke jerked his thumb over his shoulder at the hotel. "I'll meet you at the store. It'll only take a minute."

"The grocer's on the way. Down the block and around the corner." She pointed. "I'll show you where it is, then meet you there."

Shoulders close to touching as they strolled, Luke fought for intelligent conversation. Morningstar slowed her pace. "Why are you leaving? I mean . . . really?"

Her nearness flooded his body with warmth. What could he say? She was too much of a temptation? His brothers were more than likely in trouble and truly needed his help? Besides, he knew he should be home with his wife and kids, despite Sally's dispassionate letter.

"Luke?" Morningstar stopped on the street, touched his arm. "Is it something I said? Is that why?"

He shook his head so fast the plaza blurred. "It's just . . ." He

rubbed the back of his neck. "My brothers need me. Should've been back by now. Got a feeling something's wrong. Maybe I can help."

Horses trotted by, kicking up dust. People called greetings to each other. Clouds scudded overhead, the sun playing hide and seek.

". . . we can get along without you, but it's been nice having you around. I feel more secure." She paused. "Luke?"

He snapped back into the present. "It'll only be a few days. Just a few. I promise." Was he babbling? If he didn't move now, he'd grow roots right there and never leave. He edged down the boardwalk while she walked beside him. Something about her . . . push those feelings away, he thought—again.

"Luke? If you are determined to go, be safe," Morningstar said. "Come back in one piece."

Those eyes, rich chocolate. Her skin, sun-kissed tan. The hair . . . Luke took one step back, thudding against a wall. He thought about her . . . about *them*. Morningstar. James. Sally. Trace. Hell, the whole damn family. This wasn't right. No matter what he wanted, no matter how desirable she was, still, it wasn't right. Dammit, this was James's wife.

"I have an idea, Luke." Morningstar's eyes sparkled. "Let's do some shopping before the grocer's. I'll help you pick out something for Sally. She'd like a new shawl, I think."

"A shawl?" That was the last thing he'd think to buy her. Maybe being around Morningstar and Teresa was a good idea. Maybe he wouldn't ride off and leave the women alone, although they didn't seem to need him all that much.

"There's a woman who makes the most beautiful shawls in the territory. Her house's down around the corner. Sally will simply die when you give it to her. She'll be the envy of all her friends." Morningstar bounced on her tiptoes and pointed down the street. "Come on."

She was right. The woman's shawls were good workmanship and looked sturdy enough to withstand the Kansas winds. With Morningstar's guidance, Luke bought a white one with small roses knitted together in the center. Sally *would* love this.

Maybe it would melt Sally's ice a bit when she put this around her shoulders. He had to hope.

They headed back to the post office.

CHAPTER TWENTY-NINE

Mogollon

It wasn't supposed to be this hard, this difficult. They were supposed to ride up into the cold Mogollon Mountains, he and Trace, locate baby brother Andy, then pluck him from the jaws of who knew what. It was supposed to be easy. Andy was supposed to be waiting for rescue. Waiting with that ready smile and hearty laugh. But he wasn't.

Where the hell was he? James shaded his eyes, peered into the endless blue sky. His gaze swept across the narrow canyon. During the few days he and Trace had been there, among the ruins of the mining camp, the sun had come out, shining day after day. It seemed to take pleasure melting the snow mounded on the dead, thawing the earth and, along with it, the bodies.

James glared into the sun, realizing he never hated heat until now. He turned his attention to Trace, who was crossing the stiff arms of the last of the twenty bodies they'd lined up.

"Snow's melting too fast." James's gloved hand scrubbed his two-day stubble. "These bodies gotta get buried."

Trace pried off his hat, ran a forearm across his face. "Almost wish it was back to snowing again. Leastways we'd have an excuse not to bury them."

"Dammit." James clenched his fists. "Why can't those Apache leave well enough alone? Suppose they'll ever quit killing? Suppose we'll ever just let each other be?"

"Maybe a better question," Trace peered into the forest, "is are the Indians coming back? Are we exposed out here?"

"My guess is yes and yes." James kicked at an icy patch of snow living in the shadow of scrub oak bushes. He studied the crusty white. *You're hoping the sun won't move—you know you'll die otherwise. You'll melt into the earth, never to be seen again. Never to be part of life. Never to be—*

A tap on his shoulder. James flinched.

"You all right?"

James nodded, unwilling to give voice to his demons. "Where're we supposed to bury them?" He surveyed the valley floor, then shrugged. "Nothing but rocks here."

Gliding on warm air currents, a hawk circled above the valley. Trace pointed. "Maybe up on top of the hill over there. Need a wagon to haul these men to softer ground, though." He tugged on his hat, its wide brim shading his eyes. "You ride up there and check it out, I'll see if I can get a wagon put together. My horse'll take to one, I think."

"Hope so. We can't haul a loaded wagon all the way up there by ourselves. And I'm not taking them one at a time." James scrubbed a hand over his face. He surveyed the row of bodies. "For their sake, I hope we bury them soon. Words need saying."

Pulling out his Colt, James spun the barrel. Fully loaded. He always felt better when he saw those full chambers—as if someone was up there protecting him, watching over him, caring about him. He shoved the revolver back into the holster and then swung up onto his horse. What would he find on top? He shivered, not from the cold.

A quick wave over his shoulder and he reined around and moved off.

Following a wild-animal trail, James rode past boulders, bushes, and pines. The top of the canyon was higher than it appeared from the bottom. At the top, from up here, he had an unobstructed view of the fractured mining camp below. And

Dawson's cabin.

Up and down the valley lay tent remnants, the gray canvases strewn around like a patchwork quilt sewn by blind women. James let his shoulders sag. Those men shouldn't have died. Not like that. Not at the end of Indians' lances and sneers.

He took his time scouting the area, riding across the top of the ridge and back into a small meadow ringed by trees. No signs of Indians or miners, alive or dead. More importantly, no sign of Andy. He spotted a flat quarter acre without boulders, which would serve well as a cemetery. Sharp pine scents, brought along on a soft breeze, tickled his nose. He knew he shouldn't smile, but with the turquoise sky, chirping birds, and the soothing smell . . . He thought of Morningstar. She'd like it here.

Pulling thoughts into the here and now, he reined his horse around to take another good look at the cabin. As if on cue, Dawson stepped out, slamming the door, and headed toward the mine shaft behind it. Crazy man. James gigged his horse.

It took longer to get to the bottom than he'd anticipated, letting his horse pick her way down the animal trail, around rocks and snowdrifts. After what felt like hours, he pulled up next to Trace.

Trace ran a long-sleeved arm across his forehead, then unwrapped the canteen from the horse's saddle horn. " 'Bout time you showed up." He unplugged it and gulped. "Got the wagon mended and my horse hitched. Had to talk sweet nothin's in her ear to get her to cooperate." Trace offered James the canteen and rubbed a shoulder. "Guess she's not too keen on wagons. Find anything?"

James pointed toward the ridge. "There's soft enough ground, not too many boulders. Up about three-quarters of a mile. Should suit them."

"Not too worried about suiting *them*." Trace rubbed the other shoulder while both men studied the hilltop. "I'm worried about *me.*"

Low whistling, a tune sounding like "Camptown Races," pierced the canyon's silence. Dawson ambled toward the brothers, his whistling louder.

"What d'you think he wants?" Trace asked.

"Don't see a stew bucket," James said. "Looks like he's not gonna try to feed us."

They stood side by side, waiting for Dawson to join them.

Dawson pointed a shoulder toward the row of miners. "Gonna plant 'em?"

"It's the least we can do." James couldn't imagine riding off leaving the bodies to every jackal and fortune-seeker who came near. He pointed. "Found a good place."

Trace held his gloved palms up and wagged his head. "Still can't find Andy anywhere."

Dawson stuck his bottom lip out, more of a habit than a pout. "You try the lake?"

"Lake? What lake?" Trace said.

"Oh, 'bout ten miles up the trail." He pointed due east. "Follow close to the stream. You'll find the lake sooner or later."

"Good Lord!" James swung his gaze from Trace to Dawson and back again. "I thought the trail ended 'bout a mile from here. We followed it, but with the snow, figured it ended there."

Trace peered into the cloudless blue, a breeze pushing a hint of welcome cold. "Gotta get to buryin' these men, but first thing in the morning we'll take off."

Although James wasn't comfortable around Dawson, the man proved to be a wealth of information. Maybe most of it was true. James started to speak, then stopped. He let out a slow breath. "Mister Dawson? You think those Apache will be back? Soon?"

"Nah . . ." Dawson chuckled. "Not again, 'specially since

they came by here just yesterday. Nice fellas." He leaned in close. "Fed 'em leftover stew. They was grateful for it, they said."

"Here? Yesterday?" James stepped back, then closer to Trace. "And they didn't hurt you?"

"Nah. Them's my friends. We understand each other."

Why hadn't he and Trace spotted the Indians yesterday? They had been camped less than a mile down the creek. Then again, when the Apache didn't want to be seen, they weren't. Shivers ran down James's back. Close. Too damn close.

Trace gazed east toward the lake, then back at James. He let out a sigh, streams of frost followed while speaking to his brother. "Tell you what. I got a feeling he's not there, but we need to look anyway. If we don't find him, let's head back to Birchville." He wagged his head. "What's left of it. Spend time there. See if anybody knows anything."

Anybody knowing anything, whether Andy was dead, alive, or moved on would be a help. Would they continue chasing their tails in Birchville? James nodded. "The lake and then Birchville." He looked past his brother, taking in the forest, its trees surely hiding secrets. "He's gotta be somewhere."

Dawson stared at the line of dead miners, then knelt beside a man about his size. "Shame to waste them clothes. Could use a new shirt or two, pair of britches. Good coat."

Trace stepped between Dawson and the body. "We're buryin' 'em just like we found 'em. Need to respect the dead."

"The dead? Hells bells! What about the *livin'*, Mister Colton?" Dawson jumped to his feet and stood nose to nose with Trace. "Or ain't you ever been hungry enough, dirty enough, cold enough to steal? Ever know what it's like to do without? *Really* do without? So hungry the only thing you feel is your stomach pressed against your backbone? So desperate you'd do anything? So tired you couldn't lift your head 'cause there's no food in your belly, no shirt on your back, no—" Dawson dropped his voice. "No hope?"

James chewed on the inside of his cheek and thought about Dawson's questions. "We've been through some of that, Mister Dawson. Yeah, I see what you're getting at."

Terrifying images, horrific anguish, those unrelenting memories charged across James's mind. He cringed, powerless to stop them. Rubbing his right arm, he turned away. Maybe if he concentrated hard enough the visions would fade away. Rapid shallow breaths brought a graying world.

Trace's strong hand gripped his shoulder. James blinked, turned, blew out a long breath. His world colored again. Jaw clenched, his gaze trailed over the bodies. "Take only what you need."

CHAPTER THIRTY

Mesilla

"You're awfully quiet. Something wrong?" Teresa washed the final supper plate and handed it to Morningstar.

She wiped the dish and shook her head. No way she'd tell that her thoughts were with Luke seated in the living room. As much as she wanted James back, she also wanted Luke to stay. "A little tired, I guess. And worried." She glanced at Teresa. "Those men of ours should've been back by now. Suppose something's happened?"

"Don't even think that. It's a long way up there and back, and you know Andy. He probably wandered way off in the hills. The men are just having a hard time tracking him down." Teresa picked up the dishpan and tossed the dirty water out the back door.

Morningstar stacked the dried plate on the shelf, then folded the dishtowel. "I'm sure you're right. No need to worry quite yet." She met Teresa's gaze. "They're fine."

"Uh huh." Teresa lowered the wick in the lantern. Gray filled the kitchen. She touched Morningstar's arm. "What else?"

What could she say? Or admit? Morningstar looked at a spot above Teresa's shoulder. "Just keep thinking how lucky you are to have Faith and then another one coming. Wish it was me, too."

"It will be. Just isn't your time, yet." Teresa touched Morningstar's arm.

Morningstar looked down at her hands. "Can't have kids or medical school." A glance at Teresa. "Either one. Is it asking too much?"

"You'll have to choose one or the other. I don't think you could be a doctor *and* a mother at the same time. Besides, what does James want you to do?"

"Why is it always a man's decision? Always *his* choice?" Morningstar's voice dropped to a whisper. "When's it *my* decision?" With that, she turned and marched into the living room.

Luke, seated on one end of the sofa, played peek-a-boo with Faith. He held her on his lap and both giggled, revealing similar grins. Teresa settled into her rocking chair and picked up a shirt, needle, and thread. Morningstar eased onto the sofa, sitting at the other end.

Teresa poked the threaded needle into the shirt front and addressed Luke. "You got all your supplies ready for the trip tomorrow?" She pulled the thread through. "I'll have a hearty breakfast waiting before you leave. I'm thinking flapjacks, bacon, eggs . . ."

"About that . . ." Luke crossed his right leg over his left knee. "Talked to Sammy today." He ran his finger down a scratch in his boot. "Seems his replacement deputy got kicked by a horse and can't work. He needs some help and says this town's too big for only one deputy sheriff."

Was there a chance Luke would stay? Morningstar wondered.

Teresa stopped rocking. "He offered you a job?"

"Temporary. A temporary one." Luke raised an eyebrow. "I know I said I should go, but he says he needs me here more than my heading alone up into the mountains. So, told him I'd help out as deputy-deputy until my brothers get back." He set Faith on the floor. "If it's all right with you two." He tapped the toddler's upturned nose. "And if it's all right with Miss Button here."

Morningstar beamed. "So, you're staying?"

Luke nodded again and glanced at Teresa.

Teresa sat up straighter, cocked her head. "You don't have to ask our permission. Of course you do what you think is best." A quick smile ran across her face. "You'll be mighty busy, though. Guess we won't be seeing much of you, will we?"

Luke studied his hands then turned to Morningstar. "I'm curious. Why wasn't James a deputy? Didn't he want to?"

She shook her head while a knot twisted her stomach. "He was interested. Especially since Trace is a good sheriff. He's popular."

"So I've noticed."

Teresa lowered her voice. "With James still seeing Indians and fighting them . . . the town council didn't want someone like that. Someone who—"

"It's not right. Just because an Indian takes out his hostility on my brother, the town says he's crazy? Is that what they say?" Luke clenched his fist.

Morningstar hung her head. "I'm afraid so, Luke." She met his stare. "But he's better now."

"Better, but not healed." Teresa set her sewing aside and picked up the toddler. "The town council has the right to decide who protects their city, Luke. They're just doing what—"

"Not the town." Luke's gaze landed first on Teresa, then shifted to Morningstar. "I understand that. But it's not right, not *fair*, James has to keep paying for his captivity." He stared at the door. "When will it end for him?"

Those same questions plagued Morningstar every time James shook at night, every time he cried out. Every time . . .

Morningstar lowered her voice. "There's something else."

"Something else? How can there possibly be *any*thing else?" Luke sprung to his feet. "Isn't that bad enough?"

Morningstar nodded. "As you know, James sees Indians

where there aren't any."

"And?"

"And . . ." Morningstar looked away, the familiar knot working its way to her throat. "Luke, he's almost killed four people."

"Holy damn!" Luke rubbed his forehead. "I had no idea. He never told me."

"There's a little more than that."

"More? There's *more*?" Luke shouted, turned his back on the women, took a deep breath, then turned around.

How much could she tell him? Morningstar considered, then decided. "He stabbed the former sheriff. Alberto Fuente died a few months later."

"He killed a sheriff?" Luke paced the room. "A damn sheriff? Why the hell didn't anybody tell me sooner? Why'd I have to find out now? It's a helluva thing." He slid to a quick stop. "My apologies for the language, ladies."

Luke scrubbed his face like it was on fire. "Gotta get some air." He yanked his coat off the back of the chair. "Thanks again for supper. Night."

The door slammed seconds later. Should she follow him? Try to explain? No. She'd already let her feelings go too far. Somebody would get hurt.

CHAPTER THIRTY-ONE

Mogollon

Andrew Jackson Colton huddled in the back of the frigid mine shaft and hoped he would see another day. He rested his head against a rock. Dawson and his blusterations! He was a man besotted with hatred. Over the last few days, he'd spent hours raging about his life. The landowner ordered Dawson's wife to work in the house, which was easier than outside picking cotton and hoeing weeds. But when she had a baby . . . Dawson's face had curved into a half-crazed, half-grief stricken mask when he mentioned the baby—how it looked when it was born. What had he said? White. The baby was mostly white.

Shortly afterwards, the baby died, and his wife was sold off to another plantation. Some of their children were sold with her, others to a different plantation.

Breath froze in Andy's chest. Dawson had killed the baby *and* the landowner! It all made sense. Wife gone, infant reminding him of his wife's assault. No wonder he ran away.

Andy grunted, the gag biting into the corners of mouth. How many times had he clawed at the material, wishing it would loosen? Dawson tied things tight. Andy held his bound hands in front of his face. Or so he thought. Too dark to be sure. He pulled his knees up under his chin and scooted his freezing rear end until he backed against a solid rock wall. His stomach rumbled. How long had he sat—lain—slumped in this cave,

175

jammed between rocks? How long before regaining consciousness?

This morning he had scooped up his last mouthful of breakfast stew when Dawson yanked him into the mineshaft. Fear twisted Andy's stomach at the cat-eating-the-mouse arrogance on Dawson's face. The face could change instantly. One second it was smiling, eyes dancing with friendliness. Then it brooded, the eyes clouding, brows thickening, pulling together like oxen. Still another . . . eyes wide, staring into who knows what, the mouth peaking at one end. That look—that was when Andy knew to duck. Or try to.

He remembered being tugged down the mineshaft in back of the cabin, the familiar sudden turn in the far reaches of the cave. A turn people wouldn't know was there.

But the last thing he remembered—asking Dawson what was going on.

Andy shook his focus into the present. Today, for the first time, Dawson had wrapped Andy's ankles in wire. Usually, rope or strips of material bound them, but wire was more uncomfortable, if having ankles tied with rope could be considered "comfortable." Andy jerked and kicked. Flexing stiff fingers, he ran them around the metal until he jammed his ring finger on a sharp end.

"Hmmmpp." His voice echoed off cold rock. Again locating the end of the wire, Andy bent his fingers to wedge, curl, and tug. Feeling his way along it, he guessed it was five to six inches, long enough to scratch on the wall. He'd draw the feather of an eagle. If James ever came by, and could see it, his brother would know he'd been there.

Andy remembered the time he and James concocted this idea—the eagle's feather. A couple of years ago, after being chased by Apaches for days, the two brothers had become lost in the desert north of Tucson. They promised each other if they got separated, each would draw the feather as a way of saying "I was here, and I'm all right." Right now was the time to use it. But would his brothers search this far back in the tunnel?

Contorted beyond what he thought legs and ankles could do, he used the wire end to scratch what he hoped looked like a feather. Being so dark, he wasn't sure if it resembled anything recognizable. Maybe, if he added his initials. He ran the wire across the wall. Would his rescue be too late? Would he be rescued at all? He had to believe.

A scraping noise somewhere in the distance jolted him out of his project. Peering into the ebony, he spotted a faint glow of orange. Torch or lantern? Rescuers? Maybe it was O'Malley, come back at last. It had been—what, days since he'd seen him? Where the hell had he been? Possibly looking for James and Trace? Soldiers? Maybe even sheriffs and marshals. A posse of some kind?

Andy blinked, wanting to rub his eyes, but shaking his head would have to do. He squinted. A white, almost ghostly, form knelt in front of him. Andy squinted harder. Thomas O'Malley! He'd recognize that Irishman anywhere.

Andy wanted to shout, wanted to hug his friend, wanted the hell out of there and to be warm again, but between the cold and the bindings, he couldn't move. He talked to his friend, but his words were muffled, muddled.

"Lookin' gran', Andrew, simply gran'. Ye're holdin' up well, lad."

Holding out his hands, Andy shoved them close to O'Malley. Why the hell didn't he untie them? What was wrong with this man? Andy screamed.

"No need raisin' yer voice. But 'tis bad news, I'm afraid. Came to tell ye I can't find help for ye." O'Malley sat cross-legged across from Andy. "I tried yer brothers, but they dinna listen. I even went to the constable in Birchville. He ignored me."

What the hell was he talking about? Andy's brothers would come running, guns blazing, if they knew. He whipped his head back and forth as if the movement would untie him, let him talk to his partner. Dizziness was all he accomplished.

"One more thing to tell ye, Andrew." O'Malley slipped his Saint Christopher's medal from around his neck, held it in his hands, then placed it around Andy's neck. He slipped it inside his shirt. "So Dawson don't see it."

This couldn't be good. Andy knew the medal was precious to O'Malley. He remembered the story of how his friend's ma had given it to him for safe travels across the Atlantic and across America. The necklace was everything to him. What was going on? Andy asked, but his words didn't make sense.

O'Malley eased to his feet, hunching so as not to hit the ceiling. He nodded to Andy. " 'Tis been a fine thing knowin' ye, Andrew Colton." He smiled. "True. A fine thing."

And then, like smoke, he was gone. Andy screamed, wiggled his legs, thrashed as best he could, but O'Malley didn't return. Minutes slogged by, then Andy sunk back against the rock. The Saint Christopher medal pressed against his skin. What the hell had just happened?

He wanted to rub his eyes, his whole face. Instead, Andy sat. And waited. He spent time sorting through answers to the O'Malley questions but came up with nothing. Then, a hint of lantern glow lit the tunnel's walls.

Within minutes, he squinted up into the towering figure of his captor, lantern in hand. The runaway knelt by Andy, dropped what looked like a heavy coat, then set the lantern on the ground. He unwrapped the bandana from around Andy's mouth.

Jaw stiff and aching, Andy moved it back and forth. Golden

light haloed Dawson's body, much like O'Malley's.

"Cold." Andy hoped the word made sense. He eyed the pile of material on the ground, then swung his gaze to his captor's coat. Different from his other, this one was of deer or calf. It sported deep pockets and a high collar, good for standing up against wind and rain.

Dawson's breath clouded as he spoke. "I'll untie these ankles if you promise you ain't runnin'."

Andy nodded. His muscles were much too cold for any running. Walking, at this point, would be challenging. He wanted to take advantage of the lantern's light to check his drawing, but if Dawson saw what he had done, no telling the reaction. No, Andy wouldn't chance Dawson finding it. He looked the other way.

Dawson unwrapped the wire, coiled it, and shoved it into his coat pocket. Binding around his ankles now gone, Andy flexed his legs, knees screaming while his hips grated against the frigid ground.

A slow sneer curled both of Dawson's lips as he slid his fingers down Andy's cheek tracing yet another blood ribbon. "Good thing 'bout freezin'. Dries fast."

Jerking at the touch, Andy held his hands out in hopes of release. They trembled, shaking with the damnable mixture of cold and fright. How could he get the coat?

Dawson's face melted into a combination demon and angel. Strong hands, a hint of a smile, yet relaxed body. What game was Dawson playing? Scenarios bolted through Andy's mind, then one gripped his innermost fear. Now he understood. The man kneeling beside him would keep him. Forever. Death would be the only release.

But Andy wouldn't give up. No matter what plans Dawson had in store for him, he'd never give up. He'd fight, kick, scream, plot, and plan. No, he'd never surrender.

"Time to get a move on." Dawson tugged Andy's arm.

Dawson's breath in Andy's face. Breath that would bring down a grizzly. On the other hand, Andy's breath was likely as bad. What he'd give about now for a hot bath, shave, haircut, and good teeth brushing. Something to look forward to after he escaped.

"You move slow, 'bout like molasses in winter." Dawson chuckled, his grip tightening. "You ain't as sweet, though." He yanked harder. "Come on. Gotta get you outta here 'fore you freeze to death."

Dawson worried about Andy freezing? So unlike him. What was wrong with this man? Besides being crazy? Andy anticipated pain, waiting for a slap, for his cheek to burn. If it happened, and it probably would, at least his cheek would be warm.

Using bull strength from a lifetime of work, Dawson yanked Andy to his feet. Both men stood hunched in the cave, Andy's head brushing the ceiling. His rigid legs refused to bend, to move, but somehow, probably with sheer will, they kept his weight.

"Brought ya somethin'." Dawson wrapped the coat around Andy. Its wool lining rubbed soft against his shirt. A faint smell of tobacco wafted with each movement. No way would he ask where he got this coat, or why Dawson gave it to him. No, Andy would simply be grateful.

"Thanks." And he meant it. Between the cold and his broken jaw, Andy produced grunts and groans. Hopefully the meaning came through.

"Let's go." Dawson shoved Andy.

Moving like a wooden soldier he'd played with as a child, Andy shuffled down the tunnel, prodded by a man who would kill without much provocation.

Andy stumbled down the narrow shaft and then into the fresh air. Thankful to be outside, he squinted at a blue sky paling in a setting sun.

A push from behind. A strong one, but not what Andy expected from this mad man. But, he was still on his feet. And most importantly—still alive.

Dawson pushed again. "Gotta get a move on or we'll stick freeze to the ground. Been warm today, but it's coolin' off quick."

Skirting bushes and slogging through thawing snow mounds, Andy picked his way across the field toward the cabin. Near the door, he hit a patch of ice. Andy slid into the wooden door frame, his face slamming against the rough planking. Dawson grabbed the back of Andy's coat.

"Watch where you're goin', Andrew. You wanna be in one piece to see them brothers of yours, don't ya?" Dawson cackled, pulling Andy out of the way, and then opened the cabin door.

Andy held the door edge, found traction for his boots, and then stepped inside. All the pieces fell together. He knew for sure what he'd expected for days. He fought to make words. "My brothers . . . still here?"

Dawson's yellowed teeth showed under the snarl. "Already told ya. Them ol' boys stayed 'round three, four days." He pushed his face closer to Andy's. " 'Parently decided to head on home." He shrugged. "Guess dey tired of lookin' for you."

As if reading Andy's thoughts, Dawson cackled. "Even if dey do come back here, you ain't gonna be 'round for that tearful family reunion."

"You're leaving?"

"Leavin'. Yessiree, we is. You and me. Together." Nodding, Dawson plucked the new coat from Andy's shoulders, then pushed him into a chair at the table. He poured water into the coffeepot, shoved kindling into the stove, struck his knife on a piece of flint. Sparks shot across the kindling, then sputtered into flames.

"Us leaving? Why?"

Dawson centered the pot on a burner, lifted the top, and spooned coffee into it. He took care measuring and then setting the pot just so and turned to Andy. "Why? Seems plain 'nuf to me. Those Apach' is done gone, but seein' as it's dead a winter, ain't much game around."

Andy swept his gaze across the room as if expecting a chicken or rabbit to pop out of a pot. No meat hanging or sizzling in a pan.

"All we gots is vegetables, and those're runnin' low." Dawson scratched his chest. "No, 'bout time to find someplace else to live. 'Specially since your brothers done took all the fresh meat around here." He cackled a second time.

Meat? Brothers? None of it made sense. Maybe the crazy person would listen to reason. Maybe there was hope yet. Andy worked his jaw back and forth. Would the words be understandable enough?

"I can help. Doesn't have to be like this." Andy waited for strong hands to grip his throat, squeeze. Instead, Dawson blew into two mugs and set them on the table.

Obviously, he wasn't listening. Andy raised his voice. "There's people in town . . . who can help. Good people. Even a few colored folk—"

"I could kill you tonight."

Dawson's reflective delivery was not lost on Andy. But, ignoring the threat, Andy leaned forward, gaze riveted on Dawson. "We could ride back together." Nothing left to lose. "I'll get you a job. Livery stable's always looking for good hands. I'll tell 'im you're a friend." He searched Dawson's face, hoping he listened. "They'll hire you for sure. You'll earn money and can—"

"But I ain't gonna kill you. No siree. Not tonight." Dawson measured Andy with his eyes. "Havin' you ride upright's easiest."

Jaw on fire, Andy's shoulders sagged. He'd tried running, he'd tried reasoning. Now he'd have to find another way.

Dawson poured coffee in a cup and plopped it in front of Andy. "Drink up. Get ya nice an' toasty warm." He pointed toward a pile of rags in the corner. "You gonna sleep in here tonight. Floor's warm 'nuf for ya. Got an extra coat. You'll sleep good."

CHAPTER THIRTY-TWO

It certainly felt like a race against time. Two trips around the lake, nothing but frozen feet on both horse and man, and a nagging, something close to a knot of panic in James's gut. It was a familiar knot, one he worked to vanquish forever. At times like this—when he was discouraged, sad, close to giving up—his brother would always have the right words. James glanced to his right. Trace didn't have words now. Dark circles under his eyes, cheeks and chin grizzled with days-old stubble, and shoulders that slumped uncharacteristically—he didn't have nor need words.

Riding most of the day around the lake had given James time to think, when he wasn't eyeing the ground looking for clues. Now, he reined up at the far end, the east side of the lake. James pried off his wide-brimmed hat and ran his other hand across his face, smearing a mud glob from ear to chin.

"Enough's enough. Let's head on back to what's left of Mogollon. Nothing here worth bothering with." He pointed toward the lake, then swept his hand at the forest. "Nothing." The knot in his chest rose to his throat, threatening to strangle him. "*Nothing* to show for our wasted days. Time to look elsewhere."

Reining to a stop beside his brother, Trace squinted, the noon sun rays, like spears, stabbed through the trees. "Got a feelin' he's never been here."

"We can make it to Mogollon and the cabin tonight if we hurry." James tugged his hat around his ears and kicked his horse into a fast trot.

Full dark ushered the two exhausted men and horses into Mogollon. The stillness and nerve-biting cold brought immediate shivers to James. "Don't see hide nor hair of Dawson. No smoke from the chimney." He pointed toward the shape of the singular cabin coming into view and glanced at his brother riding next to him. "What d'ya suppose that means?"

Trace flipped his coat collar up around the back of his neck. "It means we'll stop and find out."

After tying their mounts to a nearby tree, the Colton brothers stretched their lanky bodies and pulled their revolvers. A quick spin of the cylinders revealed full loads.

Trace replaced his .44 Colt, but James kept his aimed toward the cabin. Besides, he'd built a reputation for being a good shot. Butterfield Stage Lines had hired him as shotgun guard for that reason. That and the fact Trace drove for them. Maybe he'd put his skill and hours of practice to good use.

Lowering his voice to a whisper, Trace gazed at the dark cabin, moonlight reflecting off the single window pane. "Don't know what kind of game Dawson's playing, but be damn careful." He swung his attention to James. "Don't want you all shot up. One brother in danger's enough."

"Don't worry." James flashed a wide grin. "I'm the expert marksman of the family, remember?"

Trace wagged his head. "Just . . . watch yourself."

Nodding, James knocked on the door. Twice. Getting no answer, he tried the handle. Locked. Undaunted, he vaulted toward the door, slamming his shoulder against the wood. It held tight. Clutching his arm, James reared back and kicked. *Crack!* The door swung open. He fell into the dark room as Trace also rammed the door. Both men stumbled into the silent cabin.

James crouched, listening for sounds. His own wheezing and

Trace's breathing. Moonlight threw a tenuous beam on the table, managing to illuminate shapes within the cabin.

Pacing side to side, James checked under the bed and table while Trace stepped back outside and circled the cabin. They met inside.

Trace let out a long sigh. "Dammit. Been gone a while, I'm reckoning."

"Why'd the hell he leave?" James holstered his revolver and pushed his hat higher on his forehead. Trace fired up a lantern, and its warm, golden glow flooded the room. He set it on the sawbuck table.

James opened the side of the stove. Curled bark shavings made easy kindling. After lighting it, he pushed in two sticks. Flames licked the dry wood. He glanced around the warming cabin and spotted no single clue to explain crazy Dawson's departure. Judging by the cold ashes in the stove, Dawson left two days ago, maybe three. Was it a coincidence he and Trace had ridden out right before Dawson left?

James rubbed the back of his neck, a headache rippling across his forehead. What in hell was going on? Dawson had seemed content to stay here forever. Something nagged at his thoughts. Something wasn't right. The cabin toasty, James removed his coat and tossed it over the back of a chair.

Trace perched on the edge of the sagging bed, pulled off his gloves, and unbuttoned his coat. "Where the hell is he?" He wrenched it off and threw the coat on the bed. "Andy's here. I know it. I can feel him."

"Something hot'll taste good tonight." Dented coffee pot in hand, James gripped the door handle. "I'll fetch some water." His brother sat, running his hands through his hair. After a pause, enough time for Trace to respond, James opened the door, allowing a gush of icy air inside. "Be back in a minute."

A bank of snow was a ready-made water source. James located

a mound near the mineshaft entrance, scooped and filled the pot to the brim, then turned back to the cabin. The mouth of the tunnel caught his attention. Setting the pot down, James peered into the dark, the moon casting enough light to tantalize his curiosity.

A puff of air blew past his face. Whispers of indistinguishable sounds, sighs, brushed by his ear, circling his body. James swatted, figuring he'd disturbed a bat. He cocked his head and held his breath. What sounded like *"in here"* and *"help me"* swirled.

"Hello?" Cocking his head toward the entrance, he stepped to the mouth. "Anyone in here?" He waited. Silence. Shaking his head, he picked up the pot and trudged through the snow back into the cabin's sanctuary.

Snow immediately melting, James added the coffee grounds, pushed the tin lid on, and set it over the stove's burner. James thudded into the wooden chair, studied his hands and then the chips and scratches in the table. Boiling coffee's aroma pushed panic from his mind. He closed his eyes.

Images of curlicures, Andy's hatband, curious markings marched across his dreams. As if a hand had slapped him, he jerked awake. James whipped around to his brother stretched out on the bed. "Where's a lantern?" He stood so quickly the chair scooted out from under his weight and clattered to the floor.

Trace lifted his head. "Why? There's plenty of light in here."

"Mine shaft. There's something in there."

"What?" Trace sat up. "What's in there?"

"Not sure. I heard . . ." James held up the extra lantern from the corner and shook the bottom. Nodding at the distinctive slosh of fuel, he struck a match and lit the wick. "Come."

"What'd you hear?" Trace grabbed his coat and followed into the cold dark. "James?"

Shoulder to shoulder, the men stopped at the shaft's entrance and stared. James held the lantern high and edged in. Stepping into the golden-lit tunnel, James searched for clues. Somewhere, somehow Andy had been here. Or still *was* here.

Woven baskets lining the cave's sides held a few frozen vegetables, tin containers of flour and coffee, James guessed. Rifling through the foodstuffs, they searched for a sign, something to point them in the right direction.

It came as James wandered to the end of the shaft. A sharp turn revealed another tunnel. "Trace." He held the lantern above his head and pointed. "There's more back here. Damn! We missed it the first time."

James waited for Trace to stand next to him, then both crept down the narrow abyss. Twenty yards brought the brothers to a dead end. Turning around twice, James let out a stream of frost. "Dammit, I was sure this was it. Felt it in my bones." He thumped his chest. "Right here."

"Me, too." Glancing behind his brother, Trace then squatted and studied the dirt. "Look here." He held up a kinked strand of wire.

"So?" James knelt next to Trace.

With a shake of his head, Trace tossed the wire against the rock wall. It sprung back.

Tracking the wire's path, James peered into the edge of the light. He held the lantern closer. Definite marking on the wall.

Trace leaned over his shoulder. "What is it?"

He knew it. He'd been right. James smiled. "Andy."

CHAPTER THIRTY-THREE

Trace peered over James's shoulder. "What do you mean *Andy*? I don't see anything. Just scratchings."

"Look. Right here." James squatted, his finger following zigzags scratched near the bottom of the wall. "See this? Feather of an eagle." He let out chilled breath. "Andy's alive."

"What?" Trace held the lantern closer.

"Yeah, and look here. Part of the letter *A*." James traced the angles. "He wrote most of the letter, then looks like it got smudged, or that's all he could write."

Trace ran his hand through the line. "I remember. Eagle feather. Apache sign for life."

"Andy and me agreed so we'd know where we were and that we were all right." Frost blew from James's nose. "Dammit, I knew it. He *was* here."

"But, the question is—where's he at now?" Trace stood crouching, taking a final glance around the tiny cave. "He's not here, that's for sure. Let's go, this place is—"

"Giving me the crawlies." James shuddered and followed Trace to the entrance and stepped into night, illuminated by starlight and the lantern's glow. The brothers picked their way back to the cabin.

Stepping up to the door, James halted, staring at the tunnel's mouth. "If we leave now, might catch up to them by morning." He wagged his head. "No telling where he is or what's going on." His heart sat heavy in his chest. If anything happened to their younger brother, he'd never forgive himself. He'd been so close to finding . . .

"Too dark to track tonight. Besides, horses need a rest." Trace pushed the door open. "How about you put up the horses and I'll pour coffee. Might as well have supper too, get a good night's sleep, and we'll leave at first light." Why did Trace always have to be the logical one? The one with his head screwed on tight? The voice of reason?

James led the mounts to a makeshift corral near the house, unsaddled them, then watched the horses roll in the dirt. He grabbed a handful of oats from a spare saddlebag and let each nuzzle from his outstretched hand. They'd had plenty to eat foraging earlier, so while hay wasn't around, these strong horses would do fine with only some oats.

He wiped his empty hands on his coat front and dug them deep into his coat pockets. Cold tonight. He surveyed the starry night. Clear. It would only get colder. He stepped into the cabin, grateful for its heat. Maybe a night's rest and he could think better in the light of day.

After pouring two cups of coffee, Trace handed one to James, then eased into the wooden chair. He pried off his hat, then scratched the top of his head. "So." A long pause, hesitant sip of coffee. "Where is he?"

Both brothers stared into their cups.

A full minute passed. Various scenarios paraded through James's mind. One idea stuck. He lowered his cup, held it mid-air, then plunked it on the table. "Dawson."

"What?" Trace frowned.

"Andy's with Dawson. That sonuvabitch took him." He shifted his attention to his brother's drawn face. Seething anger knotted in his chest. "That's what happened."

"Why'd he take Andy?" Trace leaned forward. "Just slow him down if he's running." He ran a finger across his mustache. "If he didn't kill Andy, why'd he take him?"

More possibilities roamed across James's thoughts. Good question—why? One idea grew until it demanded voice. James surrendered. "Since Dawson was a slave, maybe he wants . . ." He brought his shoulders back, his breath held. "You think he's gonna sell him some place? Dawson's crazy enough to do it."

"But who'd buy—" Trace jerked his head up and met his brother's stare. "Good Lord in heaven! The Apache."

A fist plowing into James's face couldn't hurt as much as this revelation. Sudden coldness hit his body; he waved his hands, fending off Trace's words. "The Apache? The Apache?" His voice rose, shaking. "Dammit! I've heard Negroes and Apaches trade and barter with each other." Throat closing, he struggled to speak over it. "You and I both know a white slave would be a feather in any Apache's hat."

"Especially Standing Pony's."

"Dammit! Should've known." James pounded the table. His cup shook. "Dammit, I should've known."

Trace ran a hand across his forehead.

Memories swam around James. "No, not . . . not *him*."

After shutting his eyes, Trace rubbed them. "Probably *his* war party raided here in Mogollon."

"Dammit!" James slid back his chair, stood gazing out the single window. Stars twinkled like eyes taunting him. Every star was an Indian's eye—staring at him. He shoved his hands in his pockets and frowned. "Dammit! Why him and why Andy?"

"Standing Pony's always hated you, especially after you killed his brother." Trace's voice turned sharp. "I remember in camp how he treated you—he and One Wing. So many times, I wanted to kill them. Too bad you didn't kill Standing Pony when you had the chance."

"I know." James drew a quick breath. "When he and I fought last year over the cavalry's freedom . . . and even though I won,

I figured sparing his life would be enough to impress Cochise. At least enough to let the soldiers go."

"It was," Trace said.

Awkward silence filled the small room. James returned his stare out the window. The moon rose over the Mogollon rim, spreading the mountain tops with icy silver. That evil sonuvabitch Standing Pony. Could he tell Trace the whole story? What he didn't know? Up till now, James had hidden his ultimate humiliation. Whored by Apaches! What Standing Pony and the other warriors did every time they'd take him out hunting was unspeakable. How much the assault hurt, not just the physical pain, but the degrading tauntings, the knowing looks every time they sauntered past. It was all there, etched in his memory. He held his breath and cringed, remembering the beatings he received when he'd throw up afterwards. Damn Standing Pony! Damn the Apaches!

"James?" Trace's voice pulled him out of memories. "You're shaking." He slid to the edge of the bed. "What're you not telling me?"

"Nothing." If he turned around to look at Trace, he knew he'd spill the story. Even as close as they were, he couldn't face the telling. Not yet. James held up a hand. Trace was right. It shook. He returned his attention to the window.

Heartbeats, heavy breathing, and skittering night critters broke the heavy stillness. James focused again on the stars. They weren't diamonds in the sky like Ma had told him; they were glimmers of hope lost—too far away to touch.

Trace's voice behind James grew flat. "I'll get him back. Rescue him before . . . before they hurt him any more. No more whips, no more pain. Couldn't get James out . . . save him. But, I'll save Andy. I'll—"

"Trace?" James turned, stunned at his brother sitting on the bed's end, rocking back and forth. Head gripped with both

hands, Trace's eyes squeezed tight. He mumbled into h

"Rode fast as the wind . . . couldn't save James. I t
tear hit his shirtfront. "He hurt so bad. God help me, I

James had rarely seen his brother this distraught. ᵀ
time, five days after James's rescue, was at the doctor's
Mesilla, when he and Trace and their two friends had ᵣ
. . . what he remembered of it. Just like then, Trace wa
edge of collapse. James pushed aside his own demons a
beside his brother. "Look at me." He paused, waiting ⸱
red-rimmed, honey-brown eyes to meet his. "Look
said."

Trace's fists tightened. "If I'd been quicker, if I'⸱
James wouldn't have been whipped, suffered like he
wouldn't have—"

"Dammit, Trace. Look at me!" James gripped his ⸱
shoulders. "I'm right here. Still in one piece." He fo
urge to scream. "Hell, yeah, it hurt. But I survived. ⸱
Right. Here."

Trace's eyes raised to James's. "I tried . . . protect
take your pain . . . get you out." His words quivered. "
do it. I . . . I couldn't do it." He gripped James's ves⸱
face against James's chest and mumbled. "I'm sorry.
sorry."

James patted the back of his brother's head. "It's a
know."

Trace's shoulders heaved.

James waited for the sobs to quiet. "We'll save A
hoped his words were stronger than he felt. "He'll be
You'll see."

Chapter Thirty-Four

Andy rode on Dawson's left and a few feet behind. The man's hand, callused and gnarled, gripped the rawhide reins of both horses, plowing across cold ground.

The ever-expanding sapphire sky, birds soaring above distant trees, and a wispy cloud pushed by winter wind created a canopy of calm. Despite the easy feel to the day, Andy rode straight upright, shifting his weight every few minutes. The Saint Christopher's medal under his shirt lay warm against his skin, a constant reminder of better times. He pushed aside questions about O'Malley.

As he rode, he blew out short breaths, his gaze darting left to right.

They picked their way down out of the Mogollon Mountains, then crossed an open plain into a boulder-strewn valley. Andy kept both eyes wide open sweeping the terrain for any sign of movement. Apaches could pick off both him and Dawson, and no one would find their bodies for months, if not years. Andy itched for a gun.

Every nerve in him strung to perfect tune, he tried not to think about his future. What gnawed on him was demented Dawson. Where were they heading? And why was he so hospitable all of a sudden? Other than keeping Andy's hands tied, he'd made sure Andy wore the heavy coat, so as not to catch "some rheumatiz," as Dawson had said. And he'd been well fed. In fact, Andy's stomach was still full from a long mid-

day break. The man had even mentioned stopping early today so they could catch a rabbit or two, cook a real feast.

They rode out of the valley and up into the hills, always heading west. How far from Birchville were they? If he figured right, it would be about ten miles north. Ponderosa pines trembled with a breeze. Out in the flats with the sun beating down, he'd been warm. But now the shade brought a shiver to his body. Despite bound wrists, Andy managed to button his coat.

"Best be findin' us a good stoppin' place." Dawson tugged back on his reins and turned around to Andy. "How 'bout here?"

Andy shrugged. One place looked a lot like the others. "Fine. Campfire over there?" He used his chin to point left. Besides, a get down would feel good. His legs would enjoy supporting his weight for a while, and his back needed a good popping. His bladder urged him to find a bush. Soon.

Campfire blazing, rabbit turning crispy brown over the flames, Andy sat near the warmth and thought about his brothers. Were they still looking for him? Most likely. Would they find him before it was too late? No answer.

Stomach full of rabbit and a handful of turnips Dawson had brought along, Andy's eyes threatened to close. He fought the urge. He needed to be awake until Dawson fell asleep. Then he could escape. Run farther up the hill and deep into the forest. Run until he found help. Run to Birchville. He peered across the fire. Dawson sat, wide awake, humming *Camptown Races*.

Behind him, a twig crunched. Andy sat bolt upright and twisted. A hand grabbed his throat, lifting him to his feet. Dark eyes, a wide bronzed face glared at him. All air blocked, Andy's world turned gray. He clawed at the hand killing him.

Before Andy blacked out completely, the hand released its hold. He doubled over, sucking delicious air until his world colored again. Strong Apache hands clamped around each arm, yanking him upright.

He jerked at the grips, but the struggle only caused the clamps to tighten. Apaches, their faces streaked red and white, stood on each side of him. Heavy breaths in Andy's ear, and he realized another Apache stood behind him. How many more were out there?

Directly across the campfire from Andy, Dawson and an Apache, more than likely the leader, stood nose to nose, looking like two bulls about to charge.

"You are either very brave or very foolish, Gray Man." The Indian leaned in close to Dawson. "My warriors could slice your throat, hand you your head before your body hits the ground."

"Wondered when you'd find us, Standing Pony. Been couple days since we made our arrangement." Dawson pointed over his shoulder toward Mogollon.

Standing Pony! Andy's brothers had mentioned *his* name over and over. And he'd seen him last year when he was in the army. It was Standing Pony who, along with One Wing, had tortured James and Trace, whipped James—giving him so many scars.

The Apache leader folded his arms across his chest. "You said to come. What do you want?"

Dawson stared up into Standing Pony's face. "Like I told you back at the cabin, wanna do some business with you. Brought somethin' t'sell. Somethin' I know you'll like."

Treatment similar to his brothers' lay in wait. If Standing Pony took him, he'd be beaten, too. Although trembling, Andy's legs were strong enough to run. Give him one chance to escape. One. With dark ready to cover the world any moment, he could break away from his captor. Soon. He studied the faces of at least five Apaches and Dawson. Maybe later tonight.

Standing Pony raised an eyebrow. "What could you have that I want?"

"Just wait." Dawson held up a hand and swung his gaze to Andy.

Bravado in place, Andy jutted out his chin, threw his shoulders back, and stared straight ahead. He tried to mask the terror and uncertainty raging across his heart.

Then, as if presenting royalty, Dawson pointed at Andy. "Standing Pony, you gonna be wantin' him." All eyes turned on Andy.

He was being given to the Indians? What? Why? He tried to stand straighter, to push his chest out, to look unafraid. Dawson walked around the campfire and poked Andy's chest. "This here's prime stock." He stepped back allowing the Apaches room to inspect.

Standing Pony cradled Andy's face in his hands and turned it side to side. A sneer curled his lips. "You have been in Cochise's camp. I know your face—and that of your brothers."

Andy jerked his head from the grip.

Standing Pony stepped back, studied Andy boots to head, then swung his gaze to Dawson. "How did you come into possession of this boy?"

"Don't matter. I have him, and that's all you need t'know." Dawson cocked his head toward Andy. "You wanna barter or do I go t'the Pima?"

Andy fidgeted with the thick ropes around his wrists. Somehow, if he worked free, he'd run.

Standing Pony frowned into Andy's face. The warriors raised shotguns and arrows, all aimed at Andy's heart. Using both hands, the Apache leader gripped the front of Andy's jacket and shirt, then yanked. Buttons flew. In one fluid motion, both coat and shirt ripped off of Andy's shoulders. Standing Pony pulled the material down around his elbows.

Andy shook so hard his teeth chattered. Maybe he'd stay on his feet before the Apaches killed him.

The Indian punched Andy's bandaged, healing shoulder. Nausea boiled to the surface. He leaned over ready to vomit, but the tight grip on his arms kept him on his feet.

"Careful with my property!" Dawson elbowed Standing Pony out of the way. He glared at the Indian. "I takes proper care of my things." He dropped his voice. "You buy 'im, then I don't care how you treat 'im."

"Buy?" Andy, surprised he could speak, mumbled at Dawson.

"What's this?" The Apache poked Andy's stitched shoulder, yanked off the bandage, then spun around to Dawson. "You try to sell me damaged property?"

"Well, hell, Standing Pony. He ain't hurt for good. Day or two, he'll heal up. After all, it was *your* arrow what damaged him." Dawson ran his hand down Andy's other arm. "He's strong, but if you don't want him—"

"How much?" Standing Pony held up his hand.

Dawson's gaze ran up and down Andy, who followed the stare. The former slave gripped the Saint Christopher's medal. "What's this? Where'd you get it from?"

Andy scrambled for a believable answer. "Found it in the coat pocket. The coat you gave me." Would Dawson believe him?

"How much, I say!" Standing Pony moved in closer to Dawson.

Medallion forgotten, Dawson turned to the Indian. "Them gold nuggets you took off'n the miners? I want five bags—full."

Standing Pony let loose a whoop and threw his head back. "You're a thief, Gray Man." He circled Andy, running his hand across his bare chest and back. "Strong. Young." He pried open Andy's mouth and peered inside. The Indian leader stepped back and nodded. "Make fine slave. Two bags. And one pony."

Dawson pulled Andy's shirt up around his shoulders, slipped

his coat over his arms. He yanked Andy toward his horse. "Let's go."

"Four."

"Three. No pony."

"Done."

Chapter Thirty-Five

He should scream. Or fight. Or run. But nothing would change his situation. Nothing. A slave? For the Apache? The Apache who held and tortured his brothers? The same damn Apache who wiped out an entire mining camp?

This was a dream. Of course! Surely that explained the insanity of it all. Andy closed his eyes, tight. If he took a deep breath and opened them, he would find himself back at camp, the miners preparing for another day of backbreaking work. The sun shining at the prospect of today being *the* day. The day they'd become rich. A tug on his arm opened his eyes.

Scowling faces glared. Not a dream, a nightmare. Captured and sold like castoff livestock. Only his life wouldn't be as easy as a horse's. No, his would be . . . whippings every day, like brother James. Work before sunrise, arms loaded with cut wood, killed game, tanned hides, like brother Trace. One bowl of rabbit stew at sunset. Kicks, beatings, ropes digging into flesh, tethered tight at night like a wild animal. All of it rose in his throat.

He stood near the campfire and used his bound hands to swipe at a strand of hair plastered to his tender, swollen face. His eyes darted from Dawson to Standing Pony. What could be worse than being an Apache slave? Andy considered, but nothing short of death came to mind. Whatever the outcome, he'd do anything to stay alive.

Dawson's lips curled as he accepted the bags of nuggets. He

jingled them against his ear. "Since I now got me some money to *buy* my supper, don't have to cart it along no more." He nodded at Andy. "Was gonna eat you, but looks like you're one lucky bull."

Andy leaned away from Dawson. What was worse than being an Apache captive? Eaten by a crazy man. Visions of the frozen miners, then Dawson's stew roiled in Andy's stomach. Maybe being sold as a slave had saved his life.

Dawson raised both eyebrows at Andy. "I know just how you feel, White Boy." A deep chuckle. "Yeah, I does. But now it's your turn to beg for mercy, be separated from your family. Be sold." He cocked his head. " 'Ceptin' we ain't got no big ol' river to sell you down to!"

Dawson threw his shoulders back and pointed one bag at Standing Pony. "You got more of those nuggets, I got more boys look just like him."

Standing Pony's grip tightened around Andy's arm, but his expression didn't change. "Explain."

Heart racing, feeling as if it would explode from his chest, Andy feared what Crazy Man would propose before Dawson opened his mouth.

Dawson jerked his thumb over his shoulder. "His brothers be chasin' his ghost up around d'lake." He glanced at Andy. " 'Bout now they should've figured he ain't there. Turns out, I knows 'xactly where they is."

Standing Pony studied Andy. "Cochise's white-eyed prisoners." He nodded. "The younger one cut me. Now I find him, cut his throat!"

"Ain't revenge sweet?" Dawson cocked his head at Andy.

"No!" Andy tugged against the strong grip on his arms. "Leave my brothers alone." He turned to Standing Pony. "Keep me. I'll work for you . . . hell, kill me if you want." He tried not to stammer over the aching jaw. "But don't touch them. They've been through—"

"Ain't up to you, boy." Moving within inches of Andy, Dawson's rancid breath blew in his face. "Nothin' up to you now." He chortled. "Don't fret none. You'll be seein' those brothers of yours soon."

"Not my brothers!" Andy ripped out of the hands holding him. His eyes narrowed to a pinpoint of white light on Dawson. Using his head as a battering ram, Andy smashed it into Dawson's nose. Blood splattered both shirts. The men hit the ground, Dawson *whumping* onto his back. Andy landed on top.

Dawson bucked, flipped over, taking Andy with him. Andy lay on his back now, Dawson perched on top. Again and again, Andy's face and his broken jaw took the impact of Dawson's fists. Pinned against the hard ground, Andy's shoulder burned, and his head snapped side to side, each punch stronger than the last. His world shrank.

"Not . . . my . . . brothers," Andy hissed.

If he couldn't escape the Indians, by damn he'd take down Dawson. More punches. His. Dawson's. Andy's bound fists found shoulders, an occasional ebony cheek. Strength dredged up, Andy reared, toppling Dawson, who rolled like a top-heavy toy. Once again on top, Andy straddled him and, using his bound hands as a club, struck. Once. Twice.

Apache hands gripped Andy's coat, pulling him off Dawson. Other Apache hands lifted the former slave. Andy fought the hands, fought the blurred images, fought for his life and that of his brothers.

And then, it was over. All energy drained, Andy slumped in the arms holding him. He couldn't fight back, couldn't fight Dawson, certainly couldn't fight these Indians. Knees buckling, he sank to the ground.

Sweat, mixed with blood, dripped into Andy's eyes. He gulped air and ran a sleeve across his face. His stomach churned, bile rose in his throat. Using his last bit of energy, he spit at Dawson. It hit his boots.

Wiping blood off his lip, Dawson stood between two Apaches.

Standing Pony plucked the bags of gold from the ground, then slid the pouches into his waistband. "Mine," he said. A thin smile spread across his face. He turned to Dawson. "As are you," he said, "and you." He pointed to Andy. "Mine."

Dawson started forward, but the Indians' grip stopped him. "Wait a minute. We had a deal. I sell 'im, you buy 'im." He pointed at Andy. "I found 'im. He's *mine.*"

"No." Standing Pony snapped. "*He* belongs to me now. *You* belong to me now."

Andy's heart pounded; his world spun. Icy coldness hit his core. He massaged his throbbing cheek. This couldn't be. Had to be dreaming. Dawson a slave again? Blinking back sudden tears, he studied the face of his brothers' enemy, their tormentor. Standing Pony sneered back.

Nothing could save him now.

The Apache leader strode toward a horse, stopped, then walked back. "This boy brings me his brothers," he said to Dawson, then stood over Andy. "Then I kill you all."

CHAPTER THIRTY-SIX

Mesilla

Deputies Luke Colton and Sammy Estrada hurried toward the crowd gathering in front of the Mercantile. In the past few minutes, from the time Luke had peeked out the office door until now, twenty, perhaps thirty people had collected. While Saturday crowds were known to congregate around the store's bench facing the plaza, there was something ominous about this group.

"What's all the fuss here?" Sammy spoke to a man on the crowd's fringe.

"Indian attack. Again."

Sammy and Luke pushed in toward the man who seemed to be the center of attention. A few of the women and all of the men muttered but moved aside as the two deputies shoved past. Luke recognized the postmaster in the middle.

"*¿Qué pasa, Señor Ramos?*" Sammy wrestled a blackened envelope from the man's grip.

"*Indios.* Hundreds of *Indios.* Mean, fearsome killers. On the warpath, *matan la gente,* killing innocent people."

The crowd drew a collective breath, and women clutched children to their skirts. Men's mumbles grew distinct as the crowd's crescendo built.

"Kill them stinkin' Indians."

"Only good Apache's a dead Apache."

"Shootin' em's too good. Hang 'em!"

Sammy held up his hands and the letter. "Simmer down, all of you. I'll find out what happened. No need gettin' all lathered up over something that might not be." He turned to Luke. "Break this up right now or it'll get downright ugly."

Luke's badge burned against his chest. "You heard him. Go on about your business." No one moved; a few even turned their backs.

"Hey!" Luke shouted above the crowd. "Time for home. Now go!" One woman, two young boys in tow, tsked at the new deputy and dragged her reluctant children down the rough boardwalk.

"Señor Ramos." Sammy shouted to be heard. "My office." He slid his hand under the man's elbow, guiding him through the crowd and out into the plaza.

Passing Luke, Sammy dropped his voice. "I said get this crowd broke up."

His face heating, Luke coughed, then shouted. "Get on home. Nothin' to see here. We'll let you know if anything's happened."

One man grumbled and wandered away.

"That's it. Go on now." Luke pointed.

Two men muttered, threw a disgusted look his way, then wandered off. With the most vocal of the group gone, Luke trotted to catch up with the other deputy. He pushed past growling ranchers and businessmen, sidestepped worried women, and ignored curious children. Luke trotted toward the office. If dresses rustling and low chatter was any indication, the throng had followed him.

Reaching the door just as Sammy and Ramos slammed it, Luke's empty hand curled into a fist. Bringing it up to smack the closed door, he thought better of his action. Instead, he turned to a renewed, growing crowd, his back against the door.

"Best go on about your business, like Deputy Estrada asked." A surge of power simmered in Luke's brain. He was the man in charge. He had the badge. And the gun.

Shoulders squared and standing just that much taller, he pulled his revolver. He pointed it over heads. He barked a final order. "I said go on home. Don't rile me. I'd hate to arrest you all. But I will. Plenty of room in those cells back there."

People turned and ambled across the plaza. Murmurs of "Crazy like his brother," and "Indian lover," drifted behind them.

Hoping his disdain didn't show, Luke let down the hammer and eased the cold metal back into its warm holster. One corner of his mouth drew up as his heart rate returned to normal.

"What the hell's goin' on, Colton?"

Luke jumped at the voice in his ear. He spun around. *Mesilla Times* editor Thomas Littleton stood at his elbow. Luke flung his hands up, thumbed over his shoulder.

"Ah, hell. Postmaster thinks Apaches attacked again. He's got a letter all burned up." Luke stared at the newspaperman's stubbled face; a shave would have been in order yesterday.

"Gawd dammit, boy. What the hell you standin' out here for? Get inside and find out what's happenin'." Littleton pushed the door open and stepped in. Luke wedged his foot in before the rest of his body was crushed by the slamming wood.

"I still don't see how you made the connection." Sammy's voice echoed doubt tinged with impatience. "Yes, this letter is from the town of Walker. But it went through Santa Rita before it got here. Right? That's where it got burned."

Roberto Ramos smacked the desk. "*Sí*. But that's not what happened. Walker's been hoorawed, and that's that!" He snatched the singed envelope from Sammy.

Littleton rested his rear on the sheriff's desk. "Both towns've been attacked, boys. 'Member Mogollon got it just before Trace and James left? Apaches were heading on down to Santa Rita."

The three men nodded.

"A smart leader such as Cochise," Littleton continued, "or his pathetic boot-licker, Standing Pony, would come back and attack again. The town wouldn't be expecting to be hit twice, so soon."

Luke pulled up a wooden chair, planted his right foot on the seat, and leaned into the conversation. "But what would it prove, Tommy?"

"Good Lord, boy, what the hell've you been usin' for brains all these years? Damnation, you're as dense as that hardheaded brother of yours. Hell, even James would've figured it out by now." The editor took a deep breath and glared at Luke. "And don't call me Tommy."

Luke clenched his jaw and studied the "wanted" posters on the wall behind Sammy.

Thomas Littleton took a deep breath. "It proves they can do it, Luke. Those Apache now control the entire Mogollon basin." Littleton pointed north. "It means . . . everyone up in the Black Range is in a helluva lot of danger."

Chapter Thirty-Seven

Standing at Teresa's front door, hat in hand, Luke smoothed his hair. His fingers hit that damn upright sprig on top, the prickle familiar as his hand struck it. Cowlick, Sally called it. Licking his palm, he ran it over the offending spike. Maybe if he didn't part his hair down the middle, and maybe if he'd used a handful more of pomade this morning, it wouldn't stick up like a hedgehog's. He knocked. Waiting, he used the time for another quick lick and swipe. Morningstar opened the door.

"Good morning, Deputy Colton. What a pleasant surprise."

Lovely this morning. As usual.

Morningstar cocked her head to one side. "Luke?"

Mouth refusing to form words and feeling like a moon-struck calf, he smiled, stomped dust from his boots, and stepped into the warm house.

"Teresa, look who's here." Morningstar took Luke's coat and draped it over the back of the sofa. "The new law in town!" She turned to him with schoolgirl innocence. "Is there a problem, officer?"

"No, ma'am." Luke dropped his voice to a bass timbre and hooked his thumbs into his pants waistband. "Just makin' the rounds, checkin' on the fine citizens of Mesilla."

Morningstar, standing less than a foot away, wiped her soft hands on her apron, smoothed her raven hair.

Luke caught Teresa's stare from the kitchen door. She brushed back a stray hank of hair, fixing it back into the rest pinned on top of her head. "Breakfast dishes're already done, Luke. Not close to meal time, I'm afraid." Teresa thumbed over her shoulder. "But I could put on a fresh pot of coffee . . . if you're gonna stay a while."

He marched across the room to hug her. "Didn't come for your delicious food, Teresa. Not this time." Behind him, a squeal and giggle, and then two little arms wrapped around his leg. He looked down into big, sepia-colored eyes. Faith.

Picking her up, he tossed her into the air, which produced more squeals. He cuddled her, his own son and daughter's images bumping into his memory. "Hey, Buttercup. How's Uncle Luke's favorite niece?" He ruffled her light-brown hair.

She returned his hug with a grin and then wiggled out of his grip. He looked at Morningstar. Just the nearness of this woman sent fire throughout his body. Why exactly was he here? Plenty of town matters to keep him busy. To occupy his thoughts. Thoughts that kept reverting to forbidden territory. He shoved them aside. Sally should've received the shawl by now.

Teresa interrupted his thinking. "So, Luke, I understand Señor Ramos stirred up the town this morning." She pointed to the sofa. "Please sit."

Luke sat at the end of the medallion back couch, its needlework fabric soft. "Yeah. Lucky no one got hurt. Ramos sure knows how to round up a crowd. He's convinced Mesilla is next on the Apaches' list." He leaned on an elbow, glad his sister-in-law spoke civil to him. "But I kept things under control."

Morningstar sat across from him in the rocker and leaned forward. Her sparkling eyes narrowed. "Any truth to the rumor the Apaches control that entire area? I mean . . ."

He knew exactly what she meant. Luke refrained from grabbing Morningstar's hand, holding this sensuous woman in his arms. Instead, he raised both eyebrows at Teresa. After all, *her* husband was in just as much danger as James. "This Indian trouble, from what I understand, is a last-ditch effort on their part." He shrugged. "I don't think it'll last long."

"Why's that?" Teresa sat at the other end of the sofa.

Luke stumbled on his reasoning. He hadn't spent much time thinking this through, just formulated ideas from rumors around town. But he wanted to sound thoughtful and intelligent. "The tribes aren't united, like our states before this fighting started. If they banded together against the settlers and miners, they'd be unstoppable. But they fight among themselves."

"Quite a soapbox speech, Mister Colton." Teresa picked up Faith.

Something dark, a thought, maybe a memory, changed Morningstar's face. Her eyes shifted downward, and her lips did, too.

Did he speak out of turn? Maybe he insulted her because of her Apache background? Luke eased to his feet, both women's eyes on him.

If neither woman wanted him around now, maybe he should quit being a deputy and head out to find his brothers. Teresa wouldn't mind. And Morningstar? He'd miss her. He plucked his coat from the sofa. Threading his arms through his sleeves he considered: what kept him in town? He stared back at the two sets of eyes watching him. The answer—simple. While they didn't depend on him for their safety exactly—Sammy checked on them regularly—he knew his brothers would appreciate his staying in town. He made sure the women had enough chopped wood, and he kept them company, entertaining them with stories about their husbands as children.

He'd enjoyed his time here so far. But it would be better when his brothers rode into town.

Remembering the excuse he'd used for stopping by, he reached into his coat pocket. He looked at Morningstar. "I apologize. Nearly forgot. Missus Ramos asked me to bring this to you." He handed her an envelope.

Furrows creased Morningstar's forehead; then a smile erased the lines. "It's from my folks in Tucson." She glanced at Teresa, then Luke, and ripped open the envelope. Unfolding the letter, she scanned it, then read again.

Teresa stood, setting Faith on the floor. "By the look on your face, I'd say it's good news?"

Morningstar's eyes sparkled. A tear in one corner? Joy? Luke stepped closer. "I hate to sound like the postmaster, but . . . I'm dying of curiosity." He peered over her shoulder.

Morningstar beamed. "My pa says a doctor in California, San Diego, will take me as a medical student. And since he's a friend of my pa's, he'll teach me without payment. All I have to do is get out there!" She clutched the letter to her chest. "I wish James was here. He'd be so excited for me."

"California? That's . . . far." Luke was pleased for her, yet she was slipping away. Then again . . . "Will James go?"

His question had no effect on Morningstar. She hugged her sister-in-law, dancing Teresa around the room. After a turn or two, a few giggles, she released Teresa and turned to Luke. "James? Why not?"

Because I'll miss you! Luke's heart pounded in his throat. He stammered and hated himself for it. He spread his arms wide. "It'll take too long. California's too far."

Teresa ignored Luke's concerns. "Just think. We'll have a doctor in the family. First a sheriff and now a doctor. The Coltons are doing fine!"

Luke struggled to rein in his bad mood. No need to spoil Morningstar's glorious news. He grinned, but the smile didn't reach his eyes. "Congratulations. We're all proud of you!"

Morningstar hugged Luke and beamed. "Thank you." She took a breath of utter anticipation. "I'll work hard."

"So proud of you," he whispered, then released her. "I best

be going. I'll stop by later."

Luke busied himself dusting his hat. Anything to avoid Morningstar's eyes. Those black diamonds seemed to follow his every thought, his every move. They pierced his soul and spun his world into possibilities, then ripped his heart apart with reality. He could never have Morningstar.

She belonged to his brother. And he belonged to Sally.

"I'll see you out." Morningstar's sweet voice followed him.

A thought hit him as he opened the door. As he stepped into the chilled air, she followed, closing the door behind her. He turned back, leaning into her warmth. "Want to have coffee? To celebrate your good news."

She nodded.

"Great!" Luke fought to reel in his thoughts. "How about in an hour at Lupe's Café?"

Morningstar nodded a second time, then opened the door. She stepped through, closing it with care.

CHAPTER THIRTY-EIGHT

Standing on the boardwalk outside the sheriff's office, Luke peered at his reflection in the window. Straightening his vest, he smoothed his mustache and mentally polished his badge. Not bad looking for a man of twenty.

What was he doing? And why did this feel wrong? All he was doing was having coffee with Morningstar . . . to celebrate, for Christ's sake. On the other hand, instead of celebrating, maybe he should have a wake. After all, her good news . . . which they were celebrating . . . meant she would leave.

Shaking off the misery, he considered: this was a meeting of friends. Family even. Pure and simple. Nothing nefarious going on, no under-the-table dealings, no clandestine meetings or a tryst. Nope. Nothing but good, old-fashioned coffee. A cup or two, conversations about nothing, and it would be over. Simple.

Still, why did this feel wrong?

Checking the timepiece he'd fished out of his vest pocket, he pulled back his shoulders. Almost time. A stroll around the plaza, a stop or two to chat with the good citizens, should place him at Lupe's Café right on time. "Just coffee," he mumbled. "Just coffee."

As he'd predicted, he arrived at Lupe's doorstep to the minute, if not seconds early. Butterflies tickled his stomach as he pushed on the door. A quick sweep of the room—tables mostly empty—no Morningstar. Which was fine. Women tended to be late to everything. Last minute primping and whatever the hell else they did, always made them late. Sally was the exception, always punctual if not early for everything. But all the other women he knew, including Ma, ran late.

He took a chair facing the door, ordered coffee for two from Lupe's teenage daughter, and waited. Coffee cooling, he sipped and wondered. Had Morningstar changed her mind? Had second thoughts about celebrating her good news? Had Teresa finally come between them? Wait. There was nothing, no *them,* to come between! Luke sat appreciating the daughter's coming and going and wondering about Morningstar. Pulling out two dimes, he tossed them on the table and had pushed back to stand when the door flew open.

"Deputy Colton! There you are!" A woman stood in the door pointing outside. "Trouble! Come now!"

Half mad he'd now miss Morningstar's company, the other half feeling important, Luke stood so quickly his chair scooted back, toppling onto the floor. "What's wrong?"

"Come!" She waved her pointing arm. "She's being attacked! Hurry!"

"Where?"

"The alley! Come!"

Luke raced across the plaza to where she pointed, sprinting down an alley's opening. A woman's screams set Luke's nerves on fire. Someone was deeply in trouble. Pushing into the dark, narrow passageway, he fell over a crate. He clambered to his feet, gaining his balance and sight. In the shadows, the cowboy in Littleton's office last week! Tall, skinny, black duster.

He recognized the woman. Morningstar! She struggled, fighting, kicking, but the man was stronger. Before Luke could reach them, the man threw Morningstar on the ground, landing on top of her. Her muffled cries mixed with sounds of fabric ripping.

"Leave her alone!" Luke shoved aside crates, boxes, and trash.

Heart pounding in his ears, he reached Morningstar. The man had her hands pinned above her, while he lay on top, wriggling. Blind rage thudded in Luke's chest. He couldn't breathe.

"Keep fightin', missy," the man said. "I love feisty women. Just that much more excitin' when I take 'em."

"Leave her alone!" Luke grabbed the back of the man's coat and yanked. The assailant swatted Luke like he was a fly.

Luke kicked his side and legs, then, using both hands, clutched the man's arms. He jerked the man off Morningstar. Luke knelt over the man, punching the stranger's face. Blood splattered.

The assailant pushed Luke off. Staggering to his feet, he balled his fists and straightened. With that, Luke had enough time to whip out his Colt .38 and point it at the cowboy. Luke moved to his left using a wooden crate as a shield. It covered half his body. "Told you to leave her alone!" He peered around the man, the alley so narrow Luke spotted only Morningstar's right arm. She was struggling to sit. "You all right, Star?"

"Uh huh."

The attacker sneered at Luke. "No badge-wearin' ignorant wretch's gonna tell me what to do."

"Hands up. You're under arrest." Luke wasn't sure what would happen if this man fought going to jail. He eased forward.

"You ain't arrestin' me today, *Deputy.*" He scowled at Luke. "What? The sheriff's too busy, sent a kid to do a man's job?"

"Don't rile me," Luke said. "Hands up!"

The stranger nodded behind him. "Got me some unfinished business. I'll finish that right after I kill ya." His hand hovered over his holstered revolver. Each finger twitched.

Luke raised his weapon, drawing the hammer back. "Not gonna ask again. Hands up." He aimed dead center. "Now."

The man cleared leather and fired. Luke pulled the trigger. Deep-throated cracks filled the air. Flames erupted from both guns. Streaks of orange lit the alley. White sulfuric smoke clogged Luke's nose. His ears rang.

Fire seared his head. He raised his hand to stop the pain.

CHAPTER THIRTY-NINE

Mogollon

"Ain't you got any salt for this here rabbit?" Dawson squinted at the Apaches gathered around the early morning campfire. Andy stopped eating. How could that bizarre man ask? Or demand. Didn't he realize he was being held by the feared Chiricahua Apache? Led by none other than Cochise?

The irony of the last few days brought a smile to Andy's face. Dawson had walked right into slavery again. Here he'd tried to sell Andy and ended up a slave himself. Pa's mantra came back. *"Don't go in if you don't know the way out."*

While the tantalizing smell of roasted rabbit hung in the air, Andy thought about Dawson's stew and then other meals around campfires. Most with his brothers. He chewed bite by bite as he pulled his head back into the present. As much as Andy hated to admit, salt *would* be good on this rabbit. Too bad he hadn't brought any. Andy wanted to chuckle at his silliness. Instead of food and seasoning, he ought to be thinking about escaping—from the Indians and Dawson. He should plan his way home.

Although his wrists were bound with thick, rawhide strings, he had enough flexibility to pick apart his share of the roasted rabbit. Almost enough length between wrists to put his arms around someone's neck and wrench. Meat in one hand, he pulled the other hand until the leather was taut. Maybe enough, if the head was small.

But Apache heads weren't small. Especially Standing Pony's, who stood near Dawson, finishing his stew. The wide cheekbones seemed to stretch their skulls into massive heads, and the black hair, held down with leather bands, created almost buffalo-size men. No, unless handed a miracle, his arms were not going around any Apache neck.

Sitting cross-legged by the orange flames, Indians on both sides of him and more around the fire, Andy gnawed on the meat wondering if this was his last meal. It seemed as if every meal in the past few days could have been his last. He should enjoy this one . . . just in case. Still, it would be better with salt.

Across the campfire, Dawson stood picking rabbit pieces from between his teeth. An Apache called Dancing Hawk waited next to him, drinking water from a gourd dipper. A stream ran behind the makeshift camp, and Andy considered leaping up, running into it, and heading upstream. If he followed the water, he'd get to Birchville. And help. But right now that would be suicide. He'd wait. Maybe he'd get a chance soon.

"We go now, Gray Man." Standing Pony jerked his head toward the horses.

Dawson balked at Dancing Hawk's push. "Make you a deal." His feet, shoulder length apart, reminded Andy of gunfight drawings he'd seen. The gunman poised, ready to shoot. Dawson pointed at Standing Pony. "If I lead you to those Colton boys, you let me go. Hell, you ain't gonna need me no more."

"What of him?" Standing Pony turned to Andy.

"What about him?" Dawson shrugged. "He's yours, ain't he? All you want him for is to find his brothers, anyway. What you do with him after that . . . hell, up to you." He reset his hat. "Give me your word you'll let me go, and I'll deliver those boys on a silver plate."

"No!" Andy scrambled to his feet, his breakfast, splatted in the dirt, forgotten. "Leave them alone!" He ran toward Dawson. "Leave them alone!"

Strong hands gripped his arm as an Apache tackled him from behind. Both went down, Andy face first into the dirt. A small pebble gouged his cheek. The Indian on top pinned Andy's arms. Andy squirmed, bucking this tormentor. Perched as if riding a horse, the Indian locked his knees against Andy's sides and hung on. Exhausted, Andy lay immobile. He may have lost this round, but he would never give up.

Sucking in dirt, Andy lay unmoving. Figuring he'd pass out within seconds, he was surprised when the man rolled off and sprung to his feet. The Indian gripped Andy's arm, hoisting him up. Andy wobbled as he stood.

Standing Pony marched across the camp, stopping within inches of Andy. "I will find your brothers. I will kill them. Maybe before the sun sets today. Maybe after the next sun." He stabbed Andy's chest with his finger. "But I *will* kill them."

Arguing would do no good right now. Andy knew he was the only one who could save his family. Question was—how?

Dawson, two Apaches, and Standing Pony swung up onto their horses. Dancing Hawk, who Andy figured to be second in command, waited near Standing Pony who spoke to him. Andy caught snippets of the conversation, but in their native tongue, he was clueless.

Leaning in his saddle, Dawson pointed at Andy. "Standing Pony here says you're to keep your scalp. Leastways 'til we gets back." He chuckled. "You oughta be doin' some prayin' right about now, Andrew. Might come in handy real soon."

He'd do more than pray.

A stick whipped his face. Andy raised his bound hands hoping to deflect it. *Whack!* One side of his head caught fire, a streak throbbing from forehead to chin. Another whack. This one across his right eye, already swollen from last night's beating.

Besides the knots throbbing on his head and face, thick welts burned under his sleeve. Thinking back, those had been from one final smack last night when the stick had splintered. The Apache had hurled the two broken pieces across camp and turned his furious black eyes on Andy. That had been Dancing Hawk, if Andy's memory served.

But right now, bronzed hands grabbed the front of Andy's shirt. He stared into eyes blazing like a million fires. This would be his life. From now on. Until . . .

Dancing Hawk's stale breath blew into Andy's face, turning his stomach. Spit hit his cheek, the warm glob, with the gumminess of molasses, slid downward, dripping off his chin. He glared at his captor. He would *not* be weak. Would *not* be a victim.

The Apache spun Andy around and, in one quick move, planted a moccasined foot in his backside. Andy flew forward, tasted dirt before his face slammed into rocks.

Dancing Hawk rolled Andy over and sat on his chest. He pressed a hunting knife against Andy's throat. The cold blade dug into his skin, the weight of the Indian's anger pinning Andy to the ground. Andy squinted at the Chiricahua. He lifted his chin. "Slice it, Indian. Kill me," hoping the man understood English. "Standing Pony will be proud when he finds out *you* destroyed his property. . . ."

Knowing he had a slim chance of saving his life, Andy growled at Dancing Hawk. "Will Standing Pony sing around the campfire? Sing of you killing *his* captive?" Stomach flip-flopping, Andy hoped the meager breakfast he'd had would stay down.

The blade's fire sliced his skin. Burning streaks ran up his body, while something sticky ran down his neck.

Dancing Hawk held up the glinting blade as a sign of victory. The smirk on the Apache's face bunched the corners of his eyes as his lips curved upward. Leathered skin pulled taut over high cheekbones reminded Andy of old mummies. At least the pictures he'd seen in books.

Andy stared into those fiery eyes and waited for the man to stand, or change his position so he could breathe. Neck and throat throbbing, Andy knew he'd had a close call.

After what seemed like days, Dancing Hawk shifted his weight and stood. Anger and bloodlust crowded the Apache's face. Andy shouldn't push this Indian ever again. This was his one wordless warning.

Strong hands yanked Andy to his feet. Why had he been assaulted? Even though he tried to do everything asked, maybe he hadn't tried hard enough. Then one event came to mind—dropping a newly-caught skinned rabbit in the dirt. But a quick swipe through a snow bank had it clean again. Whatever the crime was, he sure didn't want to repeat it.

More strong hands tugged him past glaring, spitting warriors. They stopped at a pine where Dancing Hawk thrust Andy back into the tree, branches scratching his face. Twigs tugged at his clothes.

"Here." Dancing Hawk produced a length of rope and mashed Andy's body against the trunk. Looping the rope through the tight bindings around Andy's wrists, the Apache ratcheted him against the tree.

Thin branches tugged and tore Andy's clothes. Several jabbed his side and back. He realized—again—Standing Pony and the other Apaches had nothing to lose if he died. Except they wanted his brothers.

Andy wagged his head. That, he wasn't going to give. Ever.

CHAPTER FORTY

James pointed to two sets of tracks in the thawing mud. "More over here, Trace. They're not moving fast, but they sure as hell never stop." Pulling rein, he swung his leg over the saddle. The leather creaked as if sighing, relieved to be free of its burden. Both feet on the ground, he twisted his back, enjoying the release. For the past couple of days, all he'd done was stop and inspect tracks, stop and inspect, stop . . .

Chilled top to bottom, James shook his legs, then squatted by the hoof prints. Two horses, one shoe missing a nail. Dawson's. Very distinctive, very trackable. Both had riders, the prints' depression in the ground staying consistent. Good news—based on the depth of the indentation, Andy was still in the saddle and still, hopefully, alive.

"Over here, James!" Trace stood by a small circle of rocks. "They camped here." Using his boot toe, he poked at the ashes. "A day back. Maybe two."

Relief relaxed James's shoulders. He inspected the campsite. "Looks like it could've been them. Suppose there's a—"

"Eagle feather over here!" Trace pointed to scratchings under a pine.

"You sure?" James loped to the tree. "You sure it's a feather?" Pressure behind his eyeballs. Tears blurred his vision. Could it be? He knelt to inspect the marking. Hard to see, but there. Indeed, it was Andy's. At last, he knew they were close. And Andy was still alive. At least recently.

James pried off his hat, scratched the top of his head. "Where the hell are they?" He glanced up at Trace. "Don't they ever stop and rest?" James stared into the setting sun bouncing light off rocks and trees, igniting the entire forest into flames of orange and red.

"Apparently not." Trace unwrapped the canteen from the saddle horn, drank, then offered it to James. After a long pull, James ran his hand over the sign. Somehow, this simple movement connected him with Andy. He shut his eyes. Blue jays squawking overhead synchronized with the wind whistling through the Ponderosa pines. If he hadn't been so tired, so frustrated, the sounds would have induced sleep. Instead, they taunted him. A voice whispered, *"Close. You're so close. But hurry."* He rubbed his eyes, amazed birds could make sounds resembling words.

"I'd say still a day, maybe two ahead, but we're closing in." Trace pointed toward the valley floor below, the plains spreading in all directions. "And if I'm guessing right, they're heading about ten miles north of Birchville."

"Think they're headed for town?" James stood, frowning at Trace. "Doesn't make sense. Why in the hell would Dawson take Andy to Birchville?"

Another long sip of water, Trace jammed the cork into the canteen. "It doesn't. Maybe that's not where they're going. Gonna skirt around it."

"And then what?"

Like a hammer waiting to drop, the question hung in the early evening air. The brothers regarded each other, then the sky. Mountain jays squawked, a light breeze rustled the leaves, and some critter dove into fallen pine needles.

"Hurry!" the voice came again in James's ear.

"You say something?" James asked.

"No." Trace hung the canteen straps around the saddle horn.

"You hearing things?"

James shrugged. Had he? "Guess not. Probably just the wind. Or I'm tired."

"You and me both," Trace said. "Sun'll be down in about an hour. Want to camp here or get another mile under us?"

Despite the clarity of the evening and the good news finding the feather, depression drew a black curtain over James. No matter how many deep breaths he took, no matter how many positive thoughts he could muster, James mumbled into his chest. "What if we're too late?"

"What?" Trace tilted his head.

James stared into the muddy hoof prints. "What if we're too late? What if he already sold Andy?"

"Don't even think like that."

"Why the hell not?" James spread his arms wide. "Why not think he's already dead? Hell, that way we'll be surprised if we find him alive."

"He'll be alive."

"You sure?"

"We gotta keep the faith."

"Why?" James moved in close. "Hope he survives so he can end up like me? Like us? Scars and demons? Nightmares? Ghosts lurking around every corner, behind every bush? No, thank you." James turned his back on his brother and dropped his voice. "I'd rather he dies."

A clawlike grip on his shoulders made James flinch, his brother's hot breath warming his ear.

"Don't *ever* say that. *Ever*. We're gonna get him back, and he's gonna be fine." Trace shook James's shoulders. "Believe it. You gotta *believe*."

James wrenched out of the hold, so tight it hurt, and faced him. Those brown eyes glowed with what? Anger? Panic? No. James felt it, too. Experience.

Trace clenched his fists. "Dammit, James. You just gotta."

Realizing his brother was on the verge of another breakdown James reeled in doubts. "All right, Trace. I'm sorry."

"He'll be fine." Trace nodded. "All three of us will. Wait and see." He paused, picked up his horse's reins. "Let's give it one more hour."

CHAPTER FORTY-ONE

Mesilla

Luke fought to raise one eyelid. Stuck. He tried the other eye. Nothing. His head throbbed and burned, but, surprisingly, nothing else hurt. Something under him was firm, yet soft. Was he dead? Asleep? Dreaming, yet awake? And where the hell was he?

Voices floated over his head, bumping into his ears, bouncing through his brain. Whose? One male, one female. No, two male, one female. Or was that three . . . ? They made no sense. Whoever belonged to the voices certainly wasn't speaking English. *That,* he'd recognize. Maybe in heaven they spoke their own language. He reconsidered. Or maybe he'd been sent elsewhere, down to the pit of fire and brimstone to spend eternity paying for his sins. He'd try the eyes again.

"He's coming to!" The female voice sounded cheerful.

"Hell and damnation, Luke. 'Bout got yourself killed."

He knew the voice. Thomas Littleton. Luke tried muscling an eyebrow toward his hair and brought the lid with it. One eye at half mast would have to do. Luke squinted, squeezed his eye tight, then opened it as best he could. That was enough exercise for the day. Through his half eye, he spotted Littleton, Morningstar, and Dr. Morgan gathered around him.

So, he probably wasn't dead. Yet.

Using one eye, now almost totally open, he surveyed his world. Behind the blurry faces staring at him, a floor to ceiling

bookcase, a diploma . . . or was it a picture of fish? . . . and a privacy screen clued him. The smell of alcohol all added up. Dr. Morgan's office.

He smiled. Not dead.

Thomas Littleton stood at the side of Luke's bed and scribbled on a pad of paper. Finished, he pointed his pencil at Luke. "Gonna be one helluva story. Might even make the big papers like the *San Francisco Examiner*. Better yet, New York. People in the East eat up anything Western." He tapped Luke's stomach. "Gonna send this article the minute I'm done."

"For Pete's sake, Tom." Dr. Morgan straightened up as he rolled white gauze, then set it on the bedside table. "Can't you see he needs rest right now? Ask questions later."

"Paper won't wait 'til later. Few more facts, then I can go to press."

Morningstar slid her soft hand into Luke's and gently squeezed. He closed his eye, relaxing into almost sleep. The dragging of a chair, its screeching across the wooden floor, brought him back.

Littleton plunked his body in the chair, then licked the end of his pencil. "Now, Luke. How'd you come to plug this sonofabitch?" He dropped his voice. "You know you killed him, don't you?"

He hadn't meant to kill anybody. Killing ran against his nature. Last time he'd had to do such a thing was when he ran guns earlier this year. When he rode with Quantrill. His head pounded. He'd think about it later. Luke swept his tongue over his dry lips. "He was hurting Star."

Morningstar squeezed Luke's hand. "He stopped that evil man before . . . well, before—"

"He drew down on me." Luke interrupted.

"Yeah, I can see that." Littleton glanced again at Morningstar, then scribbled on the paper. "And I understand you and

Missus Colton were about to go out together for . . . coffee?"

"How'd you know where I was going?"

"Hell, son. I'm a newspaper reporter. I know hundreds of details."

"Well, it's none of your business, Tommy." Luke knew his words were garbled, slurred. Damn, he couldn't keep his eye open. The other one still refused to cooperate.

"Just getting the facts straight," Littleton said. "For the article."

Fingers, strong, masculine, gripped Luke's wrist. Had to be the doctor who muttered something under his breath. Was he counting? The hand released Luke. "Good pulse. Not too fast, not like when you came in. Think you'll recover soon enough."

Judging by the chair creaking, Luke pictured Littleton leaning back in it. Littleton asked, "Know who the shooter is? Rather—was?"

At that point, Luke wasn't interested, but he'd need to know eventually. Had he shaken his head? The throbbing intensified. Maybe he had.

"I want to know," Morningstar said. Her words quivered. He opened one eye, wishing he could hold her, tell her it was all right. *She* would be all right.

Dr. Morgan sighed loud enough for Morningstar to turn in her chair. He wiped his hands on a towel. "All right, we're curious, Tom. Who *is* the gunman?"

Littleton paused, a smile sliding up one side of his face. "What does the name Waco Kid mean to you?" When no one responded, he added, "Any of you?"

Had he heard it before? Luke considered. No.

Morningstar shook her head. "Sounds mean."

"Out of Texas?" Littleton leaned in.

Now able to raise his arms, Luke massaged his temples.

The doctor shrugged.

Littleton raised his voice. "Hell. The Waco Kid? Only fastest gun this side of the Rio Grande! Reports say he's plugged nine men." He lowered his voice. "And one woman."

"Good Lord!" Luke peered around his shaking fingers. "Damnation!"

The doctor rearranged the gauze wrapped around Luke's forehead. "Couldn't of said it better myself, Luke. Looks like you're lucky." He turned to Littleton and cocked his head toward the door. "Enough for today. He needs rest." Then to Morningstar. "I'm sorry, ma'am. You can come back later."

Thomas Littleton stood, pocketed his pencil, then smacked the bottom of Luke's feet with his paper pad. "This'll be front page. Story of the century. Hell, this time you'll be a *real* hero!"

Story? Hero? Something about a wacky kid? Luke took it all in, but nothing made sense. His eye fought to close as more words floated over his head. Sounded like Doc.

"Laudanum's taking effect. Gonna be asleep within moments. Best let him rest . . ."

CHAPTER FORTY-TWO

Mogollon

Mid-afternoon sun warmed Andy's face as he stood against the tree . . . waiting. His leg muscles quivered. It had been most of a day since Dancing Hawk cut his throat. In that time, no one came by with water or to check that he hadn't bled to death. He licked his split lips and turned his head side to side. The crackle of dried blood reminded him of what he already knew—he was the luckiest man alive.

Alive. The important word. But, had his brothers found his drawings in the cave? Or the one by the first camp? What would happen if they never came? Or if he couldn't escape?

The sun's final rays bathed the entire camp in golden light by the time Dawson, Standing Pony, and the warriors rode in. They slid off their pintos and strutted toward Dancing Hawk. One of the returning warriors gripped a lance with something brown and hairy poked through the end.

Andy peered through his swollen eyes and wondered whose scalp. Would he be next?

He eyed it and the strutting Indians and fought down rage. He couldn't help that victim now, and any backtalk to Standing Pony or his band would undoubtedly result in his own scalp paraded around camp.

As if reading his thoughts, Standing Pony turned to Andy and signaled his warriors to bring the fresh scalp. Like a pack of snarling wolves, the Apaches marched toward him, their faces, reflecting the setting sun, glowed red. Andy squirmed, fighting the bindings.

They stopped, circled him.

Standing Pony pushed aside branches, breaking several. He ran his hand down Andy's neck, poking at the recent knife wound.

Andy jerked back, slamming his head against the tree trunk.

"Dancing Hawk wanted to kill you, White Eyes. He almost did." Standing Pony yanked the scalp off the lance tip, then shoved the hairy specter into Andy's face.

The stench of fresh blood . . . the raw, feral odor of sliced meat. A bitter aftertaste in his mouth burned down his throat. Greasy hair pressed against his cheek. He turned his head, stood straighter, and squared his shoulders. Could that have been his brother's? He looked harder. No, too dark. *Thank you,* thundered in his mind.

Standing Pony cradled the scalp and stroked the hair like he was petting a dog.

Andy offered a watery smile, glanced at Dawson standing nearby, then spoke to Standing Pony. "You take more like this?"

"Many more." One last stroke of the hair, then Standing Pony handed the scalp to a warrior. He grabbed a handful of Andy's hair and yanked hard. "Yours will be next if you anger Dancing Hawk again." The Apache leader tugged Andy's shoulder-length hair until his chin rested on his chest. His entire body strained against the ropes.

Andy squeezed his eyes shut, wincing at the pain, the ropes cutting across his chest. Standing Pony shoved Andy back against the tree. His head slammed into bark again. Stars throbbed white and silver.

The Chiricahua leader pushed his face close to Andy's. "I see your spirit, White Eyes. It is stronger than your brothers'. In Cochise's camp, One Wing, my own brother, broke their spirit—

just like I will break you." His voice lowered to a whisper. "After I kill your brothers."

CHAPTER FORTY-THREE

Shafts of sun pierced James's eyes. He jerked awake, rolled to his left, and plowed into his brother's knees.

"Just gonna wake you." Trace thumbed over his shoulder toward the campfire. "Coffee's 'bout ready."

"Right." James sat, ran his hand through his hair, pushing it back from his forehead. His hat, flakes of frost spreading around the brim, made him shiver when he fitted it to his head. Would he ever be warm?

Riding all day yesterday and most of the day before had taken a toll on James's body. New aches crossed his shoulders, while his left knee felt like hens pecked at it. His lower back was sore, but that would ease when he walked a bit.

Trace ambled to the horses, his gait slower than usual. Although his leg was healed from the horse falling on it, Trace still favored it a bit. Was that a limp? James figured his brother would say something if it hurt too much. Then again, probably not. Of the four brothers, Trace was the most stoic. Not that he didn't feel pain; he just didn't show it—or admit it.

Aroma of boiling coffee sailed over the campfire. Nothing better than that smell. His mouth curved at one end, anticipating the bitter fire that would soon be flowing down his throat. He spoke to Trace's back. "Got any more beans, or is it jerky this morning?"

Trace yanked the cinch strap on his saddle. "Jerky, I'm thinking. Want to head out pronto. Those tracks look like they're heading to Birchville. Should be there mid afternoon. Give us plenty of time to check around."

"I vote we start asking in the Buckhorn Saloon. Glass of beer would taste good." Pouring a cup of steaming coffee, James blew on it before trying a sip. While he waited for it to cool, he thought about yesterday and the decision he'd made. The slow ride following Dawson's trail had given James time to think, really think about his life. His and Morningstar's. Whatever he was doing, it was wrong. He wanted his wife to be happy, but she wasn't. She wanted to be a doctor, but she couldn't. He wanted to give her children, but he wasn't able. Would anything make her happy?

While up at the lake days before, he had watched a trout break through the thin ice covering the water. Sticking its head barely out of the surface, the fish's mouth flapped open and closed, hoping for a fly or bug to happen by. Obviously, it needed something the lake wasn't providing. His wife was exactly like that fish, and he was the lake. Morningstar needed something he wasn't providing. And he knew what that was. Maybe a change of scenery would change him.

James warmed his hands over the fire, staring into the flames, and waiting for Trace to join him. " 'Bout decided when we get back, I'm gonna move on."

Trace's cup stopped halfway to his lips. "What? Move on?"

"Yeah. Nothing really holding me in Mesilla. I mean, you and Teresa and Andy are there, but I think moving on would be a good idea."

Trace sighed into his mustache, took a long drink of coffee, and regarded the fire. "What'll you use for money?"

"Thought about that," James said. "Before we go, I'll work for Bergstrom's Livery for a bit. Swede said he'd hire me. I'll save every penny. We can leave in the spring."

A long silence wedged itself between the men. Trace sighed

again. "Any idea where you're going?" He glanced sideways. "Maybe I'll want to come, too."

"No, you won't. Your home's in Mesilla." James grimaced as he stood. "Besides. Maybe I don't want big brother tagging along. What does Pa always say?"

Both men spoke in unison. "You've got to do your own growing, no matter how tall your father was."

"All right, I get the message," Trace said. "So, where do you plan to do this growing?"

"I'm thinking somewhere warm," James said. "Or plain somewhere else. I'd like to see the ocean. Neither of us have. Maybe, just maybe . . ." He pointed his cup west. "Yeah, that way's the answer."

"Just could be." Trace sipped the hot liquid.

"Besides," James said. "Lots of families have headed west with no more than bedding, buckets, Bibles, and high hopes." He nodded. "That's a pretty good start, I'd say."

"What d'you think Morningstar's gonna say? Would she want to go?"

James stared into the black liquid. "I've been thinkin' on it, and she'd probably be willing to. For a while anyway. May have to do some fancy talking, but I'm sure she'll go."

"You're good at fancy talking, little brother." Trace tossed the rest of his coffee into the fire. Flames hissed. "The way you spin your words is poetry. But that silver tongue of yours always seems to get you in trouble. Fact is, I remember a certain blue-eyed gal back home who—"

"You gonna stand here all morning and yak, or you gonna ride?" James gulped the remaining coffee, kicked snow on the fire, and ambled toward his horse.

Trace called after him. "I'm just saying the ocean's a long way. Better come up with fifty-cent words to convince her." He spread his hands out wide. "Figure out how to string 'em all together. Just be sure to taste your words before you spit them out."

"Now who's the poet?" James adjusted his weight in the saddle, slid his boots into the stirrups, and turned to Trace. "Let's go find Andy."

CHAPTER FORTY-FOUR

Mesilla

The plan: walk from the doctor's office to the hotel. Simple. But what Morningstar hadn't counted on was Luke's weakness. He'd seemed much stronger at the doctor's.

Halfway to the hotel, she regretted the decision. The trek across the plaza turned into an endurance test. Morningstar gripped Luke's arm as they walked; she certainly could use help right about now. True, he was healing, and true, he stood unaided, but his gait had taken on the appearance of a drunken man navigating a slippery riverbed. He stumbled, slid off the boardwalk, and lurched sideways into the front of the *Mesilla Times* office.

It was a miracle the editor hadn't stomped out to berate Luke for bumping into his building. Thomas Littleton was too brash for Morningstar's taste.

Ten minutes and hundreds of steps later, they paused at the hotel door. Morningstar held it open while he gripped the doorjamb, leaning against one side. She pointed her chin toward the narrow staircase. "Think you can make it?"

"Do I look helpless?" Luke turned, his red cheeks, bloodshot eyes, and gauze-wrapped head resembling more a monster than a man. "Sorry. Didn't mean to sound ungrateful."

This must be hard for him, Morningstar thought. Strange town, no brothers around.

Luke pushed off from the doorway and whispered. "I'm not

to be mollycoddled. It's embarrassing."

Morningstar smiled despite knowing she shouldn't. Men liked to be babied, but not so much as they knew it.

The desk clerk stepped out from around the counter. "Heard what happened. He all right?"

"Rest and quiet," Morningstar said. "He'll be fine in a day or two."

Nodding to the clerk, Luke aimed for the stairs across the lobby. "I'm all right." He lurched forward. Long steps, then he grasped the stair railing. Swaying, he sank to the bottom step.

"I'll get the doctor. Stay right here." Morningstar turned toward the door as the clerk handed a nickel to a child.

"Kid's gonna fetch him." The clerk shut the door and then ambled to Luke. His gaze trailed from Luke to Morningstar, resting on her. "When I saw you two come in like you did and Mister Colton, here, not looking too good, well I figured the doc'd be needed sooner or later. Didn't think it'd be quite this soon, though." His stare ran up and down Morningstar. "Gonna need lots of close attention."

Morningstar's face burned. "His other sister-in-law and I will be taking turns seeing to his injury." More her than Teresa, but it sounded better. "He'll be up and around in no time, I'm sure."

The clerk raised both eyebrows and glanced up the stairs. "I'll help this fella up to bed, get him out of the way, here. Too many guests for one to be hoggin' the stairs." He slipped an arm around Luke's chest and hauled him to his feet.

He muscled Luke up the narrow stairway to his room. In the hall, the clerk fought for breath. "If you need . . . extra blanket . . . my housekeeper . . . can fetch you one."

Opening Luke's door, the clerk walked Luke in, then turned to Morningstar. He took a deep breath, his reddened cheeks fading to pink. He twisted his face into a one-eyed squint. "Doc should be along shortly." He then stepped out into the hall, leaving the door open. His footsteps diminished as he clicked along the wooden floor.

Luke sat on the bed's edge and sighed long. "If my head didn't hurt so bad, I'd tell you I'm glad we're finally alone." He cut a sideways glance at Morningstar. "You gonna stay for a while?"

"I shouldn't. People will be talking." Her gaze trailed from the open door to her brother-in-law's face. She pulled off the boots of this man who so closely resembled her husband she sometimes forgot he was Luke, not James. They spoke alike, moved alike, looked alike, but they didn't think alike. Similarities stopped at the physical. But still, something about this man compelled her, drew her toward him.

He lay back while Morningstar tucked a blanket under his chin. She perched in a chair at the side of the bed. "You'll be fine. A day or two, you'll be back on your feet."

These past two days, she'd done a mountain of thinking. She loved her husband. That was a fact. But this brother-in-law . . . the crazy magnetic attraction, the unsolicited feelings. Butterflies, schoolgirl giddiness, endless smiles. He could give her children. How would she explain it to James? But now, she had a chance at medical school. Did she want children? On the other hand, Luke was a married man. And she and Sally had become friends. Would she do this to Sally? Could she?

"Thought I died and an angel talked to me." Luke's mouth curved at one end. He reached for her hand. "I was half right. You're the angel."

"Silver tongued just like your brothers. That part of the Colton family charm?" He *was* charming. Maybe even a bit more than James.

"You mean you've heard it before?" Luke pursed his lips. "Thought I was original."

"Oh, you're original all right." Morningstar stroked his outstretched hand, the contact raising tiny bumps on her skin. She fought the urge and returned her hands to her lap.

Luke's mouth twisted into a full grin. "Now who's got the silver tongue?" He chuckled, then winced, clutching his head.

She moved from the chair to the edge of the bed, waiting for him to open his eyes. Luke, this man who'd fought for her, this man who'd laid his life on the line for her, groaned.

"Want more laudanum? It helps." Morningstar mentally thanked the doctor for letting her take a large bottle of pain killer with her. It kept her from making several trips back and forth from his office to the hotel.

"Please." Luke's chest rose and fell twice before he opened his eyes. "Might be more like *three* days before I'm up dancing. What'd he shoot me with? A buffalo gun?"

"Shhh." Morningstar sprinkled white powder into the water glass at his bedside and stirred it. "Drink." She supported his head while he sipped. When he finished, she set the glass on the table and stared at her trembling hands.

"What?" Luke grasped one.

Avoiding his eyes, Morningstar glanced out the window. "Just wondering if I should send an express letter to Sally, tell her you got shot. Wondering if she'd come out here to take care of you. Just wondering—"

"I'll write her tomorrow, let her know so she won't kill me when I get back." His eyes fluttered open then shut. "Think it would be better coming from me."

It would be better. Morningstar swept strands of hair off Luke's sweaty forehead, as she did when James was ill. "Rest now. I'll wait here 'til the doctor comes."

Chapter Forty-Five

Mogollon

Andy tilted the wooden bowl against his swollen, split lips, and swallowed hot chunks of deer stew. The warmth slid into his stomach, bringing immediate comfort, temporary relief from the cold. A glance right and left. The Indians on either side of him he recognized. Both had contributed to the throbbing lumps on his face.

He remembered back to mistake number two, yesterday, a day he knew he'd never forget. Evening shadows had grown long, and he'd been on his horse since before sun up. Although they'd stopped once for food, the Indians hadn't bothered to feed or water him. Head still tender from hitting it twice on the tree the day before, Andy's world had grayed and then whitened with each passing mile.

The rhythm of a slow gallop, combined with fatigue and a numbed head, lulled Andy into semi-consciousness. He recalled looking over his shoulder to see how many Apaches were behind him. Spinning his head like that was all it took for blackness to overtake him. With only rope reins to grip, his horse slipped out from under him, and Andy crashed to the ground—directly in the middle of the Chiricahua warriors.

As if in a dream—rather, nightmare—the horses reared to avoid stomping him. Three Apache riders flew into the air, then smacked against the ground. Pounding hooves. Bucking horses. Furious words as he lay in the middle of the raiding party. Rage on Standing Pony and Dancing Hawk's faces. Andy sank into blackness.

Last night after coming to, he received the worst beating yet.

Shuddering, glad the incident was behind him, Andy adjusted his weight on the rock near the fire and grinned inwardly at the freedom of unbound hands. He scooped another helping of breakfast stew from the bowl and licked his fingers clean before attempting another scoop.

His right eye remained swollen shut, but his left sported only a lump. Breathing was difficult over cracked ribs, but otherwise, he was alive. The bruises and eyes would heal, and his jaw felt better, even though it'd been punched. He'd have stories to tell his brothers if . . . *when* they were reunited. A soft groan as he moved. How in the world would he be able to ride all day like this?

Dawson squatted on the far side of the campfire, the damn smug look crinkling his eyes. Looked like he'd wormed his way into the tribe. He wasn't a slave any more. Andy sat up straight, tightening his grip on the bowl. That meant Dawson had found James and Trace!

Standing Pony swaggered into the center of the group and caught the eye of every man. "Gray Man tells me the White Eyed brothers are near. We ride to Birchville, my warriors. They will not be expecting us. When the sun shines tomorrow, we destroy the White Eye settlement, kill the people, run off the cattle, burn the houses." Standing Pony glared at Andy. "Tomorrow, we take back what the white man has stolen!"

The raiding party leaped to their feet, makeshift bowls clattering to the ground. Chanting, whooping, hollering set his nerves on edge. A few lifted their lances, shaking them to the awakening sky.

Celebration of imminent victory stretched into stomach-clenching minutes. Andy wolfed his stew, figuring it might be the last food he'd see today . . . maybe ever. This brief time gave him a chance to think, plan how to save his brothers' lives and maybe his own. He came up with little.

Still perched on the rock, Andy lowered his bowl as Standing Pony's stare across the campfire brought shivers. Everything he'd ever learned came down to this: survival. Andy swallowed the last bit of stew. The Apache grabbed Andy's arm, jerking him to his feet.

"Your brothers will be in Birchville this day."

"How d'you know that?"

Snorting, Standing Pony glared. "This warrior knows many things." He pulled Andy closer. "Many more than you."

Andy felt more than heard Dancing Hawk hovering over his shoulder. The Indian's hot breath raced down Andy's neck as the brave's barrel-chested body pressed against his back. Dancing Hawk pinned Andy's arms behind him, the strength impressive. Standing Pony held up an eight-inch hunting knife, glinting in the early morning glow.

Vowing not to be afraid, to make his family proud, Andy pushed his chest out. Searing fire tore across Andy's left cheek. He gasped, jerking back into Dancing Hawk's chest. Knees threatening to buckle, Andy swung his head back and forth, the stinging hotter than a million fires.

Sticky liquid streamed down his face. Angry hands yanked his pinned arms back harder, his sore ribs screaming as he sucked in air. Face burning, he knew to keep his head, to make these Apaches think he was tough. Real tough.

Andy brought his leg up to kick the leader but reconsidered. He was in no position to attack. Instead, Andy licked his dry lips and looked for a way out. Somewhere he could run. Nothing came to mind. Blood dripped onto his coat.

Thin lips curling on one end, Standing Pony's sneer revealed a gap where two teeth used to be. The knife waved inches from

Andy's left eye while the Apache's tight grip on the handle turned his browned knuckles white.

The leader jammed the tip against Andy's "good" eye. "I could make your life much more painful, more difficult, White-Eyed soldier."

"Not a soldier now," Andy whispered. "I left last summer."

The Apache huffed. "So, not even your own country wants you." He sneered. "Why do I bother with you? Should kill you now."

Andy wanted to explain he'd been too young to join. Sixteen wasn't legal, but no one asked questions. Under court order, James had to join either army, so chose the blue uniform. But Andy . . . he needed to be close to James, to keep him safe. Keep him safe from himself more than Graycoats or Indians.

Standing Pony lowered the knife, slicing the buttons from Andy's coat. It opened, revealing a shirt held together with one button. He clutched the shirt and, in one smooth motion, jerked the sleeves over Andy's shoulders. The Apache grabbed the Saint Christopher's medal, eyed it, then yanked it over Andy's head. He bit the icon, trying to bend the metal. With no success, he placed it around his own neck.

Ignoring the necklace, Andy sucked in a quick breath, lifted his chin to the Indian, who snorted and slid the knife tip down to Andy's lower rib cage. The Apache rested the tip there. He brought his eyes up to Andy's, then pushed.

The point poking his bare skin, Andy met the Indian's stare. What had his ma always said? *Endure what you can't.* He sure as hell was trying now.

The Apache huffed in Andy's face and ran the knife down his trousers, stopping at his crotch. The blade stabbed through the heavy cotton twill while Standing Pony grabbed his open shirt with the other hand. Andy froze, breath captured in his lungs.

Sharp metal pierced his most sensitive area. Would this Indian press any harder? Surely he'd pass out if that happened. He was close to doing so now.

"You ever want to have a woman again, you'll do exactly what I say." Standing Pony shoved the blade in farther. The knife tip hit skin.

Andy winced, then nodded.

"The fire on your face is little compared to what you'll feel here." The Apache leader pushed harder.

Groaning, Andy knew another inch and he'd pass out. He couldn't let them see him afraid. Locking his knees so he wouldn't crumple, he murmured, "What do you want?"

Standing Pony pulled the blade out and released Andy's shirt. "You ride in front today, lead this raiding party near Birchville. Tomorrow, you, brother of James, will burn, raid, and rape."

Mouth open, Andy stared straight ahead.

Standing Pony's powerful fingers clutched the front of Andy's pants and squeezed.

Andy held his breath, clenched his jaw, and fought to stay upright.

Savagely twisting the handful of man, Standing Pony spit as he hissed. "Hear me. You *will* lead the warriors. You *will* burn. You *will* kill." He pulled Andy within an inch of his face. "Just like your brother, you *will* take women."

Tears welling behind his swollen eyelids, Andy sucked in air as the entire lower part of his body burned, then grew numb. Stew surging upwards, he struggled to keep it down, not to pass out.

"You will." The Indian's eyes narrowed into cruel slits.

Andy nodded.

Releasing him, Standing Pony rocked back. "I see by your face, you did not know James raped women, many women."

Crazy. This Indian was crazy. James would never in a hundred years do something like that. Andy eyed the Indian leader and cringed every time Dancing Hawk moved. Arms still pinned behind him, but, pains subsiding, escape would have to come later. Better play along with this insane Indian.

Standing Pony snarled as he spoke. "James took a woman promised to me. She was a Pima girl, from the dirty-eyed tribe. We killed many of her tribe and captured her. Your brother took her as Cochise ordered. At first James protested, but he liked it. She fought him, but after many days, he broke her spirit." Standing Pony lowered his voice. "When he wasn't working, he was on her. His grunting, his—"

"He wouldn't do that. Not James."

Standing Pony cocked his head. "To survive, men do what is needed. Ask your brother." He paused. "Will he say the truth?"

How much, if any, was true? He knew James and Trace had done things they struggled to forget, things continuing to haunt their dreams, stealing their sleep. But, James hadn't mentioned this woman more than in passing. He said he'd married her. That was different from raping . . . but how different?

Standing Pony nodded to Dancing Hawk, who released Andy's arms. He clutched the front of Andy's coat and led him toward a horse. "You lead, we follow."

CHAPTER FORTY-SIX

"Damn! Just can't believe it!" James pulled on the reins, mopped his forehead, and glanced at Trace yards in front of him. "Where the hell'd they go?" How could they get this close, only to lose him? Tracks earlier this morning had swerved north, toward Birchville. But why? Surely Andy wasn't going with Dawson willingly. If free, Andy had enough sense to head for Mesilla or Santa Rita, where help might be available. No doubt, Andy would be found by nightfall.

Two more hours 'til dark.

Trace turned back. "How can they cover their tracks like that?" He tugged off his hat, ran a gloved hand over his hair, then fitted the hat back on. "It's like they vanished into air."

"I do know one thing."

"What?"

"He's in Birchville." Somehow deep down James knew, just *knew*. The voice that had whispered in his ear all day whispered again. *Keep going. Not far now. Hurry!* He didn't know who spoke; it wasn't Trace.

Wagging his head, Trace's shoulders rose and then sagged. "I hope to hell you're right. Don't know where else to look. We're about out of rocks." He gigged his horse. "Let's go."

He didn't bother to search the ground, turning over every leaf, looking for tracks. Any clue would help right now, but James knew they'd spotted the last of any marks. It'd been four, maybe five hours ago. Dawson's horse, plus another one, had ridden into a ravine. Trees, mesquite, and other bushes hid the indentations. But they'd been easy enough to follow until they vanished.

They'd been heading north when they disappeared. North to Birchville. And now, only an hour or two more and please, *please,* let Andy be there.

As they rode, James considered. If Dawson had come into contact with Standing Pony or other Apaches, why were they going into town? Cold shivers hit James. Maybe it wasn't Andy in the other saddle any more.

Maybe Standing Pony was holding Andy and they'd killed Dawson? But why would they want to lure James and Trace in? They were just more White Eyes, Americans encroaching on Indian land. Why hadn't they simply killed Andy when they'd had the chance?

What kind of game were they playing?

A crow squawked overhead. James stared at the circling silhouette as it glided toward safety or possibly a snack in a towering pine. Movement out of the corner of his eye caught his attention. Deer? Puma? Indian? James jerked on the reins and let his gaze trail over the forest floor. Straining to hear feet rustling, birds calling, or frightened squirrels chattering, only silence greeted him. His beating heart echoed in his ears.

Swallowing panic, James leaned over his horse and peered into the forest. Nothing moved, spoke, or attacked.

Another long look, then James urged his horse forward.

Winter sun set early this time of year, and today was no exception. Thankfully, James thought, snow and wind had held off. Today had been nothing but blue skies carrying a bucket load of worry.

The closer they rode into town, more and more tents dotted the river. Every so often, a man would stop, look up from his gold pan, and stare. James or Trace would inquire about Andy, but their answers were all the same. Andy who?

The sun hit the western edge of the world as the brothers reined to a stop in front of the Buckhorn Saloon. This place had been around since 1850 and was a mecca for thirsty miners. James swung out of the saddle. Maybe they'd know something in here.

Smoke roiled to the ceiling, hanging like thick icicles. James coughed, and his eyes stung. Trace rubbed his as he navigated around the crowded tables. A bartender, hair slicked down, a garter holding up a sleeve, leaned across the bar. A dark mustache hid his upper lip.

"Just get into town?"

"Couple minutes ago." James stood next to his brother. Odors of smoke, stale beer, and unwashed men whirled together creating some sort of haunted ballet. He couldn't decide whether to sneeze, cough, or step outside. He stayed.

Trace held up two fingers. "Beer." He leaned with his back toward the bar and surveyed the room. James glanced around. Miners stood three deep at the bar and occupied every chair at every table. A Faro game took up one corner.

By the time his beer arrived, James knew Andy was nearby. Exactly where was the problem. He pushed a coin across the bar top. "You been around these parts a while?" James hoped the bartender would have the answer.

"Sure." He grabbed a rag, mopping where the beer had sloshed. "Why?"

The pit of James's stomach boiled. "Looking for our little brother. He was in town few weeks back. Apparently had Indian trouble, but we've got reason to believe he's returned."

"Hell, we *all* had Indian trouble." The bartender cocked his head and stepped back. "This 'little brother' got a name?"

"Andy. Andrew Jackson Colton." James pointed to his brother

then back to himself. "Looks a lot like us, maybe an inch taller. Eighteen last month."

Pursing his lips, the barman's gaze ran up and down James, then Trace. A second long look, then a nod. "Maybe." He stood straight and yelled into the crowd. "Hey! Anyone seen Andy Colton? Looks like these two fellas here?"

"What?" one man yelled.

"Andy Colton!" The bartender pointed to Trace and James. "Looks like these two, only younger."

Shrugs and murmurs filled the room as the patrons returned to their games, conversations, and beer.

After a minute standing at the bar and half a glass of beer, James couldn't breathe. They'd never find him. Andy was lost forever.

"You the fellas lookin' for Andy?" A man, not much taller than the bar, shook hands with James, then Trace.

"You know him?" Trace's raised eyebrows were the hope James needed.

"Do indeed! Name's Clancy. James Clancy, but folks call me 'Stubby'." He chuckled, then hoisted an empty glass.

Was it possible? James motioned to the bartender, then turned his attention on Stubby. "You seen him recently?"

The man scrubbed his lips, scanned the ceiling, and nodded. "Few weeks back. About the time those damn heathens tried to run us off." He sipped the refilled beer glass. "Andy didn't scare, and him and O'Malley headed off for Mogollon. Said there was gold up there."

"O'Malley?" Trace stood on the other side of Stubby.

"Fella from Ireland. Friends with Andy, he was. That red-headed Irishman partnered with Andy. Fact is, they had a good stake couple miles up the river." Stubby finished his beer, holding out the empty glass to the bartender.

James snapped his fingers. "O'Malley. Right. Andy wrote

about him in his letter." He caught Trace's wide eyes. He knew what his brother was thinking, because he was thinking the same thing. Finally. A major clue.

Glass refilled, Stubby continued. "Andy said he was going back to Mesilla for the winter, but O'Malley talked him into heading up toward Mogollon and Cooney's Camp with him. Said they'd make a fortune."

James plopped his empty glass on the bar and caught Trace's eye. "Must've been that red-haired fella we found back by the cabin." Those days felt like years past, but James knew it was less than a week.

"O'Malley's dead?" Stubby gulped, his Adam's apple bobbing.

" 'Fraid so, if it's the man we found." Trace used his glass to point east. "Shot by Indians less than a mile from Mogollon. But no sign of Andy."

Stubby's gaze followed the wooden floor. "It's a helluva thing. O'Malley was a fine man." He looked up at James. "You find his Saint Christopher's medal? He always wore it 'round his neck."

"Don't think so," James said. "We buried him. Didn't find a medal."

Trace stood in front of Stubby. "What about Andy? You seen him lately? Today maybe?"

Rolling his eyes upward, Stubby thought, then shrugged. "Nope." He lowered his voice. "But . . . when he does get back, this'll be the first place he'll come. Hell, everybody comes in here."

"I hope so," Trace mumbled. "I hope so."

CHAPTER FORTY-SEVEN

Mesilla

She should stop this nonsense and hire someone to nurse Luke back to health. She would visit with him when he'd recovered enough to come calling at Trace's. On the other hand, if she was to be a doctor, what better way to learn than on Luke? Corn Exchange Hotel now in sight, butterflies swam in her stomach. Tomorrow. She'd find someone tomorrow.

Right now it was her duty to help Luke. The man who'd saved her. She knocked on his door, then entered at his soft words.

"I feel better already." He patted the bed where he lay, sheet pulled up under his chin. "Please, sit here. I won't bite."

Morningstar chuckled. "I know you won't." She stepped over his boots at the end of the bed, looked down at him. "I'll bring breakfast in a bit. Just thought I'd check on you this morning. Need anything?"

"Wrote a letter to Sally last night." He pointed to the nightstand on the other side of his bed. "You want to read it? See if it sounds all right?" Luke twisted an imaginary ring on his left hand. "I can change it if it's not enough. Or too much."

She hesitated. This was too personal. Should she get involved? Unfortunately, she already was.

"Please?" Luke's voice turned velvety soft.

Unable to resist his pleading eyes, she sat in the chair, opened the envelope, extracting two pages of carefully written words.

252

Her eyes trailed down both pages, then she started at the beginning, studying each word.

At first, he spoke of the shooting, how he was going to be on his feet in no time. Nothing to worry about. His head was thick, Doc had said. Farther down, heartfelt pleas to take him back. He'd changed. Saw things her way. He missed the children. Missed her more than life itself.

Pressure pushed against her eyes. Tears threatened to fall.

She sat, gripping the paper, trembling. Morningstar knew what she should do next. Would James be willing to move to California?

CHAPTER FORTY-EIGHT

Mogollon

Everyone was in grave danger. With no way to warn the town, Andy stood, hog-tied to a pine within shouting distance of the Birchville Catholic church. On his left stood the church and the yard, on his right the graveyard, unfortunately expanding by the day.

Pink and gold sunrays spread their fingers across the world, erasing the dark. If it wasn't for the bandana tied around his mouth, he would shout, holler, and scream. But he hadn't seen anyone not Apache this morning. And even as close as he was to town, he couldn't be seen. Not easily. The chokecherry bushes hid most of him. He wiggled, figuring the bark would wear out the rawhide securing his hands and ankles. But it held fast. He wasn't going anywhere. Regrettably, he'd have to stand and watch people be slaughtered.

And it would be a slaughter. Late last night as they'd ridden to the town's outskirts, no sounds were made, no one spoke. Even the horses were quiet, as if they'd been trained to trot silently. The Apaches blended into the trees and shrubs like they'd grown there. Andy knew where to look, but could not distinguish man from tree. No, the good people of Birchville had no chance.

"Gotta stop 'em. Stop 'em. Gotta stop . . ." Andy repeated his mantra this morning, same as he'd done yesterday while riding in the middle of the warriors. White tents had glared against the greens of pine trees while the horses galloped through the outskirts of the growing mining community. The closer they had come to Birchville yesterday, the closer the good citizens were to dying a horrible death. A death by Apache hands.

This morning, before true dawn, Andy knew the town of Birchville would never be the same. Men would die. Maybe even him. He vowed he would do everything in his power to prevent that, but lately, power slipped through his fingers. No matter what he did, he couldn't stop anything or anybody.

What about his brothers? He'd heard conversation pieces among Standing Pony, Dancing Hawk, and Dawson. One confirmed James and Trace were in town, another said no, they were merely near by. That bit of information should have stretched a smile ear to ear on Andy's face. Instead, he frowned and fought a tightening building in his chest. They were dead men if the Apache leader had his way. This morning would be the turning point. Some would die, some would live. Andy pulled his shoulders back as far as he could, the bark scraping his coat. He sucked in crisp mountain air.

But what about Dawson? Would they let him go, keep him as a slave or kill him? Did Andy even care? The runaway slave was a crazy man who'd gone from helping Andy . . . hell, maybe even saving his life . . . to trying to kill him or sell him. As he stood, knees shaky, Andy considered Dawson. Yes, he was deadly, and yes, certainly he was insane. But with good reason. Parts of him were to be pitied. He'd had a hard, sad life. On the other hand, it didn't give him an excuse to kill people or enslave them. There were other ways to keep your feet on the ground without turning into a madman.

His brother James had nearly fallen all the way, but with family help he was healing. Eventually, he would be all right, normal. Maybe Dawson didn't have that kind of support. Andy considered; in many ways he felt sorry for Dawson.

As brighter light cast its warm hue around the churchyard, Andy distinguished Indians from trees and bushes. Only because he knew where to look. Heart pounding in his throat, he now stood on the brink of disaster. Because of him, his brothers had been lured . . . into the spider web of Indians. And death.

CHAPTER FORTY-NINE

A person who has complete power over others becomes wicked. First Dawson. And now Standing Pony. Andy thought about the definition of "wicked" and what made these men who they were. What in their lives caused it? Andy fidgeted against his tied wrists, and the waiting evolved into an endurance test. What the hell were the Apaches doing? Why weren't they attacking the village? When would they untie Andy, let him go? The answer was obvious. When they found James and Trace. When the Indians knew they could kill almost everyone. When the time was right.

Gray skies gave way to blue. Birds called, flitting from branch to branch. A rabbit scooted across the graveyard mere feet from Andy. He wanted to shout at the animals, warn them of the impending destruction of their homes, but with the rag tied around his mouth and bound the way he was allowed only squirming. Even the air seemed happy. Smells of juniper, carried by a slight breeze, filled the churchyard. Under different circumstances, he would have smiled.

A sunray pierced his eyes. He shut them, turning his head. A voice in his ear made him flinch.

"Funny how life turns out, ain't it, boy?"

Dawson. Andy opened both eyes.

Dawson danced in front of Andy and held up his unbound hands. "Looks like dem fellas done let me go." He jigged from headstone to headstone. "I'm free! I'm free!"

"You don't know the meaning of the word," Andy muttered into the cloth cutting into the corners of his mouth.

"Free at last, free at last!" Dawson twirled over to Andy. He stopped, leaning in close. "Ain't never been free—truly free before. Don't know what to do."

"Home. Go home." Andy hoped he understood the words.

Dawson leaned back, eyebrows mashing together. "Home?"

Andy nodded.

A shrug from Dawson, who stared into the forest. After a long pause, he turned back to Andy. "Ain't got no home. Got nowhere to go." He threw his hat onto the ground. "Now ain't that a damnable thing? Here I is, *free,* and I gots nowhere to go to."

Instead of fear and hatred, Andy pitied the black man. Maybe when this was all over, when he was free, too, he'd help Dawson . . . Memories of beatings paraded across Andy's mind. No, Dawson could survive on his own.

Burning wood smells captured Andy's attention. Campfires? He sniffed again. No. Smoke much too thick and heavy. Dawson turned toward town, which sat over the hill.

"You smell smoke?" Dawson pointed.

"Untie me!" Andy screeched, knowing his words were mushy. He wiggled.

Screams.

More screams from town.

Smoke thickened.

Rifles fired.

Men hollered.

"Untie me!" Andy strained against the ropes, but instead of stretching and giving way, they seemed to tighten.

"Ooo-eee!" Dawson hopped on one foot then the other. "Looky there, white boy! Looky what them Indians be doin'! Got the whole damn town stirred up!"

"Stirred up" was an understatement. How in the hell could Andy convince Dawson to release him? Maybe together they could help stop the massacre. Or at least find Trace and James and save them.

Shouting and shots, both rifle and revolver, marched closer up the road toward Andy and the church. The few Apaches who had remained hidden near him emerged from the forest like snakes from under rocks. Arrows nocked in their bows, they readied themselves for battle.

Dawson moved back toward the trees. *Coward!* Andy wanted to shout. *Stand and fight like a man!* But then again, what did Dawson truly have to fight for?

A warrior slid in behind Andy, shoving a knife against his throat. Someone else untied his legs. Free! Free, but not free. Only his hands were tied, but the gag remained around his mouth. He had to appreciate the small things. Now he had a fighting chance. He could run, and there was enough rope between his wrists that he could use them.

Braves on either side gripped his arms and marched him closer to the churchyard's center. A glance right to left. His captors sported war paint, white and red streaks from nose to chin. Bloodlust glinted in their eyes. After several steps across the field, strong hands yanked him to a halt. He stood, locking his knees to keep them from buckling.

If he lived through this, he knew he'd never ever be as scared as he was right now. He fought to keep from shaking. His teeth chattered. Standing Pony swaggered over to him, a damn sneer crinkling his eyes.

"You have served us well, Andrew Colton. Your brothers"—he cocked his head to the right—"wait behind those trees. However, they will die before you can greet them."

Despite the gag around his mouth, Andy screamed, fighting the hands clamped around his arms.

Standing Pony chuckled. "It does no good to fight. We have won." He eased behind Andy, throwing his arm across his chest. The Indian leader's chest warmed Andy's back. He held a hunting knife at Andy's throat.

"James Colton! I know you are there. See your brother here?" Standing Pony took a long breath, then continued. "He dies today. Like you."

And then, like saviors charging through the enemy line, James and Trace emerged from behind trees, gray smoke billowing into the air. Damn it was good to see them! Heart in his throat, Andy squirmed, but the knife blade dug into his skin. A growl from the Apache froze Andy.

"What do you want, Standing Pony?" Trace hollered.

"I want James. I want your brother to face me like a man. Not like the coward he is. Not like the rapist, murderer he is. Not like—"

Thick smoke erupted from the whitewashed pine church, its steeple turning black. One stained glass window shattered. Apaches whooping, rifles firing, flames warming his right side, Andy fought to stay upright. With each passing second it was harder to breathe, to keep his head up. But by damn, he'd come this far, and nothing would stop him from saving his brothers.

"Here I am!" James moved in closer, revolver in hand. He held both arms out wide. "Come take me. Leave Andy alone! Leave Trace out of this. It's between you and me, Standing Pony." He edged toward the Apache.

More than irate, James's face reddened, turning it into a snarl. Throaty, animalistic growls emanated from his brother. James glanced at Andy. A nod, his eyes looked heavenward. He sighed. Andy spotted Trace a few yards off to the right. His narrowed eyes, pursed lips, tightened fists—yes, Trace was truly angry. Angry and worried.

Ignoring Standing Pony, James asked Andy, "You all right?"

Andy couldn't nod without the blade digging into his skin. Blinking like a crazy person was all he could do. Without warning, his knees refused to keep his weight. He sagged in the Apache's grip.

"Don't move, Andy. Stay still." James held up a hand and turned to Standing Pony. "He's no use to you now." James stepped closer. "Promise to let him go. Then I'll fight you like the man I am."

"I promise nothing." The Apache leader threw his shoulders back. "You all die, James Colton."

Standing Pony barked orders as his men scrambled out of the way, forming a circle around James, Trace, Andy, and Standing Pony. The Apache leader grabbed a handful of Andy's hair and yanked his head back until their eyes met. "Your brother is correct. You are no good to me." He yanked harder. "I kill you now."

Standing Pony removed the knife from Andy's throat and held the tip to his chest. Andy pressed back against the Indian, frantic to avoid being stabbed.

"I'll fight!" James screamed. "I'll fight! Leave him alone!"

Snorts and grunts behind him. Shoved hard, Andy flew forward, the Apache behind him. Andy's face plowed into dirt, pebbles scraping his cheek. Standing Pony, lying on top of him, released his grip. Andy tried to roll, but what felt like a boulder squashed him.

"He's mine! He's mine!" Dawson's words didn't make sense. Andy squirmed under the weight. Sucking in dirt, he managed to roll onto his right side. Arms, legs, and hands tangled together, Andy was unable to do anything except breathe.

An arrow whipped past his face, plowing into the ground not three feet away. Gunshots exploded in the air. Shouts and grunts—his brothers', Dawson's, Standing Pony's—mixed into a whirlwind of sounds.

Andy pushed, squirmed, struggled. A weight lifted. He spied Dawson, rolling to the ground and then rising to his knees in front of Andy's eyes. "You're mine, white boy!" Dawson hollered, sweat streaming down his face. "Nobody gonna kill you but me!" He grabbed Andy's coat sleeve and yanked.

Hands and body parts mashed Andy until his world spun. Dawson yanked harder. Andy slid out from under Standing Pony. Andy kicked and pushed.

"Run, Andy, run!" Trace's voice from somewhere above.

"Go!" James's words, not making sense.

Dawson tugged until Andy scrambled to his feet. Focusing on Trace, Andy loped toward his brother. Dawson ran inches behind. One step. Two.

Andy glanced over his shoulder in time to to see Standing Pony plunge a knife into Dawson's back. Dawson fell into Andy, pushing him forward and down.

As the ground raced up to meet him, Andy twisted, taking Dawson's dead weight with him.

Andy's head thudded like an overripe melon. His world exploded into darkness.

CHAPTER FIFTY

"Sonuvabitch! You'll burn in hell for this! You sonuvabitch!"

Andy startled. He moved one arm, his hands still bound in front of him. Men shouting, rifles clicking, burly voices encircled him. One eye opening, his world, sideways, blurred. From this position on the ground, he watched legs and feet scuffle in the mud. Farther off, men pointed knives and guns at each other. Bright light hitting his face, he squinted, tried to roll, but something heavy draped across him, squashing his body into the ground.

"You killed my brother, you sonuvabitch!"

Trace's voice? Andy wiggled under the weight. Sounded like him. Andy bit at the cloth around his mouth, then gave up. He focused on the world. Did that mean James was dead?

Couldn't be. Not James! Heart pounding in his chest and throbbing in his head, Andy pushed up. Dawson's body rolled off, flopping to the right. Legs tangled with Dawson's, Andy pried his from under his captor's and scrambled to his knees. A glance at Dawson, then he turned his attention to the living.

From far off, timbers groaned, crashing to the ground. Nearby, a church wall collapsed, sending a mud spray over the gathered Indians. Andy's world took shape, focusing piece by piece. Trace stood a few yards in front of him, facing away. Dancing Hawk, knife in hand, charged Trace. Sidestepping, lunging, thrusting, the two matched each other in a dance of death.

Not truly understanding, but knowing his brother had been killed, Andy vowed no one would kill Trace. One dead brother was one too many. Legs still wobbly, Andy careened toward Dancing Hawk.

One step. Two. Another couple and he'd be on that Indian, take him down before Dancing Hawk could get to Trace. Legs weak, Andy pushed them harder. He hollered, hoping his word was understood. "Trace!"

His brother spun around, eyes wide. "Andy?"

Dancing Hawk pounced. His knife thrust into Trace's side, blood pooling on the shirt. Trace clutched the wound and sank to his knees. Andy stood over him muttering through the tight gag. He clawed at the material. "All right. You'll be all right."

Trace sagged to the ground and sat, looking up at Andy. "You're alive?"

Nodding, Andy turned his attention to Dancing Hawk holding up his knife like a trophy. Out of the corner of his eye, Andy spotted two men wrestling on the ground, rolling over and over, exchanging punches. James! He was alive! The other, Standing Pony. He would not let these Indians kill his brothers. Would *not*.

Gag removal forgotten for the moment, Andy bent over and rammed into Dancing Hawk's chest. Both men went down, the knife flying out of the Apache's grip. "No!" Andy kicked Dancing Hawk's face, and, in return, the Indian kicked Andy's stomach. Grabbing each other, they rolled across the churchyard.

Plowing into a mound of muck, Andy somersaulted, scrambled to his knees, and searched for the dropped knife. He spotted it stuck in the mud too far away, outside his reach. Before Andy could get to his feet, Dancing Hawk jumped on his back. Fists pounding Andy's cheeks, a finger tried to embed itself in his eye.

Determined to beat this enemy perched on his back, Andy twisted, turned, bucked. He threw himself into the mud, taking his attacker with him. The Indian lost his grip but stayed on top, riding Andy like a wild bronc. Using all the strength he possessed, Andy flipped over, glaring into the Apache's paint-streaked face. "No!"

Still on his back, Andy wriggled, the Apache wobbling on top like a toy. Andy thrashed harder until Dancing Hawk slid off. Andy scrambled to his feet and, using his head like a spear, rammed the Indian a few feet back into a tree. Wind knocked out of the Apache, Andy used this advantage to headbutt the man. The Apache's head crashed into the tree over and over. Using his bound hands like a bat, Andy swung, the sickening *thwack* somehow satisfying. A minute later, Dancing Hawk slumped to the ground and lay still.

Andy pulled in air and turned his attention to James.

Now on their feet, Standing Pony and James crouched. Knife shoulder high, Standing Pony's eyes locked with James's. "I have waited long, James Colton. Now I kill you . . . like you killed my brother."

"Your brother died a warrior," James said. "There's no shame in that."

"You took my woman. Dark Cloud was promised to me." The Apache inched forward.

James stepped right. "How's that?"

"Cochise promised the Pima captive to me. She was mine. After your marriage ceremony," Standing Pony moved left, "I stayed by your wickiup all night. Should have been me." He lunged.

James jumped back. "I didn't know." He shrugged. "Cochise . . . Remember Cochise insisted I—"

"Three dark moons of rutting." The Apache circled James. "I listened, ear against wickiup, heard her moans, your . . ."

Not willing to chance James getting hurt, Andy charged, tackling the Apache at the knees. Both men slammed into the ground, somersaulted across icy rocks, and then plowed into the church wall.

Thrusting his legs upwards, he pushed the Indian's body over his head. He twisted and scrambled to his feet. A glance at James, who nodded. Andy spotted the knife on the ground not too far on his right.

James followed Andy's gaze and dove for it. Before Andy took a second breath, Standing Pony plowed into him, both men again splatting against the ground.

Tumbling over and over, the men crashed into a mesquite bush. The sudden stop gave Andy the advantage. He straddled the Indian, giving James time to kneel beside Standing Pony. James jammed the knife into the Apache's side.

The man under Andy shivered. Frantic hands grabbed Andy's face, fingernails raking down his cheek. Two long breaths, then Standing Pony's body relaxed.

Andy squeezed his eyes, curled forward, then slid off the Apache. He sunk to the ground as Standing Pony's last breath struck his face.

"You all right?" James's words in his ear.

Andy opened his eyes, tears blurring his brother's face. He waited for his brother to pull down the gag. He worked his mouth around. "I will be. You?"

"Fine. Where's Trace?"

Where was he? Andy sat upright. Was Trace dead? After James cut the ropes around his wrists, Andy pointed to the other side of the churchyard. "Got stabbed. Over there."

James was on his feet and running before Andy could swipe at his eyes. He managed to stand, taking time to survey the area. The remaining Apaches had vanished. In their place, townspeople appeared, silent witnesses to the end of a long-standing grudge.

Andy lurched across muddy ground and knelt by both brothers. James produced a half smile. "Alive. Don't think the blade hit anything important."

The weight of the world lifted from his shoulders. Andy sagged back onto his rear, sitting in mud. But he didn't care. His brothers were still alive. And he was still alive. Now it was time to go home.

CHAPTER FIFTY-ONE

Mesilla

Home. Andy sighed, leaned back against the soft folds of Teresa's tufted couch, and closed his eyes. The warmth of the Saint Christopher's medal lying against his chest soothed him. He remembered the feeling of satisfaction and pure triumph when he pulled it off from around Standing Pony's neck. Sweet revenge, indeed.

The murmur of his family's voices surrounding him mixed together until it resembled happy bees gathering at the hive. Although they'd been home over an hour, the women still doted on the brothers—many hugs, plumping already-soft pillows, filling cups with warm, freshly-boiled coffee, listening to every word they said. And there were many words. Even little Faith had gotten in a word or two. Trace's face lit up, the contagious Colton family grin on full display, whenever he caught sight of her.

Stuffed into Trace's living room and squeezed onto the sofa on both sides of Andy sat Luke and James. Trace occupied his favorite rocker, while Morningstar took the single chair. Teresa hurried from living room to kitchen.

Why had he decided to search for gold in the first place? It was his damned indecisiveness. He'd have to work on that. Mentally, he smiled. He had more wealth right here than he'd ever get freezing his rear off in the mountains. Or swishing water in a pan for days on end. No sir, the riches from family were precious and not to be taken lightly. If he'd learned anything, it was that.

Teresa stood in the kitchen door wiping her hands on an apron. "If you boys go have a bath, maybe a shave, I'll bet Star and I can have a meal you'll never forget ready when you all come back."

"I'd settle for anything that wasn't Trace's cooking!" James nudged Andy's arm. "Sure got tired of his burned jerky." Chuckles filled the room.

Holding his side, Trace leaned forward. "I, for one, could use some hot water and soap. A good long soak down at Pedro's might soften these sore bones." He eased to his feet, eyes squinting and one hand fisted. Andy knew his brother hurt. Hell, they all did, even Luke. Down at the soaking tubs, maybe the brothers would share stories, stories they wouldn't share in front of the women. Like why the hell was Luke here?

Teresa held Trace's arm, guiding him to the door. He fitted his hat and kissed her. She stepped back. "Don't you go getting too pretty. Might not recognize you when you come home."

James stopped at the door. "Don't worry. Ma always said Andy's the prettiest."

"Am not," Andy grimaced as he pushed off the sofa. "She said it was Luke."

Luke shrugged. "No, I'm the tallest."

"*I* am." Andy stepped through the door and into chilly December air. Damn, it felt good to be with his brothers but, just as importantly, to be free. They limped down the dirt street, crossed the plaza, and entered Pedro's Barbershop.

A single barber chair sat in the front room, occupied by a bearded man long in need of a haircut. Pedro stood behind him, scissors in hand. He nodded and then flashed a grin at Trace.

"Señor Colton! *¡Bienvenidos!* I heard you had returned." Pedro stepped aside and shook hands with Trace. He scanned the brothers. "After your adventures, you want a bath? Maybe a shave, too?"

Andy held his shoulder. Despite the stitches being out over a week, it still hurt. "Sure do. Wouldn't mind getting rid of some of this dirt first."

Pedro pointed over his shoulder to a doorway. "*Bueno.* I got enough tubs for all of you." He hollered to the back. "Consuelo! Hot water for four!"

Andy had been here only once before, preferring to bathe at Trace's house, enjoying the privacy of the kitchen. But today, he'd take pleasure in being with his brothers. Five wooden tubs, looking suspiciously like old whiskey kegs, filled the room. There was enough room to strip down, a hook on the wall to hold towels and clothes, and a bar of soap and washcloth on the floor by the tub. No frills, just warm water. And a row of filled whiskey bottles. For half a dollar, a bottle was yours.

Luke bought two.

The men eased out of coats, shirts, trousers, socks, and boots. Down to their longjohns, they stood, waiting. James ran his hand through the water. "Warm, fellas. Think they knew we were coming?"

Luke held up a bottle. "How about a toast first? Here's to us!" They passed it around, each taking a slug. Luke drained most of it.

Unbuttoning his cotton undershirt, Andy grinned. "I'm gonna be first in, last out." Shoulder on fire, he eased out of the shirt. The old arrow wound was healed, but a zigzag scar glowed dark red. Marks and bruises all over his body reminded him of his good fortune—to survive it all. He shucked out of his longjohns and stepped into the tub, its warmth soothing the aches. He eased down until he sat and held the Saint Christopher's medal hanging around his neck. He regarded it. Where was O'Malley now? But the burning question—why didn't he manage to free Andy? He had pondered over it many times, but anything logical had escaped. Somehow, he'd lost track of O'Malley.

Andy dunked his entire body twice then, with water up to his chest, leaned against the side. "Trace, James?" He picked up the washcloth and waited for his brothers to quit splashing and look at him. "While you were out looking for me, you ever come across or heard of a red-headed Irishman named Thomas O'Malley?"

James stopped, soap in hand. "He a friend of yours?"

"The one you went to Mogollon with?" Trace asked.

Nodding, Andy figured this wasn't going to be good news. "Yeah. Good friends. We partnered for a while, then decided to head to Mogollon." He looked from James to Trace. "Why? You meet him?"

"Kind of," James said. "We buried him."

"Buried? O'Malley's dead?" Andy cocked his head. "Can't be. He gave me this medal, said it'd bring good luck."

"Sorry," Trace said. "Found his body near a campsite about a mile from Mogollon. Indians."

Cold shivers ran over Andy. "Can't be. He gave me this medal back in the tunnel where Dawson kept me. *After* we fought those Apaches." His gaze trailed over to Trace. "How can he give it to me when he's dead?" Maybe that was why he didn't help.

Silence bounced off the walls. It was James who broke it. "Suppose it was *his* voice I heard? Telling me to keep looking? Keep going? That we'd find you?"

More silence.

Luke splashed Andy. "Hell, little brother. You seeing spooks?" He splashed James. "And you're hearing them?" He rose from the tub, soapsuds dripping from his extended arms. "Oooohh-hhh, I'm a ghost! Oooohhh!!!"

"Settle down, Luke. This is serious." Trace sat up straight, holding his side.

"Serious? I'll give you serious." Luke gulped half of the second bottle, then returned to the water. He used the washcloth to point. "What about Star being a doctor? What about James leaving and going all the way over to California? Hell, Trace, you're a big bad sheriff, and Andy's gonna be deputy. I *was* one. But now I'm a nobody. Again. Replaced by my own brother. And even if I wanted to leave, I can't."

"Why not?" Andy wiped suds out of his eyes.

Luke huffed into his mustache. "Nothing's lining my pockets, except the piddly deputy pay." He huffed again. "Hell, that ain't enough to even buy me a beer."

James scrubbed his face, speaking around the cloth. "Hell, Luke. If you'll work, you can have the job Swede Bergstrom's holding for me at his livery stable. Needs somebody who knows how to shoe and can make deliveries." He held the cloth. " 'Sides, I've saved a bit."

Luke nodded. "Might suit me for a while."

"I'll talk to him tomorrow," James said.

"You do that, big brother." Luke waved the bottle toward town. "Tomorrow, I'll take your job and your wife, thank you."

Andy looked at Trace, who was glaring at Luke. This wasn't going to be good. Andy bit his bottom lip. James turned in the tub. "You can have my job, but Star's mine." He waved the soap at Luke. "She wears my ring."

"She'd rather wear mine." Luke finished off the whiskey.

"Shut up, Luke. You're drunk." Trace stood and grabbed the empty bottle out of Luke's hand. "Time to go."

"Mine!" Luke waved toward the bottle. He turned to James. "Star's lonely, and I kept her company, while *you* were gone."

He stepped out of the washtub. James stood, grabbing Luke's shoulders.

"You sonuvabitch! You slept with Star?" James pushed him backward, both men sliding on the wet floor.

Trace jumped out, grabbing at slippery arms. "Stop it! I said stop it!"

This was not the homecoming Andy had envisioned. Had Luke really slept with Morningstar? She would never, ever do such a thing! Or would she? Had Luke forced her? Questions flew through his mind as he gripped a leg and pulled.

Within seconds, all four brothers wrestled on the floor, slipping and sliding, somersaulting one over another. Curses, grunts, then someone kicked a washtub, the water sloshing over the floor. Andy clutched James's body, tugging, trying to pull him off of Luke.

"Hold it!" Baritone words flew overhead. "I said hold it!"

Andy released his brother and located the source of the voice. At the door stood Pedro, then behind him a half-shaven man, drape still wrapped around his chest, and Sammy Estrada, deputy sheriff. Sammy spread his arms out wide. "Trace? Andy? What the hell're you all doing?"

Trace rolled onto his back, Luke pinned in a chokehold. Andy sat, surveying the room. It would cost a small fortune to pay for the damages. But if what Luke said was true, he had damaged much more than wooden barrels.

Scrambling to his feet, Trace grabbed a towel off the hook, wiped his face, then wrapped it around his waist. He shrugged. "Just a misunderstanding, Sammy. Sorry you had to come in here."

Sammy's shoulders relaxed. "Hell, Trace. Heard you from outside, down the street. Pedro thought for sure Indians had attacked. Didn't expect to find four soapy, naked brothers, though." A thin smile slid up one side of his face.

"Thanks to my back-stabbing brother here." James swung at Luke, his fist missing his face by an inch. Andy pinned his brother's arm.

"Listen, I don't know what this's about, but it stops now." Sammy pointed his finger at each of the men. "Get it figured out. Quietly and quickly. Would hate to have to arrest you all." He turned to Trace. "See you in the office tomorrow, boss." A long slow scan of the Colton brothers, then Sammy, Pedro, and the stranger walked away, heads wagging.

Thankful everyone had calmed, Andy released James's arm. Luke snatched towels off the peg, tossed one to James, then another to Andy. The last he kept for himself.

Mostly dry and with the towel wrapped around him, Luke pulled in air, then let it out. He looked from Trace to James to Andy, who braced himself for the worst. What could Luke possible do or say now that wouldn't totally destroy what was left of the family?

Luke studied the floor, the ceiling, the tubs, his hands. "Look, James. I'm sorry." He shrugged. "I had no call to be saying what I did. It was the whiskey talking. Hell, we're nothing but friends, Morningstar and me." He combed his hair with his fingers. "I saved her life, that's true. And she nursed me back to health. That's true too. But . . ."

"But what, exactly, Luke?" James, fists clenched, moved within inches of Luke's face. "Exactly what happened?"

Luke's shoulders rose and fell twice. "Nothing. Absolutely nothing. She loves you and wants nothing but my friendship." He held his palms up. "Ask her. She'll tell you. We're friends, and that's all. Hell, James. She helped me pick out a shawl and write a love letter to Sally."

Another long, agonizing silence filled the room. Water dripped onto the floor, muffled conversation from the front room, horses clopping in the street. No one moved.

Gaze sliding to the floor, Luke stuck out a hand toward James. "I'm sorry as hell." He looked up at James. "Still brothers?"

A long slow pull of air, James cocked his head, then flashed Pa's Colton family grin. He gripped Luke's hand. "Yeah. Still brothers."

Andy smiled. This was the best day ever. Yep, it was good to be home.

ABOUT THE AUTHOR

New Mexico native **Melody Groves** has a deep love for anything Old West. Winner of numerous writing awards, Melody is a member of Western Writers of America, SouthWest Writers and New Mexico Press Women. She writes for *Wild West, True West, New Mexico Magazine,* and other regional publications.

Author of *She Was Sheriff* and the award-winning Colton Brothers Saga series: *Border Ambush, Sonoran Rage, Arizona War,* and *Kansas Bleeds,* Melody is a contributing editor of WWA's *Round Up* magazine.

Non-fiction books include: award-winning *Hoist a Cold One! Historic Bars of the Southwest; Ropes, Reins, and Rawhide: All About Rodeo,* and award finalist *Butterfield's Byways: The First Stagecoach Line and Overland Mail Route Across America.*

When not writing, she's busy playing rhythm guitar with the Jammy Time Band.

The employees of Five Star Publishing hope you have enjoyed this book.

Our Five Star novels explore little-known chapters from America's history, stories told from unique perspectives that will entertain a broad range of readers.

Other Five Star books are available at your local library, bookstore, all major book distributors, and directly from Five Star/Gale.

Connect with Five Star Publishing

Visit us on Facebook:
https://www.facebook.com/FiveStarCengage

Email:
FiveStar@cengage.com

For information about titles and placing orders:
(800) 223-1244
gale.orders@cengage.com

To share your comments, write to us:
Five Star Publishing
Attn: Publisher
10 Water St., Suite 310
Waterville, ME 04901